Precious

AND

Fragile Things

Debby Kruszewski

ISBN 978-1-64300-050-3 (Paperback)
ISBN 978-1-64300-051-0 (Digital)

Covenant Books, Inc.
11661 Hwy 707
Murrells Inlet, SC 29576
www.covenantbooks.com

I lay with my back on the concrete wall that separates the park from the harbor, with my leg dangling off the edge. The sun has already come up, but you can't tell because of the thick fog that hangs over us. Gusts of rain and wind pick up throughout this morning, but I don't move. I lay there and listen to the silence; listen to the wind. I still feel nothing.

It may be cold. It may be wet. It may be too windy to sit here off the edge, but I don't care. No one is here. No one can see me. No one will notice me, because I am invisible.

As I lay here, I open and close my eyes. The fog is getting thicker; not a day for boats to leave the harbor. The trees sway back and forth, leaves fall and scatter across the park. I keep one eye open and watch as a leaf falls in slow motion toward my face. It tosses from side to side. It lingers around in the air. It gives away drops of rain and slowly finds its perfect spot, landing on my face. I close my eyes and hope to feel it, but I can't. I still feel nothing. I take a deep breath and wait for it to fade away.

I don't know how I got here. I don't understand why my life ended so soon. But, as I lie here, I feel less and less. Eventually, it all fades away. I grasp to go back, and fight to go back. I resist the darkness until it takes over me.

*   *   *   *   *

If God has a master plan,
That only he understands,
I hope it's your eyes he's seeing through.
—"Precious," Depeche Mode

We laid on the floor with everyone dancing around us. All I could see were your hazel eyes. You were smiling which only made me laugh back. It was loud. Starlight's twinkled. The music faded into the background. You held my hand so tightly. I could remember your smell, a fruity musk. Your fingertips were soft as you brushed away hair from my face. I will follow you anywhere. I saw my future in your eyes; our house, our children playing in the yard, our kisses after dinner, and the fireplace lit and calming. He rejoined our hands and, again, held so tightly.

"This is it, kid. You and me forever," he said with a smile.

"I love you."

"I love you too." That was all I could remember. Everything else flashed before my eyes. Then it was over, just like a blink. I was so tired and lost after that. It was so dark, I couldn't see. It was so quiet; I couldn't hear. It was so warming; I didn't want to leave. All I wanted to do was replay that memory over and over. It made sense. Then it didn't. Pieces faded and faded.

Where was I again? For what? Was it light or dark? Was I old or was I young? What was I wearing? I can't remember. Those pieces are gone. More kept fading. But I never forgot your eyes, your smile, your grip, your fingertips on my face; I never forgot you. Until then, you were gone. Your eyes became brown; or were they green? Who are you? You were a man, a woman. There was no smell. Then you became a cat. Then there was nothing. All I could see was me, alone on the floor. I don't remember why I was there at all. It was over and erased. I don't even know that it occurred; but somehow, somewhere, to someone, it did. It happened to us. Then it faded to black. I don't remember if your name was Devin or Ryan; or was it maybe Brian? I don't know, but I will never forget you.

The lights were bright and hard to adjust to. I don't remember seeing illumination for so long. It was comforting. I literally said, "What?" out loud, once I opened my eyes. I don't know if anyone was listening to me. Who are these people? Why can't I get up and move? Wait, why . . . I . . . no, no, no, no . . . I am not doing this again; no way!

"Nooooo!" I screamed again and again. People stood over me, and smiled and laughed, and giggled. They stuck fingers at me and tossed me around; I cried until I couldn't cry anymore. I still had my voice, I still had my sarcasm, but I had a new body. I became me, again, in someone else.

"Why?" I closed my eyes and was back to being me. My brown locks, my favorite dress, my favorite heels. I always wore heels. I sat in a white room, a waiting room of sorts. I waited. Patiently, I waited. The silence was deafening. The time felt long. But I expected to grow patience, and waited so patiently. I wanted to study my body and remember each piece, but I couldn't see me. Were there freckles on my back? Did I have wrinkles in my eyes? I didn't know, I couldn't see me. I saw a white room with a white light. No defined walls, no defined seating—just a white room and me. Who am I? Who do you say I am?

After some time, a man appeared. He was dapper. I want to say Italian, or some form of European. He was tall and thin, and wearing dark blue, pleated dress pants with a blue button-down, a navy, fitted, V-neck, cashmere sweater. His hair was dark and wavy. He kept it long enough to pass his ears. He conserved his scruff to a minimum as it started to turn to an excellent salt and pepper.

"Hello," he greeted me with a smile and a handshake.

"Hello," I replied in skepticism.

"Why are we here today, miss? I understand you have a problem?"

"Ugh . . . why am I doing this again? Why? I'm so tired. I am so tired. I am not ready."

"No."

"But why? I just don't think I can; I don't have the energy."

"You will."

"Yeah, see, I still miss my old life. I want it back."

"You can't have it back. It's over. So tell me what is it that you remember that you miss so much?"

"Ummm, I, well, um the thing . . . wait that time . . . the place, ummm."

5

"Let me stop you here, honey," as he sits down next to me and places his hand on my knee. "You don't remember. You are going back to this new life."

"Who are these people? I don't know them; I don't want to know them!"

"They are new people—well, new to you in this life. They will love you. It's a new life, trust me, the old was . . . it was not a good one. You will start new, fresh; you will be happy. The energy will find you. There will be rough patches. No worries, you will have a new life. God wants this for you. You got this."

I took a deep breath and felt the blood rush to my head. "I'm so tired."

"So, sleep."

"This is it; I don't want to do this again. But I will do it for God."

"Good, then it's settled." He slapped my knee and got up, fixing his belt as he turned away.

"By the way, you don't have a choice. I will be waiting here when it is over. Have a nice life, my love, and stay beautiful."

"Wait, what is your name?"

"Peter."

*　　*　　*　　*　　*

Don't waste your time on me,
You're already the voice inside my head.
Missing you,
Missing you.
—"I Miss You," Blink-182

I am back, but I don't remember that it happened. I am here with my voice, my sarcasm, and mainly, at this moment, that is all I have. But I lay in silence; there is a twinkle in the background. I ignore it. I'm here; I'm doing this; I don't know why. Can I hurry up and become an adult already? I want a cigarette and a stiff drink.

I am here. I am playing the game, following the rules, being obedient. I'm doing it. I'm in it. I sit in silence. Then, there she is. A pair of eyes that giving me an intense stare through these bars that feel like prison bars. She tries to stare me down. I stare back. I don't blink. I found my rival. My sister. Suddenly, I am intrigued by her angry eyes. I will follow behind her. I will wear her hand-me-downs. I will put gum in her hair. She will steal my favorite bra, my favorite heels, my boyfriend. I guess you can say we have an understanding. That moment, that first encounter, is where the agreement begins. She doesn't crack a smile or even move her lips. She is studying me and sizing me up. I feel like prey through her eyes. I don't know if I love her, hate her, or want to kill her. But she is my sister. The only choice is love. That is what God wants me to do—so I choose love.

I put the rest of the emotions away. They may never go away. I reach out my hand to touch her. She reaches back. We press fingers. She never breaks her stare. She may have been here first. But, I am older and wiser. Just you wait and see.

"Mom! The baby is awake."

"Ashley, don't call her 'the baby.' Her name is Valerie."

"She's a stupid baby."

"Stop it, Ashley! No TVTV today for you. Please, just stop!" The stare is still there. I wink at Ashley as she walks backward. I smile. She runs away. She feels my strength. She is afraid of it.

"Oh, Mom, I want to hold the baby, can I? PLEASE?" He came in and grabbed me from the crib, my current prison cell.

"Yes, Todd," she screamed from the other room. He didn't even wait for permission. I was already in his arms. My sudden need for scotch and soda faded away.

"I got you now, Valerie!" he said with excitement and kissed my forehead. He was so kind and warm toward me. I felt so safe and comfortable in his arms. I touched his chin; he smiled as he kissed my hand. I fell asleep that day in his arms. Suddenly, I slowly relax for a bit.

"Valerie?" I said to myself. "I like it."

Every morning, Todd would come in for a visit. Todd made my day. I felt like we had conversations without saying a word. He told me about football, dungeon and dragons, Legos, what he wanted for breakfast. Pancakes, he loved pancakes. He loved Joe Namath, Mookie Wilson, and wanted to build a rocket-ship with Legos. He had big dreams.

Todd would bring me on the porch when the weather warranted. We sat on the swinging bench, where he read to me, or we would just play little games. When I became older, we moved into the yard to play catch with whatever ball the season warranted.

He taught me how to read, how to write, and how to gamble off watching ESPN from learning about sports scores. We spent late nights watching TV, and falling asleep on the couch. Sometimes we even fell asleep playing cards in his room at night. I was his shadow. We played gin rummy for pennies. As years went on, Todd taught me poker and, soon enough, Texas Hold'em. He gave me quizzes.

"Valerie, what is a straight flush?"

I answered like a game show. "A straight flush is the fifth highest hand. It consists of five cards of the same suit."

"Beautiful, Valerie, beautiful! What is a straight?"

"A straight is the sixth highest hand. It consists of straight numbers; the suit doesn't matter, i.e. 7,6,5,4,3."

"You're on fire, Valerie. Let's play!"

I smiled. I had gained his attention. The more attention I had, Ashley didn't. It felt wonderful. I memorized all the information I could get out of the books he gave me. We played for hours after dinner, and sometimes, into the middle of the night. It was a rush; I wanted to learn the game to be closer to him, to bond with him, and not to be alone.

"You beat me again, Valerie! How are you only eight years old and a poker shark? We need to get you to a casino!" I just smiled at Todd. I was pleased with myself and had to keep my game tight; I didn't want to lose the game. I didn't want to sacrifice losing his affection. I needed him. I watched his football practice, soccer in the spring, and then, over the summer, lifeguarding at the beach. Todd was someone people wanted to be around.

"What a sweet boy," ladies would say to my mom on the soccer field. She never knew how to respond, but politely smile back.

"Where is Todd's father? He must be so proud of how good a player he is." That question would get to my mom every time it was asked. They did it to bully her. The women on the field were mean. They knew that Todd and Ashley's dad disappeared from their lives, right after Ashley was born. They saw him on random holidays and on birthdays. Then he vanished. It pained her to give that to her children, as she never intended that he would leave and never come back.

Now my mom is with Tom, my dad, and that is not working out so well. She will not admit that out loud. Mom—Shelia—acted solid in public. She held her own. Shelia wanted a new beginning with me, but it was quickly failing. Todd was the star. She tried to keep him the prince. I lived in his shadow.

"Todd's dad is out of the country. We will call him and send him the updates. Where is your husband again?" The women quickly scattered. Mom knew who in town was not sleeping at home. Thankfully, no one had a cellphone with photos at this time.

Todd was the star forward in soccer, and star quarterback in football. Todd was everything. I was so proud that he was my brother. He had clout in lots of places. That helped me through my young, school years. I got the best seat in the cafeteria, and got invited to the best pool parties. Cute, young boys wanted to know if they could meet my brother, the town's star athlete. It was kind of cool.

Once Todd got a car, he wasn't around as much. I didn't understand why he didn't want to play with me. I waited and waited for him. I became dust as he discovered girls, parties, and college. When Todd turned eighteen, I realized he was growing up so fast, and at ten, I wasn't quick enough. I cherished our time together. I still needed him. I missed him. As he found independence, I became "Hey, kid," in passing. Suddenly, instead of his best friend, I became his little sister. My heart was crushed. The morning wake-up's dwindled, as they became "sneaking girls out of the house." Our homework and late-night card games became me sitting alone in his room, mourning Todd and not understanding why. My brother became my acquaintance. I was hurt. He turned me away. He was fulfilled and happy. I was the president of his fan club whose tickets got lost in the mail. It changed me; it hurt.

As Todd was ready to go to college, my mom noticed how hurt I was. That was a hard summer for me. I stared out the window, and sat on the porch in a daze. I was always waiting for Todd.

"Go play with Ashley," Mom would say.

"No."

"Noooo," Ashley replied, as she ran out of the room and slammed doors. She was good at that. This game was our usual. I turned to the wall before I took a swing at Ashley. She was so horrible toward me. It was easier just to avoid her.

Shelia wasn't the best mom in the world, but she was the only parent we all had. Todd and Ashley's dad left years ago. He didn't want much to do with Shelia. They would stop seeing him through time. My dad was Tom. He also became an occasional acquaintance.

I would try to get close to Mom, but she would push me away. After Tom left us, she put up a wall. Every couple of months, I had lunch with Tom. He always paid his child support on time. I didn't know him very well. I gave up on being interested in what he was about, and where that side of the family came from. I stopped searching for answers. I learned to be just like my mother. I pushed people away. I kept my wall up. I didn't want to get close to anyone. I was always searching for something lost. I didn't know what it was. I just kept searching.

One day, I was wandering around the house, looking for something to do, and a place where I could avoid Ashley. I found myself up in the attic, where I found old photos in a dusty album, tucked in the corner of the room. It was moms. Also knowing very little about that side of the family, I wasn't sure if anyone existed.

I studied them and tried to know the people in these photos. I came across a picture of my grandparents from when they were first married. I considered their eyes, and tried to read them. I wanted to know them, who they were, what they were thinking, and especially, what they would think of me. I put together a vision from the pieces I knew of them. The deeper I got, the more they made sense to me. The more I felt a sense of my search for answers.

Perhaps I am just like my grandfather. I believe Cal to be loud and outspoken, then he would be quiet and angry. It must all be over his heartbreak from losing the love of his life before they ever had the time to think of their extinction. They said they would be together forever; they made promises to start a family after the war was over, have children, buy a house, and build a garden. They had a plan, a sacred vow to be together forever. They took this pledge, then she left this world and entered the next. Then he was alone. The message became clear. He was missing the same thing I was—love. We shared a loss; I could feel his pain and didn't know why. I drown myself in understanding their story and exploring them. It became my obsession.

My obsession grew deep. The time I spent to avoid Ashley, and my lack of time with Todd, was spent in the attic. My new friends became Madeline and Cal. This place, this memory creation, became my haven.

Are they all together in heaven watching over us? Some say there is an evolution of your soul. That we float in circles along each other. Maybe my grandmother and I were sisters, friends, lovers, or maybe even neighbors. I know her, but I don't know her. I feel her presence and have a scent that I believed to be hers. She is within my circle. Whatever it is that I have, I have the grief and pain of never knowing her, or understanding why she left us so early. I felt the pain within of losing something you can no longer touch. I mourned them without even knowing them, but they were family, and right now, I needed them.

When Todd was ignoring me for girls and being allowed to take the car out at night, I headed back into the attic and searched for more photos. I drilled my mom with questions, answers to stories she didn't know the answers to. She didn't care about them as much as I did. I grew mad at her for it. I found a photo that I couldn't let go of. I studied it as I laid on the dusty floor in the attic. There it was—a story behind the photo, something I needed to know. My feelings were hurt. I needed answers.

The photo had a white frame around the edges, warped from the heat of sitting in the attic for so many years. There were cracks, the shot was a bit faded, but it existed. My grandmother was there with her sister, my uncle on the other side, my grandfather with an arm around my grandmother's sister, Carrie, my aunt—great aunt. He has a cigarette hanging out of his mouth. He wore a button-down shirt, and a tie. The top shirt buttons were opened. His tie was loosened. He was relaxed and very familiar with his arm around another woman, very comfortable. My grandmother was smiling with her eyes looking down, as she was disappointed. There were glasses on the table before them. I am sure the scotch was heavy that evening.

"Mom! Have you seen this photo before?" I hand it to her as she is cooking dinner.

"Hmmm, Valerie, I am cooking. I can't look at this now."

"Do you know when it was? Do you know where it was?"

"Valerie! I don't know. Why is this so important to you? Did you do your homework? Ashley, dinner is almost ready so wash your hands; and you, missy, put that away and go wash your hands too."

"I need to know," I demanded and stood in front of the sink, as she was moving toward me to drain the pasta that was steaming on her face.

"We can talk about it after dinner. Now go!"

We sat, the three of us, for dinner. Ashley was staring at me, as usual, and my mom was preoccupied with some thoughts or worries that she would not share with us. She diverted to the TV as the nightly news was on. "Gas is going up again." she made these statements that, of course, had zero relevance to us.

"Mom, tell me more about grandpa." She pretended not to hear me, sipped her white wine and stared blankly at the TV.

"Mom!"

"Valerie! Don't scream at me. Please, why do you want to know? Eat your broccoli, dear."

"I just feel connected to him, and want to know more about him. I want to understand him; I want to understand YOU." She kept her eye on the TV. Her face became red, and she sipped her wine a little longer. The long-lasting gulp was used as her defense; again, her tears were about to pour out. I had touched a nerve.

"Are you girls done? Valerie, please clear the table."

"It's Ashley's turn," I said as I stared back into her evil eyes and walked away. I went outside to sit on the porch, and hoped to catch Todd at some point coming in or out. I could hear Ashley screaming and whining about having to put dishes in the dishwasher. You'd think she was sticking needles under her nailbeds; she was that dramatic.

"ASHLEY, PLEASE!" Mom screamed as she raced up the stairs and slammed the door to her bathroom.

*   *   *   *   *

The night was crisp as it turned into fall, and the neighborhood silence started earlier than usual. All the neighborhood kids were in their dining rooms doing homework, instead of riding their bikes in the street. The worst time of year for me was when I couldn't ride my bike. I couldn't take the continued draw toward cold weather, and further isolation of winter; maybe I was a warm weather person. I craved the heat. Maybe that was why my dad moved to California to hide away from us; perhaps that was it.

I sat on the porch for hours, and watched the lights in each house on our block go out for the evening; it was way past 11:00 p.m. I went inside because I needed to use the bathroom, and the chill was too much for me to bear any longer. I never let the picture out of my mind of Cal, Madeline, and the rest of the clan; and I just dreamed about it longer and longer. As I went past the kitchen, the bottle of wine my mom started at 5:00 p.m. was now empty and lying on its side. The new bottle was vodka. The bottle was on the counter, almost half empty. There was no glass in sight. Neither was my mother. After I used the bathroom, I went upstairs to see Ashley sleeping in her goddess room, my brother's door opened—he had never returned home. I went into my mom's bedroom; she was lying on her side with the TV blaring. I crawled in next to her; she needed me.

"He was horrible," she said. "He was horrible after my mom died. You don't know how cold he was to me, and how he made it my fault." She was crying; it was my fault. I didn't know these were memories she didn't want to re-open; I brought them back to her.

"I was so young; I didn't understand what happened. I came home from school one day, and then she wasn't there anymore. I was twelve years old. Cal came home, and he backhanded me across my face. I bled as his ring cut my face. He slapped me again and pushed me away. I didn't understand why she didn't come home. I crawled into my room, and sat between the wall and the bed, and cried in silence. I became afraid." Mom was shivering and crying, but she would not look at me. I came in from behind her and eased my arms

14

around her to hug her as mighty as she would let me. So far, she didn't budge; she needed me. I wanted to be there for her.

"He didn't talk to me for days. Aunt Carrie came over and helped me get ready for school, and she was very comfortable in our home. It was weird and made me uncomfortable in the home where I grew up. They took me to see her in the hospital. She was so frail and daunt. I don't know what happened to her. She held my hand and, with tears in her eyes, she told me that she loved me and that I needed to be a brave girl. I didn't understand."

"I'm sorry, Momma, I didn't know. I am so sorry," Shelia said out loud to Madeline. "Valerie, she died the next day. I didn't understand; I don't even think I said goodbye. I miss her so much! It hurts, Valerie, it hurts."

She continued to cry. I could feel the pain. As much as I wanted to cry too, I couldn't. I understood her distance; her cold domineer she shows in her pain. I broke the wall for the moment, and for the first time, I felt comfort from my mother. I held her as tight as I could, and rocked her to sleep.

"I love you, Mom." She may never have heard it, but it existed.

*　*　*　*　*

It is now 1:00 a.m. Todd is still not home. It was now Thursday morning. I got on my bike, put on a warm sweater and headed out. I knew all his spots. I knew where all the girlfriends lived. I went first to the Dunkin Donuts where his friends hang; no Todd. I headed to his make-out spot in Manor Park, all five of them; no Todd. I proceeded to the cute cheerleader's house, and no Todd. I headed to the football field. There he was, sulking in the bleachers. I went over to him and sat next to him.

"You found me, Poker shark. Why are you so wise amongst your years?"

"Just luck, I guess. Why are you sad, Todd?"

"Same reason you are. Just lost myself. Mom wants me to be perfect, my dad doesn't care about me. I have any girl I want. I am killing myself to do good in school. What is next? I'm scared, Valerie."

"I know. It's okay to be scared." I hugged him from the side. "Todd, you can do anything you put your mind to. Don't give up."

"I don't know if I can do it."

"You can."

"You are the best, Valerie; I need you in my life." I smiled. I had my Todd back. He took my bike, put it in the car, and we drove home.

"Night, Poker shark."

"Night, Rockstar."

*   *   *   *   *

That morning, Mom was not too happy to be awake and was a little out of sorts. No one said anything. I made breakfast and a strong coffee for her.

"Ashley, do you need me to pick you up after school today?"

"No."

"Don't you want to pick up those sneakers?"

"The ones you told me I couldn't have? The Nike grey with a pink swoosh?"

"Yes, you have been on your best behavior lately, so good about doing the dishes after meals. You deserve them." She looked out the window as she sipped her coffee, and I slaved over eggs. I felt the dagger in my back.

"YES!" she screamed and ran to hug her.

Those were MY sneakers that I wanted. She knew that. They BOTH knew that. I did her chores most of the time, they both knew that. I felt so hurt. I turned to Todd to stick up for me, but he sulked in his cereal, headphones, and *Sport Illustrated*. He never heard a thing. I was there again, back alone, back to team Valerie; I felt so alone and betrayed for wanting to know more about Cal. I decided to stick up for myself. I was now a team of one.

"Wait, I told you I wanted them, not Ashley."

"Hmm, I am pretty sure it was Ashley. She deserves them, you are bad. You left the house last night in the middle of the night without asking. You are grounded."

"Are you serious? Todd, Todd!" He was ignoring me. My mother continued to look out the window with her coffee, as Ashley hugged her from behind. Now I'm punished for loving my mother, and ignored for saving my brother. Today, I am being punished for being there for my family. What would Madeline do?

I ran upstairs to the attic and pulled out the photos. As I took them out of the box, I scattered them all around the floor. I studied them and hoped I could find some relief and wisdom from looking deep into their eyes. The hurt was low, so shallow. I cried in my haven. I held the pictures to my chest before I placed them before me.

"Love me, Madeline; love me, Cal; I need you," I said to hope I could feel a hug back from them.

*   *   *   *   *

I don't exactly know how Cal and Madeline met. I can't grasp anything other than Madeline had been replaced when she died. Cal was mean to Shelia when she left this world. I guess they both never mourned Madeline's death.

I want to believe it was pre-war, and she played hard to get. I picture Cal being sculpted with a dashing smile. From pictures, I can see his hair slicked back. I bet he would run his fingers through his hair slowly, as he gazed into a lady's eyes. I bet he was hard to chase, but they all tried. I can tell he enjoyed it. I didn't think their seduction went that deep, but I want to picture it as such. I didn't know if there had been another woman, before or after Madeline. I didn't want to believe that there could be. I made up stories; I could feel the emotions. The stories had the same ending.

"It didn't work out." He's push her away.

They would all be mesmerized by his deep, brown eyes. Did he know his power? Was he the confident man I wanted him to be? Maybe he told himself he wasn't good enough, didn't have what she needed; he would just push everyone away. But one thing I didn't want to believe was that he had an affair with someone else.

I tried to place the pictures in chronological order, but as I became frustrated with lack of dates, I just grouped events and timeframes.

My favorite photo was of Cal and Madeline on the beach. Madeline was wearing a 1920s black bathing suit that was a full, one-piece halter top. Her boobs gave perfect cleavage; she wore red lipstick, with her hair up in curls. Cal, with his slicked-back, black hair, had his signature cigarette in his mouth, and trunks. The picture was vague. They must have been just about twenty years old, but I could see his perfect pecks and lines in his stomach. If I were in that time and place, I wanted him to be mine. I couldn't blame Madeline for falling for him.

I laid on the floor in the attic and drown in these pictures—these moments—and tried to feel the memories. I wanted to be Madeline's best friend, a girl at the party; I wanted to be there with them.

"Who are you, Cal?" I asked out loud. I was drawn to concentrate on the pictures grouped around the holidays. I imagined Christmas after they got married. I could see my grandmother cooking a perfect roast with potatoes and green beans. I pictured the fear and horror when Cal went off to war. How Madeline sat at home with her rosary, and prayed for his safe return. I bet he was a bad ass. They would have one child, Shelia, but always wanted more. I believed, by the concerning look in her eyes, that the struggles to have further children were not successful, and left Madeline, at times, in a deep depression. I wanted to have lots of kids to make Madeline happy.

Madeline was in a perfect, lace dress with a red bow in her hair. Her curls just touched her shoulders. She wore Mary Janes with white socks folded over, trimmed with lace to match her dress. Madeline did everything to make Shelia the perfect child. She believed in a white, picket fence. She had no doubt that Donna Reed could do no wrong. She would mimic her every move. Dinner on the table when Cal came home, dressed impeccably, pearls with everything. Every photo, Madeline had pearls on, except for when she was at the beach.

I wanted to feel Madeline. I went downstairs and into Shelia's room. Shelia was on the couch, still working on the evening wine. I found Madeline's pearls hidden in the closet. I took them and wore them with everything. It made me feel close to her. I kept touching them when I needed comfort. They made me feel safe and warm.

I know that Madeline died when my mom was young and didn't get to see through her duty of making Shelia the perfect daughter. Did she regret it? Did Madeline create the person Shelia is today? Is she ashamed of who Shelia has become? Oh, Madeline. How I wish I were your daughter instead.

* * * * *

After hours in the attic, my haven, I heard a noise from downstairs. The curiosity caught my attention. It was at night, maybe about nine-ish. I had missed dinner; no one bothered to call me down, they forgot that I existed.

I went into Shelia's room. She was in bed with Ashley watching TV.

"What are you guys watching?"

"Something you don't like, so beat it," Ashley replied, as she snuggled a little closer to Shelia. "I think I heard Todd come home. Why don't you go see what he is doing? Maybe he wants to play with you?"

Shelia stopped looking at me since the night I spent with her. Each day, she did something to push me away. I sat on the edge of the bed, and I watched Ashley push herself closer to Shelia. Shelia was distant to her, but let her stay. Why wasn't I allowed just to hang out? I held my tears, and with my head bowed down, I walked away.

As I walked down the hallway, I could hear giggling coming from Todd's room. I looked back at Shelia's bedroom and nobody budged. I felt the need to creep slowly as I went to the wide, opened door. The giggles became more profound, and then I heard a moan.

"Oh, Todd!" the voice screamed. I moved to the door and held my hands to the outside door frames to keep from falling in. There was a blonde girl on the bed with her cheerleading uniform opened, and her bra was on the floor. Her breasts were perky and full, and moved gently as Todd had his hand under her skirt playing with her. He was kneeling on the bed with her legs opened before him. His button-down was opened, and the black, argyle sweater I gave him for his birthday was on the floor. I was in shock.

"Todd," I said softly in my head.

"Todd," I said again.

My eyes were big. My world was crumbling.

"Todd," I tried to say again. I held onto the door frames with my nails digging into them.

"Todd!" the blonde screamed and propped herself up with her elbows. She pointed at me. Todd looked and glanced back at her, taking his fingers out of her. Todd put his middle finger into his mouth and slowly pulled it out, and he kicked the door shut in my face. As I was shunned, their giggles continued.

My anxiety and breathing became deep and more profound. I couldn't gasp for breath. My stomach was beating. I think my heart fell into it. I crumbled to my knees as I used the door frame to help me from completely falling and making a loud sound. I was now convulsing. Trying to hold the tears were of no help, but I stayed silent. I curled over my bended knees, my hands on the floor that was dusty and cold. My head was between my knees. I try to gasp for air. My heart was broken. I crawled down the hall into my bedroom that was a faded, lilac color. I went into the far corner and sat on the bed. Nobody could see me. My door was shut. No one cared that I was there. It was safe to cry.

I spent much of that evening in tears, feeling drained from my toes to my fingertips. I needed Cal; I needed Madeline. I wouldn't be able to sleep without them. I tiptoed out of my room. Todd was still behind closed doors. Shelia and Ashley were both fast asleep with the TV static. I shut the TV off and fixed their covers. They never moved. I headed back into the attic with a flashlight, and found my pictures still laid out entirely on the floor where I left them. I took the blanket I kept up there, and wrapped it around myself.

I bowed before them with my hands, touching the bottom of the collage I was piecing together, with my head to the ground.

"Please tell me that you love me. Someone, please tell me that they love me." Tears streamed down my face. I didn't move. The daylight came. I was faced down to not see it. These pictures were my hug, my bond. I could relate to these faces. The "so-called" family I had now was physically close, but, emotionally, so far away. I turned my head, and the memories came back to me from birth. I could see flashes of lights. I could see the dance floor. I could hear the laughter. I could see you. I reached out my hand and there you were, so close to me, but not close enough to touch.

"Who are you? I miss you."

"I miss you. Who are you? Come to me," he replied. We laid on the floor and the flashes of light continued.

"Come with me," I repeated back. The flashes became brighter, the noise was loud. *What does he look like again?* I reached out my hand, and he reached back.

"I will follow you anywhere."

Then he was gone. I was left there on the attic floor with my dreams of Madeline and Cal, the memories of you. *Oh, I can't wait to find you.* I held my hands on the photos, and as the day broke, I was just at a beginning level of REM. I felt a chill in the air that doesn't usually rise in our attic. Soon after, a feather came falling from above and landed on my hands. I lifted my head, and saw it perfectly placed at the center of my hand. It was beautiful. It was red and had an energetic amount of bounce. It was a hug from Madeline. I could feel it. It was my prayer answered.

"Thank you, Madeline. I love you too."

*　　*　　*　　*　　*

I turned myself around, had my back on the floor, and was able to close my eyes. I held the feather, and the picture of Madeline and Cal at the beach, in my hand; it was my favorite. It was before Madeline died, before Shelia was born, before Cal's affectionate connection with Aunt Carrie. It was how I wanted to remember them. With my eyes closed, I smiled and placed myself in her shoes. Madeline wore a feather boa as Cal took her to a speakeasy during their courting session. She smoked a cigarette from a long, black stem and with her lipstick and pearls; she drank the moonshine they served and danced until dawn. Cal would be in a tan suit, with a fedora hat and a cigar. He had well-polished shoes, and showed them off on the dance floor. I bet they were spectacular. I could feel the twirls as they moved; I could feel his fingertips slide off hers. I could feel her fall into his arms as he caught her from a long spin. There was music and glasses clinking, and laughter, tons of laughter. *Oh, how I wish I knew you then.*

The morning light surprised them as they walked outside. He held her hand, and opened her car door. He drove her home, begged for a kiss, and she blow one into the air. *Oh, Cal, how I feel your desire for lust.*

My dream was abruptly broken by a kick to my shins. I woke up, startled. Ashley stood over me.

"Why are you up here? What are you doing? You are going to be late for soccer, LOSER!" She made her quick turn, and walked away— so proud of herself.

I looked at my watch. I WAS going to be late for soccer; I needed to win this game. I grabbed the feather, and picture of Cal and Madeline at the beach, and ran downstairs. I hid them perfectly under my mattress, and changed into my soccer clothes. I grabbed an apple as I was heading out the door. I bravely asked the question, "Mom, are you going to come to my game today?" I waited for the long pause for almost a minute.

"Don't call me Mom," she responded. I walked out the door. I got on my bike and took a deep breath; it became my leaving-the-house ritual to cleanse away pain from all of them.

"Valerie!" I heard a voice from down the street.

"We are going to be late!" Chase said, as he rode toward me.

"Let's go!"

I first met Chase on the soccer field during lunchtime a few years ago. We both were just swapped for the game as forwards. He was on one side; I was on the other. After a few rounds, the halfback passed the ball up to Chase, we made eye contact. Time stood still at that moment. I spoke to him just by my looking into his eyes.

"Pass to me; I can make it past him and score," I said to myself, but directly at Chase. He nodded.

Chase dribbled the ball and kicked it in my direction. I did the fake out to their defense, dropped up to the goal, and kicked into the far-left corner.

"score!"

"Ah, man, I didn't see that coming," said the sad, defensive player. I felt so good. I turned away from everyone. As I turned back, the aide blew her whistle. It was time to head back to class. Chase stood across the field and stared at me. I stood across the field and stared at him. Kids ran through us and around us, but we didn't move. I felt his stare was strong and familiar. It was so real. It was a hug I wanted, and needed. Even if it wasn't physical, it was there. As the field became empty, he walked to me and offered a high five.

"Nice score!"

"Thanks," I said reluctantly. I couldn't find the words I was feeling. It was the warmth that I needed. Chase was an adorable ten-year-old. Black hair with green eyes, he had a bright smile, wore a fisherman's cap and a striped, collared shirt.

"I'm Chase."

"Valerie," I replied as we walked back to class.

"I'm new here; I think you live down my street. I've seen you on your bike. Maybe we can ride to school together?" Chase said to me. A window opened, a light came through—a friend I wanted and needed. We joined the soccer team together that season, and played together ever since.

The day of our big playoff game, Chase and I would tag team. We were the best in our division, the best players in our league, and we scored the most goals. Together. Chase and I became our team within the team. We were hard to touch. Chase was the cutest boy in the fourth grade; I was just a dorky kid. I felt like most people looked straight through me, the same way Shelia did. His fan club sat on the edge of our turf, if they weren't on the opposing team. It was cold, the fog was still rising from the morning air. I could see my breath as I exhaled. I probably wasn't dressed warm enough, but I didn't care. I couldn't feel much, but the shin guards were sticking to my legs from the sweat our bike ride created. My coach approached me and Chase with a playlist for the game. He had his winning coach face on; he wanted to win. I always approached the game seriously. When I was in the game, I was present. We looked through his playlist and discussed the other team.

"Valerie, you are tall. You can block Mark while Chase makes his way up the field. Chase, you can get around Maria when she goes in to play defense. When she is in, you take the ball." We nodded and stayed focused. I stared at the ground and mentally prepared for the game. My arms were crossed and my uniform intact. We had no other option, but to win.

"Chase, how are you feeling on your running today? Does your leg still hurt?"

"No, I'm good. I'm ready for this."

At that moment, I stopped listening, and just took the moment to smell the fog and the wet grass. The fog was breaking. The sun was peeking its way through the clouds. I could feel the sunshine and the power it brought us. My ponytail was tight. My game face was on. My family was nowhere in sight, just like every other game. I was ready for this.

"Valerie, is your mother here?" my coach asked. He liked her, but never had the guts to ask her out after his own marriage crumbled.

"No," I responded, without looking up. I walked down the line of the field. A mom came up and rubbed black tar on my face to help my eyes from the sun.

"Go get 'em, girl!" she said as I kept walking. The game started. I stayed out the first quarter. The coach knew me; I needed to study my prey and learn their plays, so that I could strategize the rest of the game. Chase stayed out the second, so if we got stuck, we could both pick up the slack in the third and fourth. Just as predicted, Maria could not figure out Chase's moves. He instantly scored. Straight from midfield kick off, he dribbled down the field, faked her out, and boom. Score: 1-0.

The second quarter came fast; I was ready. The other team did have some new moves, but I knew how to do fake outs, left and right. As soon as I learned their favored side, I moved mine. I didn't want to score right away; I wanted it to last and linger a bit, have them relax a bit, and head in for the kill. Five minutes left in the quarter, and it was time. Boom, one in. Score: 2-0. Why not go for another? Corner shot, boom. Score: 3-0. Halftime.

Chase's Mom came over to me on the sidelines and asked, "Valerie, where is your mom?" She had a concern in her voice, but she knew that Shelia didn't come to any of my games. I gave her a look. I didn't want Shelia to ruin my game-head, my moment, especially since she wasn't here to do it for herself.

"Shelia? Oh, she's not coming," I said with my body focused on the game.

"I am sorry, I forgot. I will take some photos of you guys for her. Chase, come over. Stand together." *Click, click, click.* I regrouped myself, and then Shelia started to pop into my head.

She is not here; your mother is not here. Don't call her Mom, I repeated over and over in my head. I couldn't stop.

Shake it off. I told myself to break the cycle. I walked in a circle, yelling at myself to let her go. All I could see in my head was her lying in bed with a bottle of vodka, staring at the wall instead of watching me. I was hurt, I could no longer deny it.

"Valerie, let's go. We are getting started," my coach screamed at me. I wasn't ready, but I went in. Third quarter, my game was off. Chase was concerned and tried to pick up the slack. Score: 3-2.

"Valerie, what is wrong with you!" Chase came over to me, during a break for a crying kid who couldn't handle his head-butt. He laid his hands on my shoulders and got in close to my face.

"This isn't you. Are you okay?"

I needed to shake this. As I looked into his eyes, they calmed me. I took a few, deep breaths. His touch was warming. His approach to me made all the other girls jealous. I suddenly felt okay.

"I'm good; I am all right."

"Awesome," he said and smiled. We got back into the game. We needed to win.

The quarter was over, the fourth began. As we started, the opposition put in an aggressive player. We knew he was put into battle to intimidate Chase. Immediately, he took a kick aggressively toward me. I was strong enough to stop it, and drag it as far to the other side of the field. Then he grabbed it back. We needed to change our tactic. After a few moments, I could tell he was our challenge; then he scored another point. Who was this guy? We could not lose this game. My coach called a timeout and put me in defense. Chase was on his own. It was brutal to watch from behind. I would scream at him.

"Left, Chase. Watch your right side. Chase, heads-up!" and there it was: BOOM! Chase was on the ground. The whistle blew. All the players had to stay in place and drop to the floor. I stood with my arms crossed and watched. I prayed, "Please, God, let him be okay. Let Chase be okay."

His mom ran onto the field. He was bleeding. The ambulance came, and they put him on the stretcher. I broke the rules and ran over to him as they carried him. As I walked with them, I held his hand. We didn't need to speak, as we did through our eyes. We both held in our feelings. He had to let go of my hand. He looked at me and nodded his head with a yes.

I stared at the ambulance as it pulled away. I stood brave. When I was ready, I turned around and ran back to the game. The field was silent, and people were watching me, as I came back, wondering what I would do. I stopped to look at all of them; I was ready. I had vengeance in my eyes. I was angry. I wanted to win.

"Valerie," my coach said as he came over to me.

"Valerie, are you all right? Can you still play?"

"Put me in. Let's do this." The coach waved to the ref. The crowd gave a low clap. Then the silence started.

We had three minutes left. As soon as it started, they scored: 3-3. I moved my position to halfback. I looked into Carmela's eyes; I told her to follow my lead. She was scared and nervous. Chase and I usually held up the game. But, she did it; I coached her as we ran down the field. The big bully player who hurt Chase stood in my way. I came up to him and did my best fake out to play off his other side. He went left, I went right, and did a tripod to spin the ball around. He fell to the ground. I went into clear view of the goal. The crowd was screaming and cheering. Just like that, I scored the goal and won the game. The whistle blew. The game was over. Score: 4-3. I laid on my back, breathing heavily, enjoying the cheers from above. I needed that.

We cheered. We lined up to the opposing team and instead of a handshake we slapped high fives and had to wish the other team a good game. We took winning pictures. We got trophies. I thought of Chase the whole time. When it was time to go home, I headed for our bikes, and Ashley was standing there. I stopped in my tracks and just looked at her. She was sitting on my bike, waiting for me; this was my moment, and so unfair for her to come and ruin it. I walked toward her to grab our bikes and head home.

"Great game, Valerie," she said.

"You watched the game?"

"Yes."

"Why?"

"I knew it was a big deal, so I wanted to see it. Everyone at school will be talking about it. You are a hero." Was she serious? Did she care about me? I didn't even see her at the game. Why was she here? I unlocked Chase's bike, then mine, where Ashley sat.

"I need to take Chase's bike home; can you ride mine back?" I asked, afraid that I may never see my bike again.

"Yeah, I can ride with you," she said very willingly; she must have wanted something.

We started the ride in silence, and I was reluctant to say anything. Ashley talked most of the time and gave me highlights of the game in shocking excitement. It was the most we had ever spoken that I can think of.

"Ah man, Val, when you looked him in the eye, that crazy move, then scored—that was so awesome! He was so embarrassed. Who is he, anyway? Is he too old to even play?" She went on and on as I replayed the events in my head. It was great to hear her enthusiasm. For that brief few minutes on the way home, I liked Ashley.

When we hit our house, Ashley was riding my bike and stopped. I headed down to Chase's house to drop his off. I went to his house to see who was home. His sister, who was Todd's age, came to meet me in the kitchen.

"How is he?" I asked.

"I am waiting to hear from my mom, again, but he might just need a few stitches. I didn't see the game. Did you win?"

"We did," I said with a smile. I was proud of myself. She gave me a hug that made me feel special.

"I will check back later." As I left, she screamed.

"Thank you, Valerie! I am so happy you won!"

I smiled the whole way home. I felt accomplished. I felt good. I felt that Ashley and I might be friends. I entered the kitchen side door. Shelia stood there with my dad, Tom, and Ashley. I wasn't expecting him.

"Valerie, aren't you going to say hello to your father?"

Shelia was smiling; he was smiling. Ashley was smiling; this couldn't be good. Ashley knew all along that Tom was here. That is why she wanted to be so "friendly." I couldn't react. I didn't know how to. As soon as I tried to speak, Todd came in the door and stepped right in front of me.

"Why are you here? Bastard!"

He walked away, and didn't even wait for an answer. I watched Todd run up the stairs. I wanted to follow him. But I didn't understand why my Father was a bastard. I turned as everyone looked at me.

"Hi," I said to Tom. We pretended we never saw Todd at all.

"Let's go to dinner, you and me. What do you say?"

"I can't, I mean I want to, but . . . Chase is in the hospital. Can I go see him?"

"Valerie, Chase's mom called me from the hospital. He is going to be fine. She said you played a great game; I'm so proud of you," Shelia answered in a loving, motherly voice. *Oh, wait, don't call her Mom. Why is she suddenly sooo happy for me?*

"You can go and see him when you get back from dinner. Tom, you don't mind taking her, do you?"

"Of course, Shelia. Valerie, shall we?" He offered his arm for me to bend into.

"Can I change first?"

"Oh yes, dear, I am sorry. Go right ahead." I ran upstairs and into the shower. When I got out and looked into the mirror, the black tar was smeared all down my face and into my eyes. I looked evil; I felt evil coming over me. I took a hard look into that mirror, and told the evil to go away. I was angry that Shelia and Ashley were nice to me; Todd was angry that Tom was here. I felt the anger coming in deep, but I continued to push it away. As the tar dripped down the drain, the feeling I stared down into the mirror also faded. I put on my favorite jeans, my blue, striped Gap t-shirt, and headed out. As I walked out of my room, I caught eyes with Todd who was sitting on his bed. I went over to him.

"Can we play cards tonight?" I asked, since today I was brave.

"Yeah, let's do that. Heard you had a good game today; that's awesome, Poker shark. You are the talk of the town."

"Yeah? How did you hear?"

"We drove by and watched a few minutes. My girlfriend's sister is on the other team. Even though she went home crying, she did say you seriously rocked it. Nice job, kid."

"Thank you, Todd." He gave me a high five; I turned to head out. Todd grabbed his guitar and started to play a soft tune he made up. I stayed to hear him for a few. As I was leaving Todd's room, we heard a huge crash outside, in front of the house like crushed metal. Todd and I rushed to the window.

"Thanks, Ashley," I said as I saw it. My bike had been run over in our driveway by someone backing up to do a three-point turn. My favorite BMX, a Haro original. A hand-me-down from Todd. I went downstairs and tried not to let it ruin my joy. Not to give Ashley the accomplishment or joy. Once again, she hurt me.

"Okay, Tom, I'm ready!"

"Great, let's go! Goodbye, Shelia. Goodbye, Ashley. BYE, TODD!" he screamed. "Don't call me Tom, please call me Dad."

After I paused for a bit, I said, "I will try, but Shelia won't let me call her Mom; I don't even know you as Dad," I said to him.

"She won't let you call her Mom? Why?" He was upset by this statement.

"I don't know," I replied.

"Oh, Shelia." He seemed upset by what he just heard.

We went to Tung Hoy in its new location on Boston Post Rd. and Richbell. I hated Chinese food, and as much as I thought everyone knew that, I also remembered that no one cared what I liked and didn't like. He insisted we went there as he said, "Val, there is no good Chinese in LA like there is in New York." So I agreed on something I had no self-knowledge on. I was unaware when Tom was coming into town, as he just popped in and out. He would claim that it was all about work. I didn't know. I didn't know him. It was just dinner, and someone who wanted to talk to me. I couldn't take that house; I couldn't take Chase being hurt. I can't enjoy my victory. I won a trophy. In return, I lost my favorite bike. I needed this moment; right now, I needed Tom.

"Table for two," Tom said to the maître d. He escorted us to a booth in the middle of the dining room.

"I hope you are comfortable here. This is our best table. Great game today, Valerie!" He also touched my shoulder and was excited, as excited as I was.

"Thank you," we both said at the same time.

30

"Ms. Maher, I am impressed. At ten years old, you are well-known. Your mother never told me this," Tom said.

"Shelia, I'm not allowed to call her Mom," I reminded him.

"Yes, sorry, Shelia. My apologies." We ordered everything on the menu that my dad, Tom, liked. Pu-pu platter, scallion pancakes, Szechuan chicken, garlic shrimp—I didn't care. He was so excited to be here. I was happy to not be at home with Shelia and Ashley.

"Hey, Valerie, nice game." It was a few boys from the other team. I said my thank you, and they went on their way.

"My, my, Valerie, great soccer player, boys. What is next? You are very popular; your mother—excuse me, Shelia, did not tell me about this game other than it was a scrimmage. I didn't need to go. What is this all about?"

"It was the championship game; we won. We won the season. I WON THE SEASON. With Chase." He could tell by my face that I was upset and annoyed. I looked down into my egg drop soup.

"Valerie, she really didn't tell me it was the championship. I came from California to see you, not waste time with her in the kitchen. I am so sorry you are hurt. What else is she not telling me?" I suddenly felt him become my ally. As we continued eating, course by course, I was thinking about Chase.

Are you okay, are you okay, are you okay? I asked him in my head.

I am fine; I am home now, he answered.

"I really want to go see Chase after dinner. He is home now."

"How do you know?"

"I just do." We got through dinner. My anxiety raced him to finish his green tea ice cream; then Tom graciously took me to Chase's house. He was on the couch with bandages on his face. He looked tired. I sat next to him and we high-fived.

"Tell me how it ended. I heard it was awesome."

"It was. I crushed it. That dumb ass kid fell to the ground. It was epic."

He smiled. We sat there as our parents talked in the kitchen.

"All right, Val, it's time to go," Tom said from the kitchen. I said my goodbye with a hug, and went on my way. Today was a good day.

*   *   *   *   *

Todd went off to Bucknell College. He called very rarely. He didn't always come home on breaks. Eventually, we didn't see or hear from Todd at all. He became a faded memory.

I still spent endless hours in the attic, dreaming and praying to Cal and Madeline. I laid on the floor and pictured pieces of their life together. Cal would come home from work in his green work pants and a white tee shirt; Madeline, making dinner for him and having it ready on the table as he came up the driveway. He gave her a kiss on the cheek; she blushed. But behind their closed doors, they spent endless nights in the same bed, alone. They listened to snores that kept each other awake, and did not say a word. They lost their passion. When she got that peck on the cheek, she remembered the passionate days before Shelia came into their life. Madeline struggled with the loneliness, and hoped that one day, he would grab her by the waist and turn her around, kiss her against the fridge, and pull himself closer to her. Maybe if her noise had been loud enough. If he could hear how she felt inside. When he came in for that daily peck he could hear what she was desiring. But for now, Cal didn't. She waited another twenty-four hours for that routine encounter again.

I was sad for Madeline, and sometimes could feel how Cal stopped looking at her the way he used to. I hugged her photos, and hoped that she could feel me through them. *Oh, Madeline, if you only knew how I understand your pain. If you only knew.* As I got up that night to go back into my bedroom, I caught a glimpse of something falling in the air. It was a small feather from a bird off the pond. It was Madeline; she heard me.

It was another Saturday in Larchmont, close to Christmas; the cold air became thicker, the clothes became heavier. Each day, I awoke to a warzone of three women in the same house, with two women who had each other, and one that was in it alone. Most of the torture from Ashley was juvenile. It was hair pulling, or ripping the laces out of my sneakers and hiding them. Or it was cutting my favorite sweatshirt, taking out all the tape from my favorite cassettes, or the famous sticking out of the tongue. But today, this Saturday before Christmas, my boiling point rose—my heart was filled with hatred. My game was about to change.

I was out with Chase and some other friends, and came home to the smell of smoke. I called out in the house.

"Shelia! Ashley! Shelia! Ashley!" No answers.

I raced into each room to find where the smoke was coming from, and could feel some heat from upstairs. They were not in their rooms, or bathrooms. No sign of where the smoke was coming from either. As I turned past my room, the door between my bedroom and Todd's room, I found where the trail of smoke had started. It was the attic door, the haven I had built—the home I shared with Madeline and Cal. In my head, I heard a voice telling me not to go up there. But I opened the door and followed the smoke to a small fire that stood in the middle of the floor. I ran down the stairs, covered my face with a wet towel, found the fire extinguisher, and put it out. I saved our attic, our home, our lives from being destroyed; but I couldn't save the photographs of Madeline and Cal. Their memories and dreams were gone. I screamed in rage.

That night, after the fire department left, Shelia and Ashley came back from their day at the mall. We were all back in the house as three women, who were a bond of two, and an outsider of one. The anger from both sides grew heavier than ever. I was shaking from the anger I had in my heart. I didn't send out accusations; I didn't expect thank yous. I gave them both silence. They gave the same amount of rage back. We retired for the evening—my haven was gone. I had no choice but to go to my room. As I stood at the door, across the hall, Shelia and Ashley stood together in Shelia's bedroom doorway. As I turned, we stared down at each other.

"Tomorrow, you are getting on a plane and going to live with Tom," Shelia said sternly and without a flinch.

The powerful stare reminded me of my first moments in my crib—in my prison. The prison cell never moved, the guard was the same. The inmates were still here. Except for one that escaped. Now, make that two. I gave the long, unflinching stare back at them and slammed the door. As Shelia still stood there, she yanked on her pearls so tightly they broke. I could hear them crash and sprawl across the floor. I could hear them dance around, skipping down the stairs, flying through the railing. It went on for several seconds, and then they settled on the floor.

My heart was beating so loudly that my ears joined in on the pounding, and became red. I stood at the back of that door I just slammed, and held my hands on it. I could feel the heat coming from across the hallway. I held my head down, and as quietly as possible, I let the tears run down my face until I had enough strength to get myself to move away from them. The night turned dark, and as the light was just about to come up, I looked around the room and decided what I wanted to bring with me. Mostly nothing mattered to me anymore. I grabbed a bag, some underwear, my favorite guess jeans with the zippers, my Rugby shirt, and my picture of Cal and Madeline, along with the red feather under my bed. I took all the cash I had stashed away, and my favorite Beastie Boys tape that I had just rebought after Ashley pulled the tape out of my original copy. I wore my loafers and favorite scrunchie. I packed what was left of my makeup and favorite hairbrush. Putting the bag down, I went into Shelia's room, where she and Ashley slept together. I made sure they were properly tucked in. I went into Ashley's room, went to the other side of the bed, grabbed the pink and grey Nike's, and shoved them into my bag. I went downstairs and stood by the backdoor in the kitchen with my packed bag standing next to me. I called to Chase in my head.

Chase, I need you, Chase come over. Chase, Chase, Chase. It was after 6:00 a.m. The sun was breaking. I watched my breath on the glass door. Moments later, a bike pulled up. Chase was standing on the other side of the glass. I stood up and opened the door.

"What's up? What is going on? Why do you have a bag packed?" He was out of breath as he spoke, and held his hand to his chest. He came to sit down next to me on the cold, kitchen floor.

"I'm going to live with Tom. Shelia is kicking me out." I couldn't look at him; I couldn't bear to see him at that moment. He stayed silent and leaned his head on my shoulder.

"You can't go." He abruptly stood up. "You can't go. Just come and live with us." The thought was entertaining, but living so close to them, the horrible, cold energy would always still be down the street. My heart knew I needed to get out of here, and through that fire, I could see the path I needed to be on.

"I need you, Valerie," Chase said to me.

I needed him too. I don't know what our attraction meant, but I needed him. We hugged and hugged stronger. "Can your mom take me to the airport this afternoon?"

"Yes, absolutely." I went to his house. His mom fed me, gave me kisses, and brushed away her tears. She was such a loving, warm woman; his whole family was. We got into the car and drove to JFK. I sat in the front seat. I could see, through the rearview mirror, Chase tearing up and making himself stop; it only turned his face red. I had no emotion; my life went up in flames. Now I had nothing to lose. The confusion of emotions suddenly became a turn of excitement. I almost wanted to smile. As we pulled up to the side of the terminal, my escort was found, my ticket was printed, my bag was whisked away. I gave hugs to Chase's mom, to his sister, and finally to Chase. We held hands, and our foreheads touched.

"I will keep listening for you to talk to me in the middle of the night. I love you, Valerie."

My tears came out, and ran down my face. My stomach dropped from all the pain and anger I was holding. For this moment, I held onto Chase, touching his fingertips to mine, smelling him for the last time in a long time. I took that moment to be with him.

"I love you," I said so low under my breath, but I said it. I don't think I ever said that to anyone before Madeline and Cal. He gave me his hat, and the escort held my hand and took me to my plane. I looked back for as long as I could, until they became dots in the background.

"So, is that your boyfriend?" Irma asked me as she was escorting me to my plane.

"I don't know," I replied in disbelief, and just not understanding what just happened. I did LOVE him, but in what way? Was it to fall in love? Was it as a brother? Or was it just as a friend? I just didn't get it.

"I don't know," I said again. I just was so confused; this was so complicated for me in this moment.

"Okay, I am sorry, I am prying. Are you excited to see your dad?"

She kept trying. She was warm and sweet; instantly, I could tell she meant no harm.

"Yes and no." I wasn't sure.

This was a lot to process for me all at once. I was emotionless for so many years, and mentally challenged by Shelia and Ashley for so long, it was difficult to believe that something good was happening. When I was told to leave, I was being punished for my haven being destroyed. It made no sense to me. I wanted to see Tom; I wanted to know what he was about. I wanted to be away from Shelia and Ashley. Was this my "get out of jail free" card?

"I am just not sure," I said out loud.

"Well, Valerie, your dad must really love you. He booked a last-minute ticket, first class. You must be someone special." I didn't know what that meant, but it was something. My dad gave me something in my time of need. I didn't know what that meant, but it felt good. I was never on a plane before, had never been to LA, never outside of my Sound Shore community; I was craving for something else, something new, something . . .

Irma said goodbye to me as she left me tucked into my first-class seat to LAX. I was scared; I was comforted by the stewardess. I was offered a milkshake. It was fabulous. We took off. I said goodbye to NY through my window. I sat back and looked at the clouds, and felt I was close to heaven. Maybe Cal and Madeline could hear me from up here.

"Thank you, thank you, thank you," I repeated over and over.

I awoke to a full meal on nice china and silverware; I was hungry. Shelia didn't cook many meals for us over the past few years. I drank real coke, and ate a fancy burger. I started to devour it until I almost made myself sick. I enjoyed a hot towel with lemon that I wasn't quite sure was for.

After the milkshake, the burger, the extra fries, and some cookies, the lights were dimmed in mid-flight. I sat back in my reclined chair, snuggled up in a blanket and pillow, and closed my eyes.

"I think I am going to be okay," I said to myself, and shortly after, a voice came into my head and said, "You will be."

"Thank you."

We landed. The air was suddenly different. I sat in my seat until my escort came to pick me up. *Will Tom be mad at me? Will he scold me? Will he understand what happened, or take their side?* I didn't know what I was about to encounter. Until I saw him, I was braced for new pain and discomfort.

When I got off the plane, Tom was waiting there for me. He had a wide smile and opened his arms to me as we made eye contact. I did have a sense of excitement at that moment; I ran faster to get to him. As I got into his arms, I hesitated from a force within me.

"Come here, Valerie," he said. I went in for the hug. The warmth and comfort took over. I was able to let go of the intense pain in my body. I started to sob. He just held me tighter.

"I didn't do it, I promise," I said into his chest.

"I know you didn't; it was time to go. Whose mother tells her child she can't call her Mom? She is not well. I pray for her. You will be good here, I promise." We made promises at that moment that weren't said out loud. We promised to believe and trust in each other, to look out for each other, and to love each other. I needed Tom. He needed me.

We drove up the coast to a house that faced the beach, off a mountain. I didn't know much about what Tom did, but whatever he did, he must've been good at it.

We walked into the house. I looked up and around and kept moving forward until I eventually walked into a table. Tom laughed, then offered to show me around. I was drawn to the sound and crashing of the ocean below us. He started to take me on a tour. I veered away, walking out to the porch. I felt the sunset on me, and the ocean smacking the ground splashed an ocean spray on my face. I felt at home. Tom understood the draw and stood behind me, watching all the glory he already decided to have when he bought this house.

"We can do the tour later," he said as he brought me a coke to enjoy the moment in silence together.

That night, he took me to someone else's house that was just a few blocks inland. As we pulled up to the house, a woman came outside to greet us with a smile, wiping her hands with a dish towel as she came running from her kitchen. You could see her white smile and wavy blonde hair. She was older. Her lines defined her beauty.

"Perfect timing, Tom!" she said loudly, before we got out of the car.

"I just took the pie out of the oven. The kitchen smells so good! Hello, Valerie, I am so excited to meet you. Tom, you told me she was pretty, but you didn't say gorgeous!"

She had so much to say, and before I knew it, she drew me in for a hug. As we embraced, Tom introduced us. "Valerie, this is my girlfriend, Brenda."

"Hello," I said and offered a smile. Her house was also big and fabulous. We sat outside on the porch with Chinese lanterns to light our dinner experience. They drank white wine. We had roasted chicken and green beans with rice.

They told stories of trips they had been on, and talked about long walks on the beach. When they spoke to each other, they always looked into each other's eyes and smiled. Occasionally, they touched each other's hand on the table; that touch became a hand on the lap; then it became a long rub across each other's backs. Next, they got lost in this moment. They forget I was at the table. Their gaze and giggles continued.

It was nice to watch people in love, yearning for each other, not noticing anyone else around them. But to me, these people sitting across from me were still strangers. I was still here, alone.

I picked up the plate, cleared the rest of the table, cleaned the dishes, poured them more wine, and sat inside by the window in her living room, listening to the silence of the ocean in the distance, with the wind chimes slowly playing a ballad in the background. I closed my eyes on her couch and fell asleep.

We spent my first Christmas in California at Brenda's house. I met their friends and some relatives. Time with Tom and Brenda was fun, warming, loving. It felt good. I needed them.

I went to a Catholic school and had to wear a uniform. I wore my loafers with EG socks. My hair was, at school, a perfect pony-tail. Here I joined the swim team and became a cheerleader. I made friends, went to football games, to bonfires on the beach. Besides all the fun California had to offer, I always make sure I talked to Chase in my head at night.

School was different here, stricter than mine in New York. We had lots of homework; the expectation was to be very interactive in each class, daily. I thrived on learning and wanted to be like Tom—have a good job, make a lot of money, be powerful, and not need con-firmation from anyone. He would teach me how to play golf, tennis, chess, tighten up my poker game, and eventually, how to smoke a cigar properly. He was in California and would say, "The only thing that changes from being a New Yorker is a love for Chardonnay."

We went to the club and played twilight golf on the nights I didn't have swimming or have cheerleading practices. Tom made me take lessons until I became good enough to play full rounds, and even had me pair up with some of his friends. I would enter into amateur contests and win. Each time, Tom and I would get a little closer. He was strict. Made sure that I had strong goals, and that I stuck to them. I enjoyed the structure, and had my eye on the prize.

Brenda took me to lunches, at the Beverly Hills hotel, and laughed at overly trendy people who just seemed ridiculous, and at famous people who wanted to pretend they didn't want to be seen. I learned from Brenda and Tom that having money didn't make you something. It was knowing how to use it. How to save it. How to make proper investments. How you didn't have to flaunt it. Money was personal; it was an accomplishment, it was power, it was arro-gance, it was personal. As much as they taught me the way not to abuse money, they understood the game field. She took me to get the right clothes, and the right shoes to fit.

"She needs to be a California girl, Tom," Brenda said as we walked in the door with bags and bags of clothes, and Tom ready to open his mouth. She knew how to work her eyes without saying a word to him. She knew how to make him smile. As I studied her, I wanted to learn her tricks and learn how to win a man as strong and confident as Tom.

After school, I looked forward to swim practice. The girls loved to gossip and included me in their group; I never had that before.

"Valerie, what kind of boys do you like?" Kellie asked me, as we stood in our wetsuits, waiting for the next race to begin.

I never thought much about that before. But, as she asked me, my eye caught a small feather flying through the air in the setting sun. I concentrated on that feather as it touched the ground, and in my head was the first time I was introduced to the man in my heart. There he stood, about six-foot-one, arms folded, dirty blonde/brown hair, arms crossed, wearing a dark suit. He had a smirk on his face, wore a big watch, and right there, in that moment, he stole my heart. I could feel him and remember sitting on the dancefloor with some-one in a previous life. Right there, I knew it was him.

"I like a man in a suit, who is powerful and demanding. I want him to be charming and witty, sarcastic and mesmerizing," I answered her, as he stood as a mirage to me within that corner of the sun going down.

That was the man in my heart. It would be hard for anyone else to compare. I couldn't lose my focus on his image as I wanted to memorize everything about him. *Would he be my future? The father of my children? My husband to be? The man that would drive me crazy for the rest of my life and probably lives to come?* The whistle blew. The image went away. Today, made me happy I needed him.

My first school dance was coming up. I didn't want anyone to know that I was excited. I talked to Kellie about who was going, what everyone was wearing, and who everyone wanted to dance with. As I didn't have much time to prepare for such an event, I wasn't sure who I wanted to dance with. My eye was on my big goals, and I didn't have short-term ones yet.

"No one?" Kellie said.

"I don't know enough people yet! I am not sure who they all are."

"Oh, then this can be fun. We are going to introduce you!" Girls being nice to me will forever make me nervous.

With only days away, I wanted to be prepared. I still had trust issues. I hesitated on who I should turn to. My heart lead me to Brenda. That night, I gave her a call and explained about the dance. With excitement, she told me, "Valerie, I will take care of everything."

That Saturday came, and at 10:00 a.m., Brenda pulled up in her perfect convertible, as Tom and I watched her from the kitchen window with our breakfast beverages. She was giggly; Tom was nervous to let me go. We blasted down the twists and turns off of the California mountainside, and into the city of LA where we had valet parking. We were handed luxury spa drinks as our bags were taken from us, to hide in their own fancy space. We were whisked away to a room full of mirrors and chairs. Brenda waved. One man told me everything was going to be fabulous. I was given a magazine to read while I had people spend some serious time putting my hair in tin foil. Then I sat under a heated lamp. My nails were painted, and my toenails too. I had someone put makeup on me, and once my hair was cooked, it was perfectly dried. There I was—a California girl. I almost didn't recognize myself. I had to study what I looked like, so the next time I looked in the mirror, I would know who I was.

"I'm a blonde," I said.

"Oh yes, dear, you are in California now! You needed to lose that New York, dark hair. Boys like blondes!"

We entered the gymnasium that was set up for the typical school dance, with streamers, a DJ, and teachers standing at the wall, pretending to care, but checking their watches. The girls were on one side, and the boys were on the other, trying to be brave. Circles started to form. Not everyone was comfortable enough to dance, but it slowly became just jumping, holding someone's hand.

Kellie whispered in my ear, pointing out to cute boys as they came in clear vision. She had her eye on someone. After a few songs, we all jumped out as a group, and they went to stand together at the back wall. I stood in a circle of students jumping, but I was looking for someone specific, someone to match the man in my head. I pictured who he was at my age. Would he be at this dance? Is he dancing with someone else? Somewhere else? Then I laid eyes on him: Mitchel.

He was tall—check.

He had brown hair—check.

He had a dazzling smile—check.

He had brown eyes—it wasn't him.

We locked eyes. Although he wasn't the man in my head, he was a very close stand-in. I shied from his look. As I looked down, he didn't stop looking at me. I waved nervously; he came over. We held hands. Our smiles became bigger. I wished that I could be brave enough to kiss him, but I wasn't. My face was red; so was his. After we jumped in a group together for a few songs, we went to move over to the wall to talk. We didn't say much. He played soccer; I told him about my big game in fourth grade. He thought that I was cool. We talked about other stuff, but I wasn't listening at all. He was so cute and delicious, but he wasn't the man in my head. I wanted to be with a man, not a boy, and felt as if I waited forever. He touched the side of my face. I leaned into his hand, so I could feel his finger with my lips. I took off the lanyard bracelet I made that summer. It was blue and yellow, and it had fancy stitching that intertwined, almost braid-like. It was my masterpiece, but I wanted him to have it. I took it off and brought his wrist to my chest. His hand was sweaty. My hands shook. I tied it on his wrist, and slowly brought his hand down; I leaned on him as close as I was brave enough to. We were both nervous. Both young and naive. Both having no experience of what we were doing. I leaned in and I felt his breath. I touched his shoulder. I gave him a kiss. I wished for it. I prepared for it. I stayed focused. It happened. It was like the piece of heaven I expected, but better.

* * * * *

As high school was all business, Tom reminded me to stay focused on my goals, and what I really wanted. It was as if we had a business arrangement. We went to mass every Sunday and taught me to stay loyal to the Lord above. He made me keep a vision wall in my room as there were things I wanted short-term. I needed to stay focused on the big picture. I wanted to be a strong and confident woman; I wanted a powerful job that paid nice money. I wanted a husband who fit the man in my head, who stood tall, wearing a dark suit with his hands folded. I needed to be a good golfer, a strong athlete, someone who was well-rounded in arts and fine food. That is someone he would want me to be in return.

"Practice and focus," Tom continually said to me. We ran daily before the sun came up. We prayed each morning, each meal, and each evening before we retired for the day. We stayed at the golf range until closing, until I could hit perfectly straight. I took lessons regularly. Tom was at my side with the continuous push of, "Again." And, "Move your stance to the left, you're chipping, you're chipping, again."

I grew to be tired after two hours. I drifted away and focused on my vision board. Trying to talk to Chase. I asked him how he was, how soccer was. Most importantly, I asked him to take care of Ashley. Some days I got no response, some days I would get an, "Okay."

Somedays, I would feel like he was not even listening. I thought of Cal and Madeline, and could safely display their blown-up photo on my vision board. I kept a piece of the feather next to my pillow, and the other in my wallet, so it was always with me. From time to time, I would find myself back on the dancefloor.

"Who are you?" I would ask. Mostly, I would just get a smile, and he would fade away. I could hear a voice, then it was gone. *But I knew it was you. When will I find you?*

I looked at the wall, and cut and paste magazine pictures of houses, fabulous couples, mysterious women, and what empowered me. I admired famous women of our time that made it on their own and were extremely influential. I wanted to be strong and powerful. The vision board grew and grew. It had a life of its own. Before I had time to close my eyes again, Tom knocked on my door.

"Fifteen mins," he said, leaving a banana and water on my night table. It was time for our morning run.

When I turned sixteen, I was an A+ student and taking all AP classes. I stuck to Tom's strict schedule and did not complain. Sixteen was just a number, and I couldn't wait to get older and get my life started. I wanted to push through time, and get my goals accomplished. I was on my way.

The morning of my sixteenth birthday, Tom did his usual knock. Instead of the banana and water, he left the door open and walked away. I sat up on my pillows and just watched. He was walking downstairs, went outside and was just waiting. Confused, I got out of bed and walked to the door. There was a glitter trail through my path, and balloons lined the outside door. I made it down the stairs, and when I walked through the open door, their stood Tom and Brenda in front of a blue convertible with a big red bow. It was mine!

"Happy birthday!" they both said. It was a dream. I stood in disbelief, and not sure how to handle it. After several moments of standing there with my hands over my face, Tom opened the door and guided me to sit in it.

"Happy birthday, Valerie. You earned this," he said. It was the greatest reward. We went for a ride around the block that I carefully navigated. I was afraid of the power this BMW would give. I also didn't have my permit yet. When we parked, all I could say in astonishment was, "Thank you, thank you, thank you." I went upstairs and crossed it off my vision board under the category of *Accomplished*. The phone rang as I was fresh out of the shower, and putting on my uniform for school.

"Valerie, it's for you," Tom yelled from the kitchen. It was Chase.

"Happy birthday!" he said.

"Chase! Thank you, thank you for remembering! How are you? OMG, I got a car! I can't believe it; I got a car!"

"That is awesome, girl! What kind?"

"A convertible! Tom got me a convertible! I can't believe it!"

"That is great, Valerie; I miss you. So glad to hear your voice."

"Yes, you too."

"When are you coming home to visit? I would love to see you."

"I don't know, Chase. I didn't think about it. I had no plans to come back. I don't really talk to Shelia or Ashley." Currently, Tom was standing by the door with an envelope.

"Hold on a sec." I held my hand over the phone and walked toward Tom.

"Tell Chase that you will be there on Thursday."

"What?" I opened the envelope which was a round trip ticket to New York.

"What?" I took my hand off the phone. "Tom just gave me tickets to NY!"

"Awesome! Tom and my mom have been talking. You can come and stay with us. It will be great, Valerie. You will have so much fun seeing everyone again."

"This is such a great birthday! Okay, I have to go. I will call you later!"

I hung up and hugged Tom.

"Thank you, thank you!" I even gave him a kiss on the cheek. I was so excited, and now l was late for class.

That Thursday, I got on a plane and headed back. It was my first time since I was kicked out of Shelia's house and sent on my way. It probably was the best day of my life—the last day of my old life, the start of my new. I never thought I would see Chase again; I couldn't wait! I drank the same coke, ate the same burger and fries, and had the same shake. Tom did not approve, but this was a special occasion.

I was afraid of not being able to recognize Chase, or of him not recognizing me. I got off the plane, went to the bathroom, and made sure my hair looked a perfect blonde, perfect pink lipstick, perfectly placed rips in my cut off jean shorts, perfect top to show off my cleavage, and my flannel perfectly wrapped around my waist. I clicked my heels and headed to the gate. I had on my sunglasses, because I was afraid to make eye contact with the wrong person. But as soon as I turned the corner in JFK, I knew who he was. I saw the tall boy with dark hair, dark eyes, and bright white smile. There was Chase. He held a sign with my name on it.

"Valerie!"

I walked to him, and dropped my bags. He picked me up for the biggest hug. I was in heaven for seven seconds.

Chase was a year older than me; he was a senior and able to drive to pick me up. He talked a mile a minute, giving me updates on everything in town, and all that had gone on since I left. Through these years, we had only spoken on the phone for brief moments, and occasionally through letters and pictures. But we continued to send a message, where no one else could hear us, no one else was listening, and where no one else could come between us.

We got back to Larchmont. He took me through all the towns, and pointed out what had changed, what had stayed the same. We went to Manor Park. We went to the far south gazebo where we could watch the city line and all the bridges to Long Island.

"You look beautiful, Valerie," he said, after he built up his courage.

"Thank you, you are not too bad yourself," I said to him back with confidence.

"My girlfriend is jealous of you." The trip was set on a new tone. I never knew who I was to Chase. It would be my first real lesson in what it meant to DTR (define the relationship). I was crushed, but California Valerie would not let New York Valerie bring me down.

"She should be," I responded and didn't even look his way. I stared out into the skyline, and he stared with his jaw hanging at me. That weekend was homecoming. I was afraid of running into Ashley. I was afraid of who Chase's girlfriend was; I was afraid that I did not fit in.

Be California Valerie, I repeated over and over in my head. I needed to keep up my confidence. Chase drove us to and from several parties at the beginning of the evening, to see which would be the best one to plant ourselves in. One keg, two kegs—I became tipsy. I went to parties at home, but I had to stay focused on school, my goals, my future. In New York, time stood still. There were people I recognized, people I didn't. I had the attention of most of the boys I encountered either way. I was California Valerie.

After much of the "tour d'parties" was done, we had the bonfire and rally. I was left alone as Chase was part of the ceremonies. I took out my portable camera, and took pictures of him as he ran through the entrance gate with the rest of the team. His hair flowed in the wind. He smiled so brightly, all the girls blushed and giggled as he ran by them. I took the time to gaze into the fire to watch the crinkle of the fire flow into the skyline, and the smoke that gathered around us. The noise was loud, the cheers were vivacious, and the sudden desire to be with Chase overcame me. Once the ceremony was over, the badges were presented, and we went on our way to the after-party; and I went with Chase.

It was crowded and unsupervised. Girls were tipsy; boys were eager to take advantage of that moment. I sat on the top of the step, and watched the party only five steps below. I saw them all enjoying the moment. I was enjoying watching Chase. He called me down to do shots. I openly obliged. I would have done anything for him that night. Anything. The night got old; the kegs ran dry. Chase and I got drunk—very, very drunk. It was time to go home.

The night air was chilly, and something I was unaccustomed to in California. The air was different here. Chase offered me his jacket, and I took off my shoes for the one-mile walk home. We sang *Nirvana* out loud to lyrics that made no sense; we danced in the air, we tripped, we took breaks, and stole rolls from morning deliveries.

We laughed as we fell to the curb. We were too drunk to laugh and walk at the same time. Close to our walk home, drops of rain started to fall. When we hit the far end of Chase's block, it poured. We ran, but we were soaked by the time we got to his house. We went in, laughing as quietly as possible—which meant we were very loud, as a laugh cannot whisper. I took off his jacket, then turned to him to take off his shirt; then, I took off mine. His skin was wet. I could feel his soft skin underneath. I kissed his shoulder and across his back. He grabbed my arm and turned me around to face him. He looked at me, and without hesitation, he grabbed me and kissed me as he hit his back to to the fridge. I pressed against him and worked my way to opening his jeans and get to his boxers. I pushed my body up on the island before him, I spread my legs trapping him between the fridge and the island. He was mine. He held my thighs, and as he was about to reach into me, he stopped.

"Valerie, I can't do this." He was upset and pushed my legs away, ran up to his room, and closed the door.

I lost him.

I sat there cold, wet, naked, and alone. I sat on the island, and looked out the kitchen window. I could see the house I grew up in, far away in the distance. I grabbed my clothes from the floor, went into

47

Chase's sister's room where I had camped out for the weekend, curled into my sweatshirt and closed my eyes. I couldn't help the tears that were silent. When morning came, they were gone, like my ego.

I stayed for the game. I went to the parties. Chase was a bit distant from me the whole time. I got drunk with his friends, celebrated a home victory—I couldn't wait to get back to California.

"Valerie, I'm sorry."

"Sorry, sorry for what?"

"I love you, Valerie, You are like; you are like . . ."

"I am like what Chase?"

"You are like . . . my sister." The kiss of death. I already had a brother that ignored me; now I had Chase to ignore me.

"Oh, thanks!" I said in my most sarcastic tone and walked ahead faster, with my arms folded.

I was heated. I was so upset, so hurt. I just turned sixteen; I just pushed myself against my childhood friend who was my childhood crush. Now I wondered how I was going to get through the next thirteen hours. I never wanted to come back to New York.

"Valerie, wait! Stop!" Chase insisted, as he screamed to me from down the street. I stopped but did not turn around. It was autumn cold. There were leaves on the ground, wet from last night's rain. Steam was rising from the asphalt, and the street light gave off a light buzz in the air that you heard after the echo from Chase's scream. I waited as I heard his footsteps and fought back tears. He came up beside me, and grabbed me by the shoulders.

"Valerie, there is something I need to tell you, something you need to know." I waited . . .

"Valerie, can we get inside the house?" He held me by my shoulders as we walked. I did not look at him. He attempted to rest his head on my shoulder; I pushed him off. We got inside, got into comfortable clothes, and regrouped on the couch, where Chase waited for me with a beer. I held the pillow to my chest and took a sip.

"Valerie, look at me," he said as he grabbed my leg and moved in closer.

"I always had a crush on you; always. I heard you talking to me at night. I think about you all the time."

I started to relax; I took another sip.

"I always wanted it to be you. I dreamed about you as my wife and the mother of my children. Then you moved away." I got annoyed and readjusted myself on the couch, but I really wanted to run away. He could see it, and kept the grab on my leg.

"Valerie, I met someone else. I kept it private, because I wanted to know my true feelings. I wanted it to be you, but since you weren't around, I found someone else."

"Chase, you are seventeen. This is ridiculous," I said to him.

"Maybe, but I just think when you know, you know."

"So, who is she?" I said, not wanting to know the answer.

"Val, you don't want to know."

"Who?"

"Valerie, it's Ashley."

There she was again, throwing out a dig, taking what was mine.

"I see. Thanks for letting me know." I went to bed. Chase followed me onto the futon on his sister's floor where I was staying.

"Valerie, look at me!"

"Why? For what? Do you know what she did to me? Did to you? Are you serious? Ashley? I don't know you anymore."

"Valerie, I missed you when you left. Ashley and I became friends. I heard you asked me to watch over her, I swore I heard you say that! One thing became another. We started to hook-up, then became a couple. She was afraid about how you would react, so she went away with your mom."

"Shelia."

"Ugh, Shelia."

So that made me feel better. I came to town, and my family left town because of me. Chase joined their team.

"I'm done with you."

*   *   *   *   *

Taylor was the football captain. All the girls in school wanted him, but I was determined he would be mine. We flirted. I got his attention. When I would walked by and ignored him, I hoped he would follow. He did.

Taylor took me to the senior prom; we followed each other to UCLA. My mind was on a business scholarship, his on a football scholarship. We were picture perfect. Our relationship was not. He was pretty, and wanted to be told so. He wanted us to match, where I wanted to puke. We never had sex, we just heavy-petted. It was awful, neither of us knew any better and saw that white, picket fence that would save us. We looked good together, so we stayed together, alone in a dead relationship. School work was more important to me than Taylor. I didn't let go of my goals, and concentrated directly on work. The college years were fast. Taylor was traveling so much with sports, that he soon just became an acquaintance.

One night, at a party, I watched him flirting with a girl. He thought I wasn't watching. I saw him take her to an empty room. He was probably doing it all along. I never was focused on him, on us. He was not the picture in my head. It was not him, so I didn't care, right? I pushed him away. He found someone else. Time to stay focused, eye on the prize.

In junior year of college, I got a call at 2:00 a.m. in the morning. It was Tom.

"Valerie, are you awake?"

"Uh, no? What's up?"

"I need you to come home. Something came up, and I need you home."

"Okay." I hung up, packed a small bag, and headed to Tom's house without question.

When I arrived, Tom had already had his coffee. He still had bed hair.

"I don't sugarcoat, Valerie," Tom said as he leaned into the counter. "I just got a call from Ashley. It's your mother, Shelia. She overdosed last night and died." I don't know what the level of shock was supposed to be, but I had none. I was blank and gave him a cold stare.

"Valerie, she is your mother. I know you have angry feelings toward her, but she is your mother. You will respect her."

"Yes, Tom," I agreed.

That night, I went to my nightstand and held one of the pearls that she dropped the night she asked me to leave. That was the last conversation we had, face-to-face. I wanted to feel something, but I had no feelings at that moment. I looked at the picture of Cal and Madeline on the wall, and wondered if she sat next to them on that beach. I wondered if she would be kind to them when they met again in heaven. Then I saw the photo. I realized she might not be going there at all. Another thing to burden Madeline with, but I believed through her prayers, she would bring Shelia home, hold her in her arms and nurture her to love again. I prayed that the pain I barred from her I could offer up, so she could go to heaven. I had to believe I went through all of that for a reason. Right now, I believe I am a better person from walking away from that relationship. Suddenly, I had a release in my heart, and felt the tears come.

"Goodbye, Shelia."

I had to make funeral plans with my brother and sister whom I no longer knew. No longer liked. No longer wanted a relationship with. I dreaded to see them, and counted the minutes on the plane.

"Why do I have to plan it?"

"Because, Valerie, you need to honor your mother. You're the smartest. You have your shit together. You have worked so hard. Besides all of that, you are the strongest."

"Why not Todd? He's the oldest."

He looked me in the eyes with a long, hard stare and said again, "Valerie, you are the strongest." I understood what I needed to do.

When I got off the plane, I was greeted by Todd's wife, Liz, who was someone I never met. I didn't recognize him at all. He seemed taller, but suddenly goofy and relaxed. His hair was longer and ung-roomed. He suddenly had a belly that I couldn't understand.

When we last left off, he was so chiseled. I saw him evolve from being a loving brother to me, mean to me, hating me, leaving me . . . now I meet Todd, the husband.

Deep breaths, deep breaths, I repeated to myself as I walked toward them. When I was close enough, I could no longer pretend I didn't see them. I started to wave.

"Todd! Hello!"

"Hey! Valerie! Hello!" He came at me with his running, pigeon toes. I thought he was going to trip. His arms were opened wide. We hugged. It felt warm like I remember him holding me as a baby. I closed my eyes, as my face was planted in his chest, and took in his smell. It reminded me of what home used to be.

We went back to the house to find Ashley on the couch, smoking frantically. She had become a hippie. the house smelled like reefer and a Grateful Dead concert. Wait, maybe that was the same thing? She perked up and, right away, came in for the hug.

"Valerie! I missed you. I am so glad you are here!" I think I stood still, almost petrified, as the hug occurred.

She still made me cringe. Even now, the horror of her beauty was tainted by this hippie fest. She was in a printed dress that tied on each shoulder, and lay over a dirty white, long-sleeved tee shirt. She had no makeup on. Although she was in her twenties, she looked like a miserable, middle-aged mom. I was disgusted by her at this moment, as if my emotions or grudges against her needed any help. I caught eyes with Todd. I hoped we could be back to allies for this moment. He didn't see it; it scared me even more.

Chase came out from the bathroom. I was shocked that they were still together. I was even more shocked that he, too, became a hippie. That, to me, was a disgrace. I was a UCLA girl. We had the hippie crowd, but mostly they were snobby blondes with daddy issues. Ashley was gross. I was so disappointed in what Chase looked like. His hair was longer; his clothes were flannel and wrinkled. He was out of sorts. They were both high as a kite. I was still in disbelief of who he became, what he threw away, and the power she shifted over him. If they really needed each other, why were they ruining each other?

"Great, so what's the deal? What are the plans so far?"

The blank stares at me were priceless.

"Ashley, where is Mom now? The hospital? The morgue? The funeral home? Where?"

"Hmm, yeah, the number is on the fridge of who you have to call. I'm not sure."

"Ashley, are you high? Chase?"

No response but a blank stare.

"Unbelievable, way to go." I made some calls, found Shelia's keys, and grabbed Todd to come with me. The arrangements were made, and I split the list between us to make the phone calls. In T-minus eighteen hours, Shelia will be put to rest.

I went food shopping, and cooked us a dinner. We sat as the dysfunctional family that we were. I cleaned up the dishes. I cleaned up the kitchen, the living room, and the rest of the house. I picked out clothes from Shelia's closet for Ashley to wear. I found the jar of pearls that I left on Shelia's dresser from when she broke them all over the floor. I don't think they left that spot for years; I could tell by the ring the jar left on the dresser. The layer of dust left a perfect circle. I opened the jar and poured a few into my hand. I moved them around as if they were marbles, and wanted to feel something from them. I felt nothing from Shelia. All I could feel was Madeline. I asked Madeline, again, to please take care of Shelia as she carried a burden we did not know. She led a life she was not proud of. She hated herself. She hated the men she drove away. I will always think she hated me.

I placed the pearls back into the jar, and went into the basement. Tom had left a bunch of tools and fishing equipment down there, and never came back for them. Sitting in the basement, I used the fishing wire I found and knotted all the pearls into a necklace. Taking sailing lessons seemed to be repurposed. I put them on. They were a perfect fit around my tiny neckline. Standing on a chair, I looked at my reflection in a high window. Not far from the window, there was a bird that sat on the lawn. We made eye contact. I was admiring my work. I caressed the beads as I looked at the bird for approval. I saw him blink and keep the focus on me. We locked eyes. My gaze took me into a blurry vision; he flew away. As I stared at the vision, and saw the outside sparkle of the night, the flying bird left a feather that came back down to the ground. As it floated, drifted, moved from side to side, it landed on the cold, wet ground. The wind picked it back up and moved its way toward the window.

I don't know if it was from Cal, if it was from Madeline, or from Shelia. I know that it was from someone, and maybe a gift from all three. I held my hand to the window, looked back at my reflection, and closed my eyes to feel their power, and maybe knew that they were all together. Shelia could now be at peace. Madeline could have her daughter back. Cal could have his perfect dinner and family, ready and waiting for him when he came home from work. Maybe the substance of what they all wanted and needed from that dinner will become complete.

"Madeline, save a plate for me at dinner. I won't be there any time soon, but the table will be filled."

The window shook as the wind grew stronger and whirled the feather into the air, and back down to the ground. I held both hands to the window to feel it; after moments, I knew. I opened my eyes to see the bird back in its spot, and looking back at me, waiting for me to open my eyes again. When he blinked, I blinked back.

"Good night, Cal," I said. I pressed my finger to the window making a permanent mark; he flew away. I went back upstairs.

My room was not the same; Ashley had ransacked it. There was no memory of me ever being there. I lay on the bed and slept for about two hours, only to find myself wide awake with no desire to sleep. I wanted to call Chase, but he was no longer available to me. I wanted to call out to Todd, but he was snoring next to his wife. Ashley was asleep by default effect from pot and beer. I went downstairs, opened a bottle of wine and brought it up to my room.

With my bottle in one hand, and my glass in the other, I came to the doorway of my room. I stopped as I felt there was an invisible fence. I didn't want to be that person again. I didn't want to go back to the upset person I was when I lived here. I was ready to move on.

I bent down, sat on the edge of my doorstep, and faced out to the open door across the open stairwell that led to Shelia's room. I could look into the dark, open door, and see it go back further in than what the walls would give, further than what our house would give, further than what the universe would give.

It was a black hole that seemed like an elevator going down.

Follow the light, Shelia, I said loudly in my head, and repeated over and over as I took sips from my glass. I kept my focus on the room. Three-fourths into the bottle, Todd came out looking for the bathroom. He didn't see me until his journey back.

"Valerie, what are you doing?"

"If I told you I was saving Shelia, would you believe me?"

"Ha ha, maybe. Can I join you?"

"Sure, but you need to get your own wine." He obliged, I kept on with my job.

"Bring more for me too," I said in my loud whisper. Todd came back up, and gave me an open bottle of wine. He took his beer and sat at his doorstep. We sat in silence for a bit; we both stared into Shelia's doorway from our separate angles.

"Wow, I can feel all the memories," Todd said as we both sipped slowly. And then deeper, the event went on. He sat with his hands hugging his knees, in his khaki shorts and an orange tee shirt. I glanced over at him, then back to Shelia's room.

"So, what do you remember Todd?" I asked in a groggy, raspy voice. There were a pause and more sips from both of us. He emptied his beer, placed it to the side, and opened a new one. He stared into the room as if he were waiting for a suspect to crawl out of it.

"I don't know. It started out good. Our lives were good. We had fun when my dad was here. He was great. Shelia was great. We ate dinner together every night. The house was clean. Mom was Mrs. PTA. Ashley was nice (we chuckled). We were a perfect family.

"Then, I don't know. Suddenly, we weren't. My dad stopped coming home for dinner. Then he came home late. Then he wouldn't come home. When he did, you could smell another woman's scent on him. Sometimes he came home with other women. My dad and Shelia fought, and then one day, he stopped showing his face and moved to Denver.

"Then there was you. Then there was Tom—in that order. Then there wasn't Tom, and you were still here. That's what I remember."

55

He sipped his beer. He was about to give up on Shelia, when he was drawn back in. He opened another beer and got back to work. I continued my job of staring into Shelia's doorway, pushing her toward the light. But as I worked, I sipped and I listened.

"I just saw it going downhill so fast. I stepped in and wanted to be a mom to you, because I was watching Shelia spiral out of control as soon as Tom came into the picture. She was so insecure. It was dangerous. Tom is a strong businessman and needed a strong woman to stand behind him. Shelia wasn't. She couldn't play the game of living here. Being a perfect mom, keeping a perfect house, belonging to a country club, being on Tom's arm looking perfect—she couldn't do it." He paused to sip again.

"Tom was strict and wanted to be successful. He wasn't going to let anyone stand in his way. At least, that is how I saw it. He really cared for you. Shelia was so jealous of you, that when Tom left, she obsessed over him and took it out on you. She lied about Tom, told Ashley and me how horrible he was to leave her. She lied about the money he sent for you, and used it for herself. She refused him to visit you—us. When he called to talk to you, specifically, she hung up. It was hard to live here. I wanted to be on her good side.

"I wanted to shield you from it until I wasn't strong enough. She turned against me the closer we became. At first, it was fine, I could handle it. Then she started to do evil things to me. She embarrassed me in front of my friends. Told them I wet the bed, and silly shit like that. Sometimes, she even hit me for no reason.

"It was crazy, but I still took it. I didn't want her to hurt you. I saw how she was using Ashley against you. Shelia grounded me, held me back from meeting my friends. Embarrassed me at school, like showing up in a house dress to give me something dumb. I couldn't do it. So, I played the game. I sided with Mom, ignored the fights between all of you, showed Shelia that I also didn't like you.

"I was weak, so I turned against you for my own selfish reasons. I was also jealous of you and your strength. I didn't have it. I couldn't do it alone. I sided with the wrong people. I should have stayed and sided with you."

The feelings all started to make sense to me. I didn't see it at the time; now it was becoming clear. We drank together. We sat separated, and I felt my connection to Todd again, but I was afraid to open into it as he was too weak to give me what I needed. I couldn't take the letdown—not again.

"I'm sorry, Valerie, I never wanted to hurt you."

I didn't look at him, but after some time, I nodded. All I wanted was to be important to someone. Todd was my first, real, healthy relationship with anyone. I thought I wasn't good enough, my strength kept him away from me. Now my strength would bring us closer. It would also keep us apart.

We sat in silence and drank on the cold, wooden floor in our childhood home, mourning a mother we grew to loathe, as she grew to loathe herself. Her silence never left the space.

We sat and reflected. If Todd kept talking, I wasn't sure I was focused.

"Follow the light, Shelia," I said. I was almost done with my second bottle of wine; I am not sure if it was out loud or not. My wine bottle was empty. It was time for another.

"I need more wine," I said, just as Ashley came out to the hallway we sat in.

"What are you guys doing?" she asked confused.

"Drinking," Todd said.

"Join us, bring more liquor."

She nodded her head. "Yeah, cool deal."

She listened to her orders and brought up what was left of the beer, wine, and vodka in the house. She handed out the stash, sat in her doorway, and lit a freshly-rolled joint, took a hit and passed it around.

We sat in our doorways. We sit in our childhood home, in Westchester, well-prepared for the evening with liquor and treats. We sit together on a tripod, staring at our mother's empty, dark bedroom.

Some have good memories; I have none. We sat as if we were prisoners, as in a movie like *Saw*. We are waiting for something to happen next, all with a loss we would take for our freedom to leave this home. We knew who the beast was. As scared animals, we were still afraid of our master that hurt us all in separate ways.

"Go into the light, Shelia," I repeated, and now out loud as I couldn't control my thoughts from my speech. Todd started to do the same. The wind shook the windows in her room as the night wind howled. We sat alone, together, and for the first time in our lives as brothers and sisters, we grew a bond.

"So, what are you guys talking about?" Ashley asked. We sat in silence.

"Memories of Shelia," Todd answered.

"Memories of Mom, you mean?" she corrected him. "Mine are all good; she was the best, always gave me what I wanted. We were friends. I am going to miss her." She took another hit from her joint. Then, she quickly changed the conversation.

"Valerie, I love your jeans. Where did you get them? They don't look like they are from the Gap."

"Since when do you like my style?" I asked her.

"Always. That's why I used to steal your clothes. But now you are soooo Cali. Do you shop on Rodeo, darling?" she said, as she was doing her *90210* mocking. We got that a lot since the show was still a running series. It was so not what life in Cali was for me.

"Ashley, I don't need it."

"What? Come on, no, seriously, do you? I don't know anything about it. Seriously, you do have nice clothes."

"Thanks. I'd like to leave with them," I said, and gave her a sarcastic stare.

"What's it like out in LA? Is everyone as blonde and perky as you?"

"Ash . . . ugh . . ."

She kept taunting. "I bet you have a Ken doll boyfriend and drive some silly convertible."

I sighed. "Ash, please."

"Oh, so you do! Hi, Ken; Hi, Barbie. Oh, you're so cute; no, you're so cute. Oh, Ken, how about I let you touch my boobies over my over-padded bra? How about I don't let you finger me, or maybe sometimes I do, but I won't let you fuck me, because it will mess up my hair."

"SHUT IT, ASHLEY!" I was enraged. She always couldn't stop until she got under my skin, and the embarrassing part was she was right. I didn't let Taylor have sex with me. I didn't, because he wasn't what I wanted for the long term. I didn't want to take my eye off of my goals with that distraction. I didn't want to mess my perfectly blown out hair, I didn't want my first time to be without Chase. I didn't want to have sex with someone that wasn't the man in the picture in the back of my head—my love—so I didn't. Hearing someone else say it to me out loud hurt. It hurt more that it came from Ashley. I took an empty bottle and threw it at her, but missed.

"FUCK YOU, ASHLEY," I said and smirked, and drank vodka straight from the bottle. Todd's wife came out.

"What is going on?" she asked. Todd pulled her down to him, and curled her in his arms.

"Don't ask." He said this, giving her a kiss on the forehead. At that time, Chase came out and sat with Ashley in the broken glass, not feeling a thing. They snuggled. We sat as a tripod that had two teams of two, and a party of one. We sat and drank to Shelia. All whispered out loud at different times, and in unison.

"Go to the light, Shelia."

Daylight broke. I could see the light from the back window in her room come through the shine against the dresser facing the doorway. I knew my job was done.

We needed to be at the funeral parlor at 2:00 p.m. I went out to restock the liquor and food we used up the night before, for the after the funeral. I checked on the caterers, came home to change, and Ashley and Chase had already left. I went into my room for a quick shower and change. My dress was gone. My perfect, black, Nordstrom's boat neck dress, with a black sash belt that flared out above my knee. She STOLE my dress.

"Ashley, you fucking ass!"

She could not help herself. Not even for a minute. I went into the shower, pissed off, and slammed the walls. I had to regroup as

I let my guard down for a weak moment; I needed to get myself together.

You are the strongest, was in my head from Tom.

I can do this, I can do this, I said over and over to myself. I got out of the shower; Todd and Liz had already left. The house was empty. I went across to Shelia's room and back into her closet.

"Listen, Shelia, I hooked you up. You need to hook me up. Send me the perfect black dress." I was in demand. I believed I deserved to be. I rummaged through what her closets had, and stuck in between hanging sweaters and suits all wrapped up from dry cleaning, a hanger fell to the ground with something in it. The closet was dark. I had to turn the light on to see it. She came through. It was her hook-up dress that she wore when she went into town to find a man. Steal a man away from his wife, if even if it was for just one night. It was the perfect send-off.

The dress was low cut and showed off my cleavage, just enough to borderline inappropriate. I put it on, dressed in my newly-strung pearls. I laced my lips red. I remember what I came here for. I came here to send off Shelia.

"*I am stronger. I am wiser. I am in control.*" I took a cab, arrived late, and made a grand entrance.

Ashley stood in front of Shelia's coffin in my black dress, with Birkenstocks and dirty hair—it was disgraceful. When someone would give me any ounce of attention, she talked loud and tried to barge in. Her game, as usual, was weak and embarrassing. I would ignore her and do my best to be the better person.

It was time for a final prayer, a final send-off for Shelia. The minister said a few words; we prayed together. He asked us to give peace to each other. Todd hugged his wife. Chase hugged Ashley. I stared into the coffin, as I could not watch the couples pair off with each other. I had no one to hug.

I stood and viewed Shelia, stiff as a board with her arms crossed at her waist. I felt the cold air that hit my skin on every open piece of cloth this dress did not cover. I felt the cold air remind me that revenge was not the best medicine, and standing here in this dress was disrespectful.

I stood there alone, and missed the mother I wanted to have, and all the attention I wanted from her. I stood there and could see her fall down the stairs, bump her head, and maybe even choke on the pills she was downing with her vodka cocktails. I stood there and could see her on the floor, in her blood, alone. I could feel her body get cold, her soul not knowing where to go, her memories fading away. I could see her drifting. Then she was gone. I could feel it. I held my stomach as I wanted to throw up, but I couldn't. I held my tears. I held in my stomach. I held in my loneliness.

"Is being stronger making you weaker, because it makes you lonely?" I asked Shelia.

They closed the casket and dropped her to the ground I stood over the open hole. I could see the dinner table forming. I could see Madeline looking out the window, nervous that dinner would not be perfect for Cal when he came home. She played with her pearls; I played with mine. Madeline glanced, again and again, to see Cal walking up the driveway. And as she heard footsteps from the sidewalk, her heart beat loud. She grabbed the roast and placed it on the table.

"Shelia! Dinner is ready!" she called.

"Coming, Momma!" Shelia's poodle skirt and saddle shoes swayed as she ran for her place at the dinner table. The door opened, Madeline's heart pumped, and she turned to him and closed her eyes for her evening kiss. Cal reached in, grabbed Madeline by the waist, and kissed her with passion. She kissed him back, and felt the warmth of his lips and knew that night, she slept in his arms instead of beside him.

She smiled as it was the peace she missed for so many years. The three of them sat down with extra plates set, but left empty. They held hands and said grace as a trinity. Cal gave Shelia a kiss on her hand. I believe that was his way of asking for forgiveness.

"Goodbye, Shelia," I said, and dropped my flower into the open hole that would now be Shelia's new home.

I cut my tears and walked away. I walked the runway, through a sea that parted, through the crowd with all eyes on me. I felt okay that my job here was done. I walked into Tom and Brenda who held their arms open to me. I fell into them, and I cried. A voice in my head whispered in a happy tearful response of "Thank you." It could only be Madeline.

"Thank you for saving a seat, Madeline."

As I walked away with Tom and Brenda, a bird flew across us and left a feather behind. Brenda caught it, and gave it to me for my collection.

"Thank you," I said out loud.

The food was serving itself; drinks were flowing. I mingled with the crowd and did my duty as the host of this quorum. Tom came over to check on me.

"How are you doing?" he asked, which seemed out of concern.

"I am okay; everything is fine."

"Can you do me a favor? You are making your father cringe. You made your point; please go change into something respectable." He was right. I made my point; I looked stupid.

"Yes, sir," I replied and went upstairs. I ran into my room to find Ashley and Chase in my bathroom in MY DRESS! She made me sick; she did these things on purpose. It was disgusting. I caught a glimpse of Chase as he could see me through the mirror. I looked dead in the eyes; he looked at me back.

"You are nothing but a fucking whore, Ashley!" I reminded her. I took my bag and went downstairs over to Tom and Brenda.

"I'm done here; I think I have done more than enough. I am ready to go back to California." Without hesitation, they agreed and put down their drinks. I looked at Todd from across the room. The stare we shared, that was as best of a goodbye I could give him. As we left the house, I turned around and promised myself I would never enter those doors again.

When we arrived in California, I excused myself to head back to school for a bit, but promised to come back the next day to spend the rest of the weekend with Tom and Brenda.

I pulled up to Taylor's frat house where they were having an afternoon session of beer and pool. I walked in unannounced, and slammed the door behind me to get everyone's attention. The house stopped for a brief moment. I could hear the slamming of the pool ball hit into one another, and eventually into a pocket. I entered the pool dining room, and looked around until I found Taylor. I walked right up to him, and kissed him with every bone in my body. The group cheered; he was stunned.

"Valerie!" he said when we came up for air. I grabbed him by the collar, up the stairs, to the left and into his room. I closed the door. I ripped open his jeans, grabbed what I wanted, and threw him on the bed. He returned the favor by tearing off my clothes.

That night we had sex. I sat on top of him, he held my waist, and beads of sweat grew on his forehead. When he fell asleep, I picked up my clothes and exited the exact opposite of how I entered—quietly.

I gave away the innocence that brought me into this world. I became the adult I had on my list of goals. I drove away. I drove back to Tom's house. I never saw Taylor again.

"Chase, can you hear me? Can you hear me? That was for you."

I was disgusted with myself.

*   *   *   *   *

New York was just not the same. My apartment was in a building on the upper east side. It was where most people my age lived, but I really didn't connect with any of them. My life was on the road. Going from city to city, spending excessive amounts of time in airports, coffee shops, bars. Every time I was on the move, I was looking for him.

Sometimes, I called him "Kitten;" sometimes it was "Pumpkin;" sometimes it was just "Him." I searched and stared at each man as they entered the bar. One martini became two martinis. Some guy would come up to me, strike up a conversation. Out of boredom, I would oblige.

I would say in my head, *It's not you, why are you bothering me?*

But I smiled, and pretended I cared. I woke up in hotels not remembering what town I lived in, if I had the blue Passat or the grey Passat; or was it a Honda Accord that I rented? I had Marriott points, Hyatt points, the occasional Hotel Indigo points. I woke up and had the same breakfast of a hotel yogurt and coffee. I got into my rental car. Drove to my client. Stood in a boardroom full of suits to give a presentation. Shook hands. Landed deals. Drank champagne and got back on a plane.

I was a nomad. I started to lose who I was because the money was terrific; but if I wasn't able to share it with someone, it didn't matter. I bought an expensive Mercedes Benz that sat in an overpriced garage. I pampered myself at the spa when I needed someone to just touch me.

I stayed home and stared at a TV, or a blank fireplace. One vodka became two vodkas. Then it became scotch, became a fireball, became a numbness. It was the only thing I could feel, to fall asleep and dream about "Him." It was draining. It was sad. It was the life I lived when I didn't know I was alive.

I was in Dallas, working with a high-profile bank. Dallas was a city I never made a connection with. It was a connecting flight, a quick stop over to a client in another city.

I started my usual routine of yogurt and coffee in the hotel. My blue Passat rental to the office, same elevator crew each morning, and then to my desk. It was meeting after meeting. It was eating of conveyer belt pizza during late nights, and going back to my hotel, where I drank endless numbers of airplane vodkas until I could feel the tingle heading straight to my toes. Until that feeling went away, then I could fall asleep and pray that "He" appeared that night in my sleep.

I see the suit. I see the folded arms. *Oh, "Kitten" what are you doing without me right now? When he touches me, will I know?*

I woke up staring at the ceiling to realize I hardly slept at all. The alarm went off. The routine recycled itself.

I spent the weekends running, and trying to learn the city. I eventually found myself at a bar with vodka that started as one, became two, and then became something else until I couldn't speak clearly. I couldn't remember who the person was sitting next to me, and I could for a few minutes go dark in my mind—and in those moments, not feel anything. I didn't realize how painful this time was as I was going through it. I didn't know how much I was in solitude. I didn't even realize I was becoming Shelia.

One Saturday, I went out for a run. I felt a sharp pain in my side, and needed to take a break. I sat in a park next to a water fountain, and hung out, waiting for it to pass. I sat and watched the families picnicking, dogs barking, kids on monkey bars. I sat alone. How did I get here? How did I stay so focused on my goals and succeed, but be so sad? Why couldn't I find someone? I just wanted to find someone to take away this pain and this loneliness.

Madeline, how do I get through this? I need help. Madeline, please help me. I said in my head, over and over. After ten times, I started to say it under my breath, and hoped that anyone would hear me. I was lost in my thoughts. I was lost, period.

"Excuse me, is it Valerie?"

I looked up to see another fellow jogger come over to me.

"Hi, I'm Richard Keller. Not sure if you remember me or not. We were at the committee meeting together. I see you in the mornings on the elevator."

"Oh, yes, Richard, hello!" *Thank you, Madeline,* I said in my head.

He was adorable. I did look for him in the elevator. He had kind, brown eyes and a white smile. You could tell how shy he was by how sparingly he gave them out. But he wore a wedding ring. My excitement and hope brought me back to ground zero. We shared casual banter; then, he went on his way. I picked up, ran myself into a bar, and started my vodka diet.

Monday came around, and I followed my mundane routine, got into the elevator and watched the doors close. I stared at the door into a new wonder. I felt something, a hand touching my butt cheek. I turned abruptly and slapped it away.

"Excuse me!" I demanded. The gentleman just laughed. No one in the elevator moved or reacted, except for one—Richard.

"Hey, watch it! Valerie, is this guy bothering you?" he asked and moved his way over to me.

"Yes, he just grabbed my ass!"

"Are you okay?" he asked, concerned. I looked at him in shock. The elevator stopped, he held my arm, and escorted me off the car. He walked me to his office where I sat on his leather, office loveseat next to his desk.

"I will take care of this," he said and handed me a bottle of water. Richard made some phone calls, sent a few emails, watched some video footage of the elevator encounter, and sometimes HR was in the room, asking me about what happened. Richard sat by me the whole time. After a round or two of questions, they nodded at Richard. He nodded back.

"He won't be bothering you anymore," Richard said.

That afternoon, Richard took me to lunch in a fancy restaurant where we ate on clean silverware, and there were men in white jackets. His eyes were so kind; they must have been from his mother's side. I felt so comfortable with him.

"So, Valerie, tell me. Where are you from?"

"Well, I am from New York, but I spent most of my life growing up in California with my dad; then I moved back to Manhattan. I am just here for this project, and then off to the next. How about yourself?"

He finished his chewing and dabbed the corner of his mouth with a napkin.

"I am from Cleveland. I moved here for this job a year ago. It is hard to live here. I am married and have three kids. We are struggling to be here, and to be honest, it is hurting my marriage."

We had a long pause of silence and chewing. I kept my focus on his hand that shook as he worked on cutting his meat. He continued his glare focused out the window, and was afraid to look at me. He was clearly struggling. He apparently was in a rough patch with his wife. He turned his focus and looked at me. I apparently was the distraction that he wanted. I really wanted it too.

"So, Valerie, what part of New York did you grow up in?" Richard asked.

"Larchmont, but now I live in the city," I replied.

"What? How awesome. I knew I liked you. My brother lives there!"

"Nice, I haven't been there since I was in high school." He continued to look at me, I felt it. We felt it. The fear was red in both of our faces, instantly. I wanted to know more about him. I wanted to know about the hair on his chest, how it felt to touch his skin, how high he could get my heart rate up. I wanted him.

"Awesome," I said with a smile. Then we sat in silence. I looked away, out of embarrassment, but when I turned, Richard was still looking at me.

We headed back to the office. I offered him my gratitude for the day, and went off to my afternoon meeting. I felt something I hadn't felt for a long time. But it hurt. He was married and had three kids. It wasn't my style to break up a marriage. I wouldn't want that to happen to me. It hurt, it was unfair. The hurt turned into pain. The cycle began again.

After work, I went to the hotel bar and ordered a Stoli orange on the rocks, and sometimes a gin martini. I watched the TV that had a sports games on. I pretended to be interested in it to make small talk with the bartender, but all I could think about was Richard. His eyes.

The lunch. The elevator that morning. The feeling I had for him sticking up for me. The feeling I had for him in the park. The sadness I had for myself, as I pictured him with his wife and kids.

I stumbled up to my room, and cried into my pillow until I just drained myself.

This is so unfair, I said over and over in my head. *Why does he have to be married? Why does it have to be like this?*

The cycle continued for days until I knew I had to get it together to keep my sanity and my job. But each day, everything slowly slipped away. Tom called to tell me how much he was worried about me.

"What is going on with you, Val? Are you losing your spark? What happened?"

"Nothing," I replied. "I am fine; it's nothing."

"Come home, Val. Take a break for a bit, and come home," he insisted.

"No, I'm good."

But I really wanted to go home and curl into him on the back deck, watch the sunrise, and have him tell me everything would be okay. I want to sit in my bedroom and stare at my photo of Cal and Madeline, and have them tell me everything would be okay; but it didn't feel okay. I didn't feel okay; I just didn't feel.

*　　*　　*　　*　　*

No Promises . . .
No Demands . . .
　　　　—Love Is a Battlefield, Pat Benatar

"Fancy seeing you here, Valerie," he said as he sat down and ordered a martini that matched mine. It was Richard; I was shocked to see him. The look on his face was also of shock—of embarrassment. After a few sips of gin, it tingled in my chest, into my legs, down to my toes. I was relaxed for the moment.

"So, what brings you here?" Richard asked.

"I am staying here. I like the hotel life; a restaurant with a bar, fitness center, different people. It keeps me anonymous."

"There is nothing about you, Valerie, that is anonymous. You walk into a room, everyone looks. Everyone knows who you are. Everyone wants to know you. I would call you a beautiful mystery," he said, and took a sip from the corner seat at the bar.

"So, what brings you here, Richard?" I asked, hoping it was to find me.

"My wife and I broke up. I am giving them a few days to pack and move out. She asked me to not be around—to make it easier? I don't know how these things are easy. I will move back to my big, empty house when they are gone. Sad enough for you?"

We both sipped and left that conversation behind us—but not forgotten.

We talked sports. We ate fries in duck fat. We had martinis. We slipped out of our professional relationship. Our fingers would get closer to the bar. As he would tell stories, I found his hand on my knee, on my waist. Getting up from the bar suddenly required us to have to touch to move out of the way because our chairs had become closer and closer. That corner suddenly formed a tight hinge.

We finished our drinks, Richard asked for the check. He kept his hand on my knee and added some strength to his hold. His hand started to move up my thigh. I was scared. I wanted to kiss him. He wanted to kiss me. I think everyone in the bar was watching, because you could feel it. You could hear the silence in the air.

"Are you ready to go?" He stood up and had to brush into me because our seats were so close. His fingers opened on my stomach just touching me, close into my bellybutton. He offered his hand to me. I nodded.

We got into the elevator, faced the doors; and as they closed, I closed my eyes, took a deep breath. I turned to him for a kiss. It wasn't a kiss that was soft. It was hard and forced on both ends because we both wanted it so badly. We moved among the car from each wall side to side as we couldn't control where to grab each other, where to get the right angle into this kiss, and where our legs should be to feel that passion we were in the middle of sharing.

I didn't move him out of the house. I didn't cause their fights, nor their discomfort for moving to Dallas. The promises that they made and couldn't keep—*I didn't create this.*

I didn't want to be alone anymore. I wanted to feel something. I wanted to be loved. I needed a few minutes to gather my thoughts, to gather what I should do. Time to listen to what my heart was telling me. I excused myself into the bathroom to get myself together.

"Madeline, what should I do?" I whispered to myself.

I saw her looking out the window at someone. I saw her touching the glass with her finger, and she had a tear. I looked in deeper and could feel her finger pressing the glass. She was holding in further tears. I watched deeper into the window and I saw her admiring a man mowing the lawn across the street. I started to understand her pain. For one night, I didn't feel alone.

That night he took off his ring. Took off his clothes. I took away his pain. That night, he took away my loneliness.

We woke up intertwined, in sadness and in lust—in need of each other. We were exactly where we needed to be at that time and moment. He caressed my arm, kissed my neck. I was warm inside from each touch, and soaked in the moment. It was exactly what I needed.

Christmas was an introduction to Tom and Brenda as we took the trip to California. We ate dinner at Brenda's. Tom questioned

Richard on politics, as they retired to the deck for cigars and scotch. Richard's phone rang. He built anxiety, retired to another room, and must have been upset after he missed Christmas with his kids.

"He's married!" Brenda said to me. I gave her a look of anger as no one needed to know.

"They are separated."

"Is he going to leave her?"

"I don't know. I mean, yeah. Yeah, of course, he is going to leave her."

"Valerie, you need to know. You haven't had that conversation yet?"

"No."

I was angry. I wanted to know. I didn't want to know. I saw the picture of us in my head, my dreams of being with him, having a life with him. But it wasn't him; he wasn't in my heart. He was just physically here with me, right now.

"Valerie, you are going to get hurt. I can see it," Brenda restated with concern.

"No, I'm not! I am not going to get hurt, stop it."

"Valerie."

"I don't need you, stay out of it," I said very hastily. She made me so angry. I took it a step further.

"You are not my mother." I couldn't look at her. I didn't want to hurt her. I wanted to keep Richard. I didn't want her to know. So, I said it. Now I wanted to take it back, and I couldn't.

"I am very aware of that, thanks, Valerie."

And just like that Brenda left the room.

*   *   *   *   *

"It would help me to know,
Do I stand in your way?
Or am I the best thing you've had?"
—"Love Is a Battlefield," Pat Benatar

I became the shiny new toy in the house. We moved out of our hotel rooms and into their home in Dallas. My dresses hung in her closet. My soap replaced her shower gel. Her spot in the bed had new indents from my body lying next to his.

We changed the sheets. We moved furniture around. Somehow, she was still present in the house. I ignored it. I had trouble sleeping there. As I was awake, I watched Richard. I ran my fingers through his thick, brown hair and imagined my future with him. I could see us walking down the aisle. Rose petals were thrown as we walked out the doors, dancing on a wooden floor laid out just for us. For that day, for that moment. I could see the tea lights above us. I could see our children with his children becoming brothers and sisters; we would get old together and hold hands as we walked in the park. It was a fantasy I played out each night. It was just a fantasy.

He was gentle and slept deeper when he touched me. He crawled into me, felt guilty and pulled away. His anxiety was destroying him, but I noticed and did not raise the flag. He crawled back to me when he didn't realize it, when he was deep in sleep. His body was shaking from the turmoil he gave himself. He would rest his head on my neck, hold my inner thigh. His breaths came back into control. His body started to settle. I could do a countdown: four, three, two, one. And he relaxed, then settled, his snoring started up again. I ran my fingers through his hair, kissed his shoulder, and enjoyed the moment until his cycle started over again.

She called in the mornings at 6:00 a.m. The phone rang, he grabbed it and walked into the other room and close the door. He missed his children. I realized he missed her too. His separation of church and state was becoming difficult. He had guilt written all over him. It took time before he could look at me again. He sat on the edge of the bed, I pulled him back to his pillow and draped myself across him. He outlined my body with his fingers, and I sat like a painting as he stroked the brush against me. He would come back to me, I could feel it. I would start the countdown in my head: four, three, two, one; and there it was. He smiled again.

"Valerie!"

"Yes, Boss, what can I do for you today?"

"I am impressed with your work in Dallas. Your numbers are going up each month. I am very pleased."

"Why, thank you, sir, I appreciate that."

"Valerie, we are offering you a promotion. It's time to leave Dallas and head back to NY."

"Wow," I said. The speakerphone was still on, I walked to the window and stared out into the corporate park.

"Val, are you still there?"

"Yes, I am. Can I have a few days to settle here and come back?"

"Of course, this is big, Val. You earned it."

"Thank you, sir."

I looked out the window into the corporate park. I pressed my finger to the window. I stared deeper into the people walking from their meetings, into new meetings. I could see Richard walk into the next building. I pressed my finger to the window; I held in tears. I saw him; he didn't see me. I heard a voice in my head.

"I thought you were waiting for me?" Then it was gone. I couldn't chase it or place it. But I knew it was you. *Where are you. I can't wait anymore—am I waiting?*

That night, we made pasta and watched the Monday night football game. I dragged him upstairs and forced him to have sex with me. It was ugly. It was meaningless. We didn't speak. We didn't stop. We shared that moment together, but it just made me feel more alone. In the moment of the act, we both grabbed for the pillow that broke; the feathers flew around the room. We had no reaction, but I knew what it meant. I just wanted to feel something. I felt nothing. When it was over, it was over. I sat on top of him, sweating and vulnerable.

"You are never going to leave her."

"No."

I decided to make a quick trip home and went straight to see Brenda. "You were right. I am a fool."

"You are not a fool; you just wanted to find someone. You got hurt. I just didn't want you to get hurt." Brenda consoled me.

Richard kept the picture of me in his head and went back to his wife. He convinced her to move back to Dallas and enter the dollhouse, tainted with my scent and feathers we couldn't clean up. She opened her arms to him and welcomed him back into the family.

I lay in my bed without him. I could smell him. I could feel his fingers outlining my body. I could feel his sleeping patterns go from shaking into a calm state. I reached out to him from California to Dallas and started the countdown: four, three, two, one; and Richard would crawl into his wife's arms. He fell fast asleep.

I stayed awake and waited for his pattern to turn again. I could no longer feel him. He was gone.

"Don't lose your focus, Valerie," Tom said to me. I was losing myself. I said goodbye to Cal and Madeline. I went through the wall. I pressed my body against it to soak it in.

Don't lose focus, I repeated to myself. I closed my eyes. "He" was there. The man in the suit with his arms folded.

Don't lose focus, don't forget about me. "He" came back for me.

"I'm waiting for you," I said to him. "I want it to be you; it is always you."

*　　*　　*　　*　　*

"Baby if I told you that you rock my world, I want you
around me. Would you let me call you my girl?"
—"Girl" The Internet Featuring KAYTRANADA

I went back to New York. I started my new position. I made
more money then I knew what to do with. My drinks went back
to vodka, my clothes became Gucci, my pearls became diamonds. I
didn't want any of it. I wanted to feel. I would go back to my vodka
diet and wait for the tingle to come over my body. After a couple of
shots, I felt something. I felt nothing.

My throat burned. My acid reflex joined me daily. I didn't feel
anything. I walked aimlessly down the street. I walked into bars and
sat in the corners, waiting for Richard. Waiting for someone. No one
would come. I was the walking dead.

"Val, my best girl, how you doin'?"

"Yes, sir; good, sir!"

"I need you to head up to Boston; I have a deal for you. It's big,
I need my best player on it."

"You got it."

I went back and forth to Boston over the next several months.
The routine was the same. Drive up I84–I90. Check into the hotel.
Go to the gym. Take a shower. Clothes ready for the next day. Back
on the computer. Check in right before my head is ready to check
out. Downstairs, I was ready to replenish the tingle on my lips, and
drown in the fact that I was there alone, again.

One TV played soccer. One TV played golf. One TV played
football. It was all the same. I didn't care. I just gazed into the screens
and faded away. There was vodka. There was amazing mac and cheese
with shredded short ribs. There was wine, and as the third inning,
second quarter, the last basket before the buzzer—there was you.

"Christopher, let's sit here," Mark said, as two bankers came in
and sat next to me at the bar. I wasn't paying attention; I didn't have
to. Christopher looked at me until I paid him any attention. He sat
patiently and waited. He waited for me.

The eleventh hole, the penalty kick, the fifth inning was back and forth in my brain as I switched from screen to screen, sipping endlessly.

"Shame about a Tiger woods, huh?" Christopher said after he received his first drink.

His sleeves were rolled back; he looked as if he put in a hard day's work. I was not interested in his comments, his questions, his striking presence. And I had no desire to look at him. I wasn't interested in his quizzing and need to know me. I wanted to NOT know him. I wouldn't take my eyes off the screens.

"So where are you from?" he asked. I stared at one screen.

"New York."

"What do you do?"

"Sales."

"For who?"

"A bank."

"What bank?"

"It's a private bank."

"Are you married?"

"No"

"Kids?"

"No?"

"What are you drinking?"

"Grey Goose Orange on the rocks."

"Hey, Ned, get us a round of Grey Goose Orange on the rocks."

I didn't understand why he was so persistent. He was annoying to me. I took that moment to take my stare off the screen, to look at him. And as he looked back at me, his hazel eyes looked at me. I lost my balance in a steady chair, holding onto a steady bar. I heard this voice before.

"It's you and me, kid, forever." I could see us twirling on the dance floor. I could see him holding my hands.

"It's you and me, kid." I could hear it. I could feel him again. I soaked him in. Mostly his intensity, his desire to know me, his feelings to find me. I have been found.

"Nice to meet you, Valerie. Mark, let's go get a table," Christopher said as he signaled Mark to finish his drink.

"How did you know my name was Valerie?" I asked in astonishment.

"You know why . . ."

He got up. We locked eyes as he walked away. Their table was out of my eyeshot. I sat at the bar and ordered water. I patiently waited for Christopher. I felt alive. I felt the dance floor. I felt my fingers running through his hair. I felt myself again.

Christopher . . . I said in my head over and over again.

Christopher . . .

Christopher . . . oh, I love to say that name . . .

Christopher . . . I repeat in my head.

"You called?" He said, as he came up from the other side of me.

"Maybe," I said as my body came back to ease.

"You are still nursing that drink?"

"Ned, another round, please." He gestured to explain another round in our now-crowded surroundings.

The man next to me was chatty, and as adorable as he was, I was not interested. The man on my other side wanted to chat with me. I was not interested. There was nowhere for Christopher to sit, no place for Mark to put down his drink. Christopher was distracted by everything in the bar. I politely spoke to the man to my left as Christopher stood behind me and acted as if he lost interest in me. I focused my nervousness, and now loss of confidence, in this new random man. I played the round of questions on him that Christopher gave to me.

"Where are you from? What do you do? Are you married? Kids? Oh, nice, really?"

I replied each time. I didn't even listen to the answers. I didn't care. When I brought my drink to my lips, I looked up to see if Christopher was listening. He was.

"Come on, kid, let's go. Ned, another round!" Christopher helped me out of the chair and he, Mark, and I went into the lounge and sat down. We did an assessment of each person at the bar. The people walking in the bar, who was leaving alone, and who was leaving with who. We played out scenarios like:

"I bet that guy in the green shirt is going to hit on the chick with the blue dress."

"I don't know. She likes the guy next to him in the blue shirt."

"No, she doesn't."

We laughed, Christopher grabbed us more drinks. Suddenly, we had a crowd starting to join us. One guy came in and tried to hit on me; our game was on. Christopher sat in the angle and as this guy came over, got snotty. Christopher stuck up for me. It was so sexy.

We didn't hold hands. We didn't look at each other We became a team. I never felt so protected by anyone. He was strong, obnoxious, sarcastic, so sure of himself and what he wanted. I wanted him. I always wanted him.

"So, what's up? That's your gig? Coming in here, and what do you got? Tell me what you got." Christopher had enough of this random man flirting with me.

"Excuse me; I am here to talk to her," the random said.

"No, you're not," Christopher shouted.

"Yeah, I was talking to her at the bar and . . ."

"Yeah and what? What happened? She left. She left you to talk to me." I was blushing from Christopher's sudden demand over me.

There was silence. He stared down this random dude. This tall, handsome, confident basketball player just got broken into pieces; moments later, he looked to me. I gave him the stare. He bowed his head and walked away. I felt Christopher's power; I never wanted to lose it.

It is 2:00 a.m.; I am drooling over Christopher as he is pouring his drink into mine when I am not looking. I am drunk from alcohol. I am drunk with this encounter. I am drunk in love. I never touched him. Never shared a meal with him. We never kissed or held hands—but I couldn't let go of my feelings for him. We exchanged cards. We exchanged a "good night," and then he was gone. I went into my room alone.

The next morning was ugly. I was still drunk; still in deep desire for Christopher. I found something I didn't want to let go of, but I didn't even have it. I went to work. The fog continued.

"Val, what is up, girl?" I sat in my temporary office cube for this deal; a fellow cubemate inquired about the impression I left that morning.

"I just had the best night of my life. I don't know if I can recover."

"Girl, you look like shit."

"Why, thank you, that feels wonderful. I will be okay, give me a bit." I dug into my computer, slammed down some coffee, and just went straight to Google. I was still wearing my sunglasses and downing coffee. I was deep into Christopher Sullivan.

I went to LinkedIn, no photo. Facebook, no account found. Went to his company's website, and there he was. There was my heart. The man in a suit with his arms crossed and his crooked smile. The photo in my head, the photo in my heart, now had a name and a physical presence. I sat back in astonishment, and here it was. *Wow.*

EMAIL: "Hello Christopher, what a night. Who was that crazy basketball player? Too funny. Looking forward to seeing you again. Let me know the next time you are in New York. Warm regards, Valerie Maher 646-867-5309."

I shed a tear and held my finger to the screen. It was him; it really was him. I walked outside with my second coffee of the morning, I walked around the campus, and I stood in a park and realized what I needed to do.

"Thank you, Jesus." I kneeled on the ground as my balance was not so well that morning. I placed my hand on the grass, still fresh from the morning dew. I could see Cal and Madeline in the kitchen as she awaited her early evening kiss. He grabbed her, twirled her around. He leaned her back, kissed her neck, and moved up to give her a long, slow kiss on the lips. I closed my eyes I opened them, just as a feather flew by and touched my knuckles. I grabbed it, stood up, and went back inside. LinkedIn request sent. Now, I wait.

Oh, Mr. Christopher Sullivan. What are you all about? Where are you now? Are you thinking of me as I am thinking of you?

After a few weeks of anticipation, I had no response from Christopher. No acceptance of a LinkedIn invitation. I decided to reach out again.

EMAIL: "Dearest Christopher, do you miss the Indigo as much as I do?"

EMAIL: "Excuse me, Valerie. Do I know you?"
Is he for real? Do I know you? What is this game?

EMAIL: "Call me Val. Don't you remember meeting at the Indigo? We had fun; we made fun of basketball players. We drank until the early a.m." I responded.

EMAIL: "Your name is Valerie. I will call you Valerie. No, I don't recall. Are you sure it's me? I do have a twin brother."

EMAIL: "It was you. Why don't we meet up? And you will remember me from that night, and from a previous life."

Then there was silence. I said too much. I felt foolish. The silence ruined me. Weeks went by; no response. I was losing myself. I wrote disturbing things on my FB wall as I was falling into a deep depression. I was failing at work. I was gaining an excessive amount of weight. I did not care. Christopher was all I wanted. Nothing else mattered. One night, and after many a glass of wine, maybe vodka, and a pizza, my phone rang. I answered.

"Val? How are you? I haven't heard from you? You are scaring me with what you are posting on your wall. 'See you in another life, my brother?' Are you quoting *Lost*? I'm so worried." It was Kellie.

"Yeah, I'm good. No worries. My relationship with *Lost* is not your business. It's extremely personal." I would respond.

"Now you're quoting *This Is 40*? Val, what is going on? Please talk to me."

"I have nothing, Kellie; I have nothing. I found him. I lost him."

"What are you talking about? Who? Who did you find?"

"The guy. The guy I told you about."

"Hmm, I'm not following."

"HIM! The man in the suit."

I sent her his picture via text as we spoke.

"It's him. The man I've been in love with since forever. He's gone."

"Oh, really? Oh, honey, did he die?"

"NO! He just doesn't want me. I suck, I am not good enough, he doesn't want me."

"Oh, Val, no, no, no! Don't say that. Please don't! I want to come and be with you, give you a hug. I'm so worried. Are you going to do something to yourself? I am on the first plane in the morning. Please, please don't beat yourself up. You will be okay."

"I'm not going to do anything."

"Promise?"

"I promise . . ."

"What are you going to do now?"

"I'm going to sleep."

"Please stay on the phone with me; I will help you sleep. Let's pray."

"Our Father, who art in heaven . . ."

I fell asleep to awake two hours later, to earbuds in my phone, and several missed calls. I went into the bathroom and threw up. I sat and threw up again. I went into the living room, grabbed my full glass of wine, and threw it against the wall. I sat against the bookshelves and wept.

"WHY!" I screamed.

* * * * *

"But I remember everything."
—"Hurt", Johnny Cash remake

I didn't want to talk or see anyone. My phone rang again; it was Tom.

"Valerie, what is going on. I am concerned."

"About what? I am FINE!"

"You are not fine. Valerie, what is wrong. Talk to me. Come home."

"I am home."

"Val, come to me. Come to California and spend some time here."

"I can't; I have to work. Big job, big goals, right? Can't give up on my dreams, right? So, rewarding . . . " I cut the call short. It rang again.

"Val, stop it. Stop being ridiculous. Take a leave of absence and come home."

"No, I will look weak."

"Val, right now, you are weak. Come home!"

"Kellie is coming here; I can't leave."

"Okay, well think about it. Please, think about it. And when she leaves, come back with her."

"I won't."

"Val—"

"Bye." I hung up the phone, turned my chair away from the window facing the hallway, and shed silent tears. I reached for my phone and sent a text to Kellie.

* * * * *

Are you still coming?

No. Doug and I are going away for the weekend. Isn't that great? I think he might propose! I am so excited! Maybe we can plan something for next month? You are okay, right?

Great. [I responded, wanting to strangle her.]

I needed a friend; she told me she would come to see me. I was weak. I needed someone. I told Tom I couldn't come when I should have said I could. How foolish to think that someone cared about me.

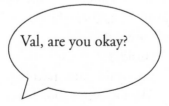

Val, are you okay?

[Kellie asked. I did not respond.]

I shut my phone off and slammed it on the desk. "Thanks," I said out loud. I shook my head in being so disappointed and upset. I then started to chuckle.

A knock at my door came, and without permission, my door opened. "Val, let's go out for a drink?"

It was my rival, of sorts, my competitor in our sales team. I was ahead but slowly slipping. He was very cute. I always had a crush on him. It was just what I needed; it was the worst thing I could do.

Say no, say no, say no . . . my Madeline voice in my head called out.

"Yeah, sure."

"Great! Ready in fifteen?"

"No problem."

Don't go, it's a trap, Madeline said to me. I suddenly didn't like Madeline. I was so hurt. I felt everyone was against me, even Madeline. Christopher was my one hope from the start of my time on this earth. He was taken from me. It was so unfair. I put Madeline aside and felt the same anger Shelia felt for her. I was starting to become her. I could feel Shelia in me. I felt the anger toward Madeline. For that evening, I did everything that Shelia would have done. I had too many drinks with a rival. He saw my weakness. He seduced me and made sure to make a fool of me in the office. I let him. He ruined my reputation which slowly took business away from me. My elite status with this company went downhill. I let him, because I was alone. I was sad. I was lost. I wanted to feel something. Hurt was the best I could find. I gave it to myself.

"Val, leave this fucking job and come home!" Tom screamed at me with each phone conversation we had. I had lost so much of what I had built and didn't want. I lost my vision, my passion, my everything. I lost myself. I wasn't careful. I went to the east river, sat on the edge and closed my eyes.

"Help me," I said inside.

"Help me," I said again and nothing. No response from Madeline or Cal, Shelia, not even God. I was losing everything. I don't know how it happened.

Christopher . . . Christopher . . . why are you in my heart? . . . why did I meet you? I don't know why . . . this is so unfair.

Go home, Val, you are a good person; it will be okay. This is just not right now. Go home, be with your family. I will be with you. It's you and me, kid, forever.

I wanted to believe that it was Christopher talking to me. I wanted to believe that he was speaking to me. Maybe he was, but it was stronger than that. Stronger than him or I. It had to be from above. It must be from God; he is listening to me. I am not alone.

"Thank you, Jesus," I said out loud. I felt the mist on my face, the cold of the ground. I took deep breaths. I knew what I needed to do. I wrote a resignation letter and went home. I dropped it off and headed to California.

"You are doing the right thing. I believe in you," Tom said as I entered his house. I sat on my bed and stared at my vision wall; I accomplished it all. All of it. All the business goals, all the money, the fortune—now what? I wanted nothing more than love and a family.

"It's time to change the wall, Val. You can keep dreaming; it's not over," Tom said as he stood in the doorframe.

I had to change the wall. I took each piece down, one by one, and said goodbye to all of them. As I took them down, I could feel myself come back again. I took a long look at the empty wall and held onto the paint on the cold wall as I pressed my face into it.

"Help me find my new dream," I said to all the visions on the wall. Madeline and Cal sat on the beach with a young Shelia, and soaked in the sun. They played volleyball, then barbecued on the beach at sunset. They sat on a beach blanket. Cal opened up a set of plans for a house—the dream house he was building for them.

"Build it, and they will come," Cal's voice said in my head.

I tore down what was currently there. I went through pictures in magazines and newspapers, and started to rebuild the wall with all-new images and dreams. I started to rebuild my life. It was going to be wonderful. It was going to have Christopher in it. *I will never give up. I believe.*

The next morning, I woke up and stared at the wall. I remember all that used to live on this wall, all that I accomplished. I reflected on all that I had become and how quickly I started to knock down my walls. I didn't recognize myself anymore. I didn't know that person. I went back to brown hair; my face was worn out, I had grown in weight. Who have I become?

"Who do you say I am?" played in my head. I don't want to be this person in the mirror. I went back to the wall and focused. I wanted to start fresh, lose the weight, go back to being blonde, back into a business, my business. *I can do this.* More than anything, I wanted Christopher. I placed his picture on the wall, and mine next to his. I placed pictures of Tom and Brenda, Cal and Madeline also on the wall. I wanted a family. *I can get it.*

"No just means not right now, Valerie," Tom said at the doorway as he handed me a coffee and orange juice.

"Ready to get into shape?" he asked.

"I am so ready. Let's do this."

We ran on the beach; it was hard. I stopped several times. Tom waited patiently. We ran five miles each morning and each evening. Tom got me into a good local gym. I worked out with a trainer, building muscle and strength. We put together a boxing gym in the garage. I hit the bag every time I got frustrated. Brenda took me to get back into golden locks. I looked like the California girl I used to be. In a few weeks, I became closer to the me I wanted to be. I sat on the deck after a run, one morning, with Tom, and we drank our green smoothies.

"So, what's the plan, Valerie?" he asked.

"I am ready; I am ready for it all, Tom. I am in love with a man I met once. I never even touched him. I want to be with him. I want to be a successful businesswoman. I have a plan for that. But I want THIS. I want to be the best wife I can be for him. I want him to want me. I want him to desire me. I want him to not be able to live without me. I want to build a happy home with substance in it. I want it for me, but I want it more for us."

"Sounds like a plan. You are very serious about this man. Why him? Why is he worthy of you?"

"I don't know how to answer that. I just never thought about it in that way."

"You need to know why."

"I do, I do . . . there is just something about him, just this over-whelming feeling I have when I saw him, when I met him. He has been the picture in my head; he has been a part of my life since I can remember."

"Why is he worthy of you? To be with you? What is he going to give you that makes him the best, and makes you the best person you can be? Can you answer that? The feelings are special. I get that. The feelings are real and mean something to you. But it needs to be more than that. Why is he worthy to be with you?" I sat in a frustrated silence as I knew he was right. *Why am I putting such a price tag on him, and not on myself? What is the tag he is giving me?* All I can see and touch is the stubbornness—silence that suddenly hurts more than ever.

"Why was it Richard?" Tom asked.

Oh Richard, oh Richard—the pain just changed into a new one. I put him in a box and hid him in an attic in my brain. For now, it is just a place in my head. I can picture his kids going back to Dallas; his wife in hesitation and tears, but welcoming him with open arms. She would move all the furniture back to where it was, throw out my sheets and all the clothes I left behind. But, she would wonder and realize that memories were made in that room—that house that didn't belong to her. Shortly, after a few months, when she had the courage, she would insist that they move, create a new home. Start a new life. Leave the memories of me in that house.

"Richard was warm and endearing. He cared about me. I loved the way he looked at me, the way he touched me; the way he slept in my arms. But he never belonged to me. I wanted him to belong to me and no one else, but he didn't. I just wanted to believe that, one day, he would choose me. He didn't. I chose to be second best. I got second best. I want to be number one to someone. I want to be number one to Christopher. I want him to think about me. I want him to desire me. I want him to not be able to live without me."

"That is a dangerous wish list, young lady. You are good enough, maybe even too good. Find out who he is, and really learn what he is about, before you pour your heart into him. I am all for you pursuing him. I know there will be no stopping you. Do what is in your heart. Don't settle for anything less. I don't want to see you be second best."

"Christopher has a good job. He is smart. He donates to charity. He is confident. He is obnoxious. I think. I feel like he can complete me. I feel so connected to him."

"Make sure he loves you, make sure he is everything that completes you. Make sure you know what that means. If you are following him, those are the qualities you want. Make sure you realize it's the journey, not the destination. God will give you what is best, not what you want."

"I will."

"Okay, now let's talk game plan. In this company you are going to build; are you ready? I am sure this Christopher will want to be with a smart and successful woman, right?"

"I am ready. I put together a business plan, now I need to raise capital."

"Let's see it." I ran into my room and grabbed my laptop and some papers. We spent the day on the deck reviewing the entire plan; my presentation for investors, where I saw the income coming from. Tom agreed to all of it and made some tweaks along the way. We strategized. Tom made some calls. In the early afternoon, Tom went into the house, came out with champagne and an envelope.

"I am very impressed with your progress and utilization of your time-off used wisely. I think you are ready," he said as he opened the champagne and the cork popped. He poured the two glasses and handed me the envelope. He stood up and faced the ocean; the sun was starting to decide to take a nap for the day. The breeze pushed his hair underneath his hat, into his face—but he didn't let it bother him. He admired the ocean and soaked in the last moments the sun's strength gave him.

"Open it, Valerie. You earned it."

I opened the letter and watched him as I feared what was behind that sealed flap. It was a picture of my house from Larchmont when I lived with Shelia, and a check for $1.5 million dollars. He never took his eye off the ocean waves and sipped his champagne slowly.

"What is this?" I asked in a high-pitched voice.

"It's for you. I sold the house. You know that house was mine, right? You are my only daughter, so now the earnings are yours. Take it. Go and start your company. Start your future. Make me proud. Make yourself proud. Everything you want within you, Valerie, go and get it." At the moment, I stood up and ran to him and held him tight. I held him so tight. He didn't budge. I started to feel foolish and pulled away. He put his arm around me and pulled me back in and kissed the top of my head. "I love you, Valerie, I am just not good at being mushy."

"Me neither." I accepted his embrace and closed my eyes.

"Thank you, Jesus," I said again, as I knew he was working in my favor.

We drank champagne. We watched the sun go down. Brenda came over and made roasted chicken. I looked at the ocean. As the waves crashed, I saw Cal chasing Madeline across the waterline. She was laughing. He grabbed her from behind and twirled her around until they became so dizzy they fell to the ground. Right before he was about to move in for the kiss, she would hold the side of his face and soak in the moment. He got closer. She closed her eyes and wished for that moment to never end.

My new office was open; business was building. I walked into the office one morning. My assistant was waiting for me as I entered the glass doors.

"Good morning, Maria, very nice to see you."

"I just booked you an opportunity in DC." I dropped my bag. She knew what DC meant to me, that I wanted this gig and how it put everything at stake. I was ready. I went to hug her. We did a little dance. I was so excited; I was ready for this.

I put together my best presentation. I went through every angle with the team. We practiced, we white-boarded each response and left field answers. We were ready. We put all hands in the circle around our conference table; we cheered for a big win. I emailed Christopher, letting him know I would be in town, and asked him to meet up.

I am sorry Valerie, but do I know you?

Christopher, yes we have been through this already. Did we meet at the Indigo? If you don't remember, then why don't you meet up with me and see for yourself?

Valerie, I am not sure. Very busy.

Meet up with me, peak your curiosity. Can we do coffee? I should be done with my presentation at 2:00 p.m.

Okay, let me know.

Here is the address: Starbucks, 901 15th St NW. See you there at 3:00 p.m.

See you then. Have a wonderful evening.

It was all coming together; everything I wanted, just like Tom said. It was all coming together.

"Thank you, Jesus."

* * * * *

I entered Starbucks at 2:50 p.m. that day. I sat at the long table next to a window where I could barely see his office down the street. I plugged in my computer and used it as an excuse to stare at a blank screen, as my hand shook and my body was right behind it. I did deep breaths without trying to look like I was having an insane anxiety attack. I calmed myself down after each time the door opened. Each time, it was not Christopher.

The clock started, then the timing. I didn't believe that Christopher was one who would stand to be late; or would he be the person who would be late, because he wanted to prove that he was important? Would his obnoxious demeanor precede him? Would I be turned off when I saw him, or would I fall into a spell? Was he just letting me sit here as he watched from across the street and laughed? The longer I waited, the more I felt like door number three.

Waaaannnwaaahhh. That noise just rang in my head, the image of opening an empty door sat in my brain. I suddenly felt worthless. A woman walked in, a grandma, a young boy, an older man, a few high schoolers, maybe some college kids, a mother, a cyclist, a man in a suit, a man in jeans, a homeless man, a blind man with a dog. Then a man with dark jeans and a blue button-down came in. He smiled and sat by me. I looked into his hazel eyes and smiled; he smiled back.

"Val, hello. I'm Chris."

"Hello," I replied with caution.

"So glad we got to meet up. Did you get something to drink? What can I get for you? wow, you are much more beautiful than your picture—wow!"

"Thank you. I will have a Grande green tea. Much appreciated," I said in as much of a subdued voice as I could.

"Great, I will be right back." He went up to order. I watched with caution. I watched for a signal. I watched to see a man wearing denim, brown shoes with black socks, and a blue shirt. The nervous twitch. The nervous energy. The nervous sweat on his forehead. I knew exactly who he was, who I expected him to be. I sat alone and waited for him to come back. After several moments, he walked pigeon-toed carrying his anxiety walked back to our spot, handed me my drink, and sat down. His nerves were still there. I looked out the window. I couldn't see the office. I felt eyes watching over me.

"Thank you, Colby," I said without looking at him. I looked at his eyes after I took a sip.

"You are welcome, Val, wait, wait, did you just call me Colby? No, silly, I am Chris. I mean, Christopher." I sat back and held my drink on the table and smirked as I looked into Colby. He tried so hard to look at me as sweat that formed on his forehead started to run down and smack him in the eye.

"Colby. Christopher would never call me Val. It is Valerie. He also would never let anyone call him Chris." He didn't know what to say. The sweat continued. I never broke looking into his eyes.

"You are more beautiful than your pictures. I like your confidence. Yes, I am Colby. Christopher is in California and sent me. He thought this was a big joke, but from the few moments I have spent here with you, I like you. I like you for Chris. You have strong wit. Yes, only I call him Chris. He always wants to be called Christopher. Are you disappointed?"

"Yes, no. Same, same, but different? I am relieved to meet you. I want nothing more than to meet up with Christopher, but I am terrified to meet him again. Sound crazy?"

"Not at all. Christopher is difficult."

"I believe that. Maybe your instant reaction and honesty make me feel that you know this isn't a joke to me. I really like him. How does this work? I have never done this before."

"Ha! I don't think I have either. We have played games like this for years; we never got caught. Well, actually, I was always playing for Christopher, not vice versa. I am married. My high school game was pretty good. I met my wife in college. I have no intention to meet someone else. I wouldn't do anything to ruin that."

"Except for meeting a woman and pretending you are your brother?"

"Well, I mean, it never gets further than this." I gave him my bullshit face; he got it.

"You are right; it has gone further than this. I never take a direction where my wife could get hurt, I promise. She knows I am here, I swear!" I touched his hand and let him know it was okay. He stopped talking. His nerves didn't know what to do; he took a sip of his macchiato. Christopher would never drink that.

"I guess I live through my brother, but he is difficult. Are you sure you like him? He is a pain in the ass and so complicated."

"I can handle it."

"I believe that. I like you, Val."

"Valerie."

"Man, you are perfect for Christopher, Valerie."

Colby told me about his wife. His two girls were off at college. He was re-learning his relationship with his wife.

"It is hard; it is hard to reinvent yourself."

"Is he really in California?"

"Yes, he really is. Scouts honor!"

"Okay." I was disappointed but enjoying my time with Colby. He was warm and goofy. I could see parts of him would be good qualities on Christopher.

"All right, we need to get you two together. I've got to plan this out. But I will promise I will get you guys together. I know he will fall for you. Damn! I wish I wasn't married. All right, this is going to work." Colby slammed the table as he spoke with determination.

"Yes, thank you so much! I am so excited! So, when do you think? I can come back to DC, just tell me when?" *Why would he rather be alone than be with me?*

*   *   *   *   *

Colby, please come through for me, I repeated over and over. After some-time, I heard *I will, I promise*. I got on a plane. I went to California to see Tom, and prayed to see Christopher in the airport. I didn't. I went straight to my room. Straight back into my depression.

"Valerie, why do you do this to yourself? What is wrong now? I thought you landed this big deal? What happened?" I laid in my bed, in my clothes on top of the quilt, and faced the wall, faced the dreams that were already accomplished—except for Christopher, he was yet to be defeated.

"He sent his brother to meet me. He didn't meet me. He sent his brother. Why doesn't he want me?"

"Val, you are so critical. Why do you want to be with this guy? Is he worthy of you if he is doing this?"

"He is in my heart. I can feel him. I don't know why."

"Please, please, please don't do this to yourself. If he is meant to be, he will find you. MAKE SURE HE IS WORTHY OF YOU! You can't fall back into a depression. You have a thriving business that needs you. The right man will find you; he will! Valerie."

"I know. I just need a day here. I will be back."

"Valerie, stay as long as you need. Fight the depression, fight the power he has over you. You are stronger than this!" He was right. *I am stronger than this. I can do this.*

No just means not right now, I said in my head. Did he have power over me? I hardly knew him. But meeting his brother was a good confirmation it was still an open avenue.

I can do this, I repeated over and over in my head until I fell asleep.

I dreamed of Madeline sitting over me in the attic, as I laid on the pictures of her and Cal. I could feel her breathing over me, brushing back my hair with her fingers, her red lipstick still intact, her pearls on her neck, and the warmth of her touch. I felt her and took her in, and forgot that my castle had burned down. But Madeline was still with me. She still loved me and for right now, I needed her. She knew how to comfort me.

"I love you, Madeline," I would say in my sleep.

"I love you too," she said. That night, I slept soundly. I woke up, went for a run on the beach, sat on the deck, and watched the waves.

"How are you doing this morning?" Tom asked as he leaned on the sliding door into the house.

"Heading back today. I am ready; I can do this. I can move on."

"Good, now go kick some ass and find someone else. He is out there. Make sure he is worthy of you."

"I will."

Cal and Madeline, please watch over Christopher for me. I got to my apartment, went straight to my computer. Went straight to work on my newly-landed assignment.

I kept my focus; I kept my drive. I went for long walks. I worked out with heavy weights. I kept focus. I worked daily, asking Christopher to leave my brain. I went to sports games instead of watching them on a multi-screen arena. I learned about the Yankees and the Giants. I learned anything about sports to help me have conversations with men around me. It was time to meet someone.

*   *   *   *   *

"Building your dream
Has to start now,
There is no other road to take
You won't make a mistake.
I'll be guiding you."
—Magic, Olivia Newton-John

The game was Yankees versus the Sox's at Yankee stadium. It was a mid-May game where you didn't know if it would be forty degrees or seventy-five. It was a chance to be outside and not have a large coat on. The smell of spring was in the air. I was feeling good. I was there with some friends in my building that I relied on for a social connection. Beers were flowing. Yankees were winning. I had the next round. I headed straight to Goose Island. The line was long, so I ran to the restroom where the line seemed shorter. I came out and saw a tall, gorgeous man, who was tentatively watching the game as he waited for some friends. The Goose Island could wait. I found my prey. I went after it.

"So, what did I miss? What's the score?" I asked without permission. He didn't look at first. I waited patiently. Once he realized I was talking to him, he stood back, a little startled, as he held his bottom lips with his left hand.

"Oh, yeah, umm, hello, yes. The score . . . umm." He was flustered and ran his right hand through his hair a few times.

"Are you sure you are watching this game?" I asked. He giggled and caught up his nerve.

"Yes, yes," he said with a laugh and a bend in his knees. "Hmm, so the score is 8-6, Yankees."

"Nice, so what is going on here? Are you a secret agent for the Yankees? Third-base secret coach? What brings you here?"

"Oh, here with some friends from work. I am the designated driver, so not having much fun. Needed a break from the silly drunks, so I came to hang here for a bit. And I am so lucky to have found you. Today is my lucky day."

"Indeed it is." We stood there and smiled as I made him more nervous. We talked about our secret lives as the third-base coach and called out plays; no one was listening to us—no one but us.

"All right, I have to go get beers for my friends." I turned away and started to walk.

"WAIT!"

I didn't stop. He came after me and grabbed my shoulder as I hit the Goose Island line.

"Hey!"

I stopped and turned around.

"Can I get your number? And maybe your name? I would really like to see you again; your charm and wit have overcome me."

"Sure, what is your number? I will send you my E-card."

713-867-5309

"Sent." His phone gave a *ding*. He opened the contact and smiled.

"Nice to meet you, Ms. Valerie, I am Dylan."

"Nice to meet you, Dylan." I turned around and grabbed my allotted two beers and went back to my seat.

"Where have you been? I was getting worried!" said one of my friends.

"I just met a cute boy . . . so, you can wait." We giggled, drank beer, and laughed the night away. It was wonderful.

(11:14 p.m.) Hello, Ms. Valerie. This is Dylan from the game, your third-base coach part-ner. Do you remember me?

(11:14 p.m.) Who? Nope, doesn't ring a bell.

(11:17 p.m.) Just kidding, yes I remember you, who could forget your eyes.

(11:17 p.m.) My eyes? No, my eyes are boring. Now your eyes, on the other hand, are beautiful blue. Full of wonder. Now those eyes are not forgettable. See, I didn't forget.

(11:19 p.m.) Hmmm, it's been a hot minute.

(11:19 p.m.) Oh, that hot minute was some well-worthy sixty seconds. You are so lovely, Ms. Valerie, when do I get to see you again?

(11:23 p.m.) When are you going to ask me to see you again?

(11:25 p.m.) I wouldn't ask you to come over tonight as that would be cheap, and I live in the Bronx. You are a fancy city girl. But if I did?

(11:25 p.m.) I would say no. I don't do one-night stands.

(11:26 p.m.) I believe that you are a classy lady. I would not want you for one night; I want you for a lifetime. I guess that is too much to ask for in one night.

(11:29 p.m.) Lifetime . . . that is quite a long date.

(11:33 p.m.) I only take a fine woman like your-self on long dates. You should pack a bag.

(11:35 p.m.) I am packed.

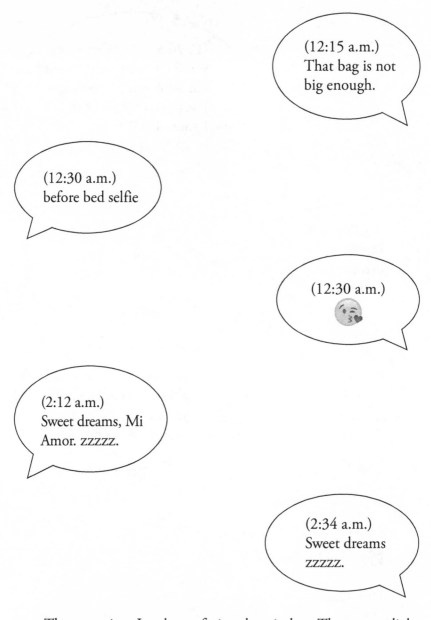

That morning, I woke up facing the window. There was a light wind and rain. I opened my eyes and watched the drops hit the window as they made a tapping noise. It rushed through and then there was be silence. The city buzz had already started even as the sun was still working on coming out behind the clouds. You could hear cab whistles blowing, buses pulling in and out of stops, cops surveying the streets. The wind and rain were trying to fight their way through the window. As I watched through my blurry vision, my mascara fighting with my eyelashes to open my eyes, I saw a feather fall slowly into the sky and work its way down. Floating side to side down the alley, and from the thirtieth floor, it continued all the way down to the ground with elegance and poise. With conviction and caution. With love and with pain, with the mission to hit the ground safely.

I walked up to the window and planted my face on it to watch. When it came out of view, I opened the window and stuck my head out to watch and hope for a safe landing. As the floating continued, it worked its way further and further, and after all the floating, all the waiting, all the hesitation and all the anticipation of the fall, it found a spot on the ground. It took a leap of faith and landed safely. I watched it and sighed in delight and comfort that it lay there. The wind picked up. The wind swirled in the air; the feather stayed put. I watched it. It seemed to be looking back at me. It kept me in comfort.

I watched it diligently. After a few moments, I saw a young girl pick it up. She studied it. Studied it in the light. The rain changed its color, its weight, its form. She hugged it and put it in her pocket. She was about to walk away when she looked up, found my eyes and waved at me as if to say, "I have it; I will take care of it, cherish it. Believe in it as much as you have." I smiled, she smiled and waved. I waved back. She walked away, and she waved the feather up to me, up to the sky, up to Madeline. I knew it would be okay.

I retired back to my bed with the window open. The wind came in. The rain came in. I closed my eyes. The text messages started to come in. Before I re-opened my eyes, I soaked in the moment and smile of that little girl.

*   *   *   *   *

Are you as beautiful in the a.m. as you are before you go to bed? This, I wondered since about 4 a.m. Is it too early for me to ask?

I snapped a quick photo of myself between the pillow and the sheets where the perfect shade made my makeup-less face look sexy; I sent it in a perfect black and white to capture the moment.

Wow, it is better than expected. Oh, I will never make it through work today, I will be distracted by this photo. Why are you so mean?

[Dylan responded.]

Now I am a mean lady? Whatever happened to old fashioned sex appeal? Oh, equality. You are so mean . . .

Fair enough, fair enough. I will be distracted by a beautiful, smart, third-base coach. Oh, I am so lucky.

I am packed. How far away is the Bronx again? Should I hold my mail?

Haha, Mi Amor, you were in the Bronx last night . . . it is not that far. I am afraid that my apartment is not fancy enough for you. I bet you live in a big, high-rise with a doorman, and someone who puts sweet mints on your pillow. I live in a cheap apartment in the Bronx; I am embarrassed.

What? Don't be silly. You don't know me at all, I mean, all of what you said is true about where I live, except for the mints. My dust bunnies are not that proactive. I think they may need a trainer or something. Do you know someone?

Hmm, I might have a guy for you.

Sweet.

Always looking out for my girl. So, can we do lunch? Maybe Thursday or Friday? I can come into the city and meet you. I work nights right now (long story). I also just moved here from Texas and know nothing about the city. Pick a place. I will bring my brown eyes you like so much.

I like your brown eyes in any part of town. Tell me where you want to go by you, the city is overrated. I can meet you either day. Just name it, I will bring my blue eyes you like so much.

Oh, see now I am distracted . . . really, fancy lady? Will you come to the BX? If you drink Tequila, then I will fall so hard, have to take all the money out of the bank to buy you a diamond ring and ask you to be my wife. I fear the answer.

Yes, but I don't need a diamond. Make it something simple. I don't need anything more than you.

Yes? So, wait, does that mean yes? I should fear the answer, or that you would say yes? I'm just nervous, I've never done this before!

Me neither . . .

So?

Don Julio Silver or just Patron Silver—I am a little picky . . . so, take me to lunch. Take the night off. Wine and dine me. Be yourself, wear that fabulous cologne you wore the day I met you. Leave all your fears out the door. Be with me. You will know the answer.

Oh, Valerie, I already know what I want the answer to be, I already know. Meet me at the cafe on 155th street at 1:00 p.m. on Friday.

Done, I will be the one in pink.

I will be the one with the goofy smile, nervous sweat, eager to see my future wife.

I can't wait.

Me neither . . .

Dylan, have a
wonderful day, and
do me a favor?

Anything for
you, my dear.

Stay lovely . . .

Oh, with you
in my heart,
that will be easy.
Wink.

*   *   *   *   *

I went into my wallet, took out my piece of the red feather from Madeline, closed my eyes for another few hours. I had dreams, of happiness, the beach, Dylan, Dylan with Tom and Brenda, of Holidays, Yankee games, laughing, having babies, dancing, laying on the dance floor and looking up at the Chinese lights, the warmth and coldness of the air, the love of the people around us . . . I felt a future. I was able to exhale without fear.

*   *   *   *   *

I sat with my back to the door. I ordered a tequila, chilled and straight with a lime. I was nervous, but after a few sips, I felt okay. My phone received a text alert. It was Tom. I never told him about Dylan. It just simply said, "Thinking about you, Valerie, want the best for you. Let me know that you are okay."

As I read the message, Dylan came in behind me and touched the back of my shoulder.

"Wait, don't move!" I exclaimed.

"Can you humor me?"

"Hmm, okay?" I snapped a selfie in the moment.

"Okay, Tom—he's my dad, is always worried about me, and is now randomly texting me. So, I just want to send him this to ease his fears? I mean if you are going to chop me up and throw me in the river, then he has something to go by, right?"

"Okay, wow. I mean, yes, please send to your dad."

"Tom," I said with conviction.

"Okay, Tom. And as for the chopping and the river thing, I am not that kinky . . . should I be?"

"No, it was a horrible joke, I am nervous."

"I am nervous too. Wait, what are you drinking?"

"Don Julio Silver . . . like you should ask . . ."

"Waiter! Hello, hi, yes, can I have what she is having? Can I have a double? I am on a date with the most beautiful woman in the world. I am going to ask her to marry me, so I need some liquid courage. Can you hook me up?"

"Yes, sir, right away. And if I may, you are making the right decision."

"Gracias. See, my peeps are on my side."

"Awesome."

"I'm awesome? Wait, that is what you said right?" He winked twice as he said this.

"No . . ."

"Ouch, no? Too soon? Wow, I am so out of my element. I just like you so much. I just . . . I'm not good at this. Is it obvious?" I placed my hand on his. My other placed a finger on his lips.

"Ms. Valerie, my heart is a flutter. Oh, you are beautiful, smart, sexy, savvy, love the Yankees . . . you are perfect, you drink tequila! If you like tacos, it is over; I will have to introduce you to my family."

"I would love to meet your family."

"Oh, they will go crazy over you. Maybe not like me, as much, as you are the best of my better half. I apologize for my lack of words. English is my second language."

"I think it is honest, sincere and adorable. I am fully enjoying this moment with you."

"Oh, Valerie, I am enjoying this more. If I could selfie this whole moment, I would. I never want this to end."

"Then don't let it."

"I won't."

My phone sends a ding just as he pulled in for a kiss.

"Your boyfriend is jealous already?" Dylan said to break the awkward pull back.

"Stop it. I don't have a boyfriend." I looked at my phone. It was Tom.

"So happy for you.
Look at the relaxed look
in your eyes, the smile
on your face. That is
what you deserve. Stay
with this and be well."

I smiled. I showed Dylan his message. Perhaps, I was growing past my depression.

"wow, I didn't even ask you formally to marry me, and I have his consent. I think we may be engaged by the weekend." I laughed.

"I am serious." I knew he was. I was scared but wanted it.

"I am down."

"Oh, Valerie, what I want to give you. I hope it's enough, but I want you and nothing else."

"Wow."

And we sipped tequila, ate tacos, danced until very, very, late. I woke up that morning in the Bronx, with a smile. I took the 4 train back to my apartment and giggled the whole way home.

*　　*　　*　　*　　*

I was in a light sleep and could feel myself dancing, dancing with Dylan. I saw Madeline and Cal dancing with us on the same dancefloor, as we both twirled at different times and different directions, I got smiles and thumbs up from both—it was the confirmation I needed.

After several dates in a row, the joking conversations of us being together forever became a serious conversation. After the short few weeks we spent together, we decided there was no reason to not move forward with making it a reality. Dylan left his apartment and moved into mine.

The Yankees won the World Series. The Patriots won another super bowl. I won the one thing I always wanted—someone who made me feel whole, fulfilled. I closed the chapter on loneliness and depression.

* * * * *

You were my cross,
My cross to bear,
But you're heavy,
So heavy to wear.

—"Golden," The Tontons

One day, in mid-February my phone dinged. After much distraction, I went to retrieve the message. It was from Colby.

I should have brushed him off. I should have deleted the message, but I didn't.

I was at work, in the middle of a big assignment and focused on it. Dylan was now a permanent fixture in my life. We are happy, content, and I had no reason to mess with that. But, I always had a weakness for Christopher.

Good, so I still want to get you together with Christopher. Are you still down? I didn't forget about you!

No, no, no, no, you are not available. Do not say yes, you are with Dylan. You are going to marry Dylan, don't do it, don't do it.

Hmm, I am, and I am not. I am with someone . . .

But you still have a thing for Christopher and want to see where it will go.

Hmm, I just can't?

Yes, you can. Come out Thursday?

I took a pause. *Don't do this. Walk away, walk away.*

No, I can't. I am living with someone. I just can't.

Come on. Ah, man. I am too late. Seriously? Won't you meet him? I can't convince you?

Sorry, yeah. I just don't think it's a good idea.

He will be disappointed. All right, good luck, Valerie, keep in touch.

Thanks, same to you.

That night I worked late. I came home and grabbed a beer. I stood in the kitchen leaning on the island. Dylan was in the bedroom in a state of REM. In his own world, asleep In his most vulnerable position. As I listened to Dylan, my mind could not stop thinking of Christopher. *How does Christopher have such power over me?*

I went quietly into the bedroom, took off my clothes and got into bed next to Dylan who laid on his back with one hand on his chest. I laid sideways leaning on my arm, and hovered over him. After some time, he awoke and was startled by my presence.

"Shhhh, go back to sleep," I said as I reached to rub his stomach and curled into his side. As we got comfortable, he kissed my head, took in a few sniffs, and closed his eyes again; I closed mine.

"Are you okay, Valerie?"

"I am okay; there is nothing better than being in your arms."

"Same to you, mi amor."

We fell asleep. I dreamed of Christopher. I dreamed of touching him. *What does he smell like again? What would it be like to gaze into his eyes again? Will I fall for him? Will he fall for me?*

"Christopher." I called to him, and when I woke up, I felt guilty from the dream and ashamed. I just wanted to hide it from Dylan.

"Come here," he said and pulled me on top of him for a kiss.

"You mumble in your sleep, you know?"

"I do? Really? What did I say?"

"I don't know, but you have such passion in your thoughts. Are you dreaming about me?"

"I don't know; I don't know what I was dreaming about."

I chuckled out of embarrassment and my inability to properly lie.

"Let me make you breakfast." I changed the topic, gave him a kiss and ran away into the kitchen. I made him an omelet with arugula, goat cheese, and bacon. I perfectly toasted his English muffin, and made Dylan's favorite Bustelo.

"Valerie, this is amazing. Very exciting for a Wednesday morning."

"Awesome, I am so glad you like it," I said as I gave him a kiss and hoped that he could not taste the guilt.

"Dylan, I have to go to DC for a few days."

"Oh yeah? For work?"

"Yes, for work. I have some friends there also that I plan on catching up with."

"Nice, so when are you going?"

"I leave for DC this afternoon. It will be quick. When I get back, maybe we can go for a long walk through Central Park?"

"Then I will stay here and wait patiently for you, mi amor."

"You are the best." I didn't know what I was doing, or why I was going to DC, after I told Colby I was not coming. I was so nervous. Thankfully, Dylan didn't suspect a thing. When I arrived in my room in DC, I facetimed Dylan out of pure guilt.

(Facetime Call)

"Si, mi amor, how is your trip going? I am in between meetings. Are you having fun?"

"I just got here, and I miss you."

"Oh, Ms. Valerie, I always miss you, I keep your photos on my phone and check them all day. You are always with me. I have another meeting, I have to go." He said in a whisper, and blew a kiss, he walked into a room and turned off his phone.

I went to visit my clients, just to pop in and say hello. The hour of pleasantries dragged on. This trip could have been a fifteen-minute conference call. But I somehow needed to be here. I was proving a point to myself.

I found myself back at the Starbucks where I met with Colby. I sat in hopes that Christopher came in and found me there. He didn't. At happy hour, I walked to a nearby bar and sat and watched the door, drowning in vodka.

"Christopher, come and find me. Come and tell me you want me. I'm waiting for you." No response. I ordered another vodka.

"Go home, Val, go back to Dylan," the voices in my head told me. I paid my bill and decided I was being ridiculous and needed to go home. In the restroom, I fixed my makeup. I looked at myself in the mirror. I felt like Shelia.

"I will go back and find Christopher. Don't waste your time with Dylan. It's Christopher you want. Find him," Shelia said to me. I spat at the mirror in front of me and headed for the door.

I miss you, Dylan.

Oh, Mi Amor, I miss you.

I took a deep breath; I walked out of the restaurant. I heard a familiar voice and stopped in my tracks. I heard giggles. My memories came back. I turned my head. It was Christopher with a brunette on his arm, laughing and slapping him as they walked into the same restaurant I walked out of. He was smiling. He was engaged with her body language. He never saw me.

It was you; it was always you, Christopher. I waited, I cried for so many nights over you, I said in my head as my heart sank into my stomach. I went up to my room, sat back on the bed and stared at the ceiling. I saw Shelia with Tom. It must have been when they first met. I saw Shelia get excited to see him. Excited to meet up with him, waiting by the phone for him to call. And when the phone rang, Tom politely declined their date for that evening.

She was nonchalant about it, saying, "Oh, no worries."

She tugged on her pearls and looked in the mirror, counting the hours she spent to get ready, to pick out the perfect dress, shaved all the right parts of her body, curled her hair as close to Farrah Fawcett that she could, the hours spent finding the perfect red lipstick that Madeline wore. She was disappointed, but she couldn't let Tom know. They hung up the phone and Shelia sat on the bed, eventually slumping over to the pillows. After she cried, she found her bottle of vodka underneath the bed and drank the whole thing.

She ignored Ashley crying, ignored Todd who needed attention with his homework. She soon forgot the whole night happened as she fell into a state of blank, a state of blur that became a state of black. She woke up angry with everyone around her until that phone rang again. When Tom was on the other line, I closed my eyes and drifted off into my own blackness.

* * * * *

(Dylan)
Hello, Valerie, are you having a good trip? I miss you, just want to say hello, busy lady.

(Christopher)
Valerie, Colby told me
you wouldn't meet me.
I want to see you.

I looked at my phone and ignored them both. I was going back to Dylan. Christopher lied to me. I was so upset with him. *How dare he lie to me!* I had a moment of weakness. I needed to see Christopher and now understood he is not who I thought he was. I needed to leave DC.

I miss you, Dylan,
I'm coming home.

(Dylan)
Well, hello! So glad
to hear. Still, want to
do the park then?

Sounds perfect.
I can't wait
to see you.

Are you okay, Valerie? You don't seem to be yourself.

I am okay, I am just ready to come home. I need to see your face.

Ms. Valerie, this place is boring without you. I can't wait.

(Christopher) I am downstairs at your hotel, come and meet me for a drink.

What? How do you know where I am?

Valerie, I saw you. I can feel you any- time you are near me. Come meet me.

No, I am going home.

*   *   *   *   *

I fixed myself up, looked at myself in the mirror. In disappoint-ment, I went downstairs.

He sat in the middle of the bar that only sat fifteen people. It was not crowded. I sat next to him.

"You made it," he said in excitement.

"I don't know why, but I am here. Why am I here?"

"Because you want to be." He ordered me a drink, he held my hand, and told me his story.

"I met her in law school. She was a nerd. She was my rival for the top of the class. She had long, brown, wavy hair, brown eyes behind wood-edged glasses. She was witty in the courtroom, she wore tight suits and heels, and made everyone in the courtroom pay attention. I had to have her. We took the bar together. We worked at competing law firms. We went head-to-head on cases. She was tough.

"I always knew there was someone else I was in love with. When I couldn't find her, or when I couldn't find you, I decided to be with her. I asked her to marry me. We got married. I was thirty-two, she was thirty-one, we had two girls a few years apart. We stopped having sex when my second daughter was born, and when she was five, we slept in separate bedrooms for a few years. And then I got my own place after that. We have been apart ever since. I see my girls, but not as much as I would like to. I love them; I didn't get a chance to be the dad I wanted to be for them." He was sincere in his story, and when he showed me the pictures of his girls now, it showed he really did love them. I consoled him with my hand on his back. He came in closer to me.

"I saw you that night at the Indigo and recognized you; I knew that you were the one. I can hear your voice in my dreams. I don't know how to handle this, but I want to be with you."

"Is he worthy of you?" Tom's voice was in my head. I finished my drink.

"I have someone at home. You have a wife. We can't do this. I have to go."

"Don't go, don't go."

I could see Dylan sleeping away the night as I continued lies about who I was. I could see Shelia crying on the side of her bed and Madeline with her finger to the window. I would be like them if I continued this. I was chasing after a man and until I wore him down, I would be miserable just like them.

"I can't do this; I am sorry I just can't."

"Valerie, I . . ."

"Please, I just can't do this." I picked up my bag and headed for the airport. Christopher didn't follow me. He was sad. I could feel it. He dropped his guard. I could see it.

"Valerie!" I heard a scream. I was trying to hail a cab.

"Can I take you to the airport?"

I nodded yes.

"I want to come to New York."

"Then come to New York. Come to New York because you want to be with me. Come because you can't live without me."

"Then why can't you stay for the same reasons?"

"Because you need to break up with your wife."

"I can't."

"Then I can't."

"Valerie, that is not fair."

"I waited forever for you; I am not settling for second best. Come because you want to change that. Otherwise, I have to move on."

"Valerie . . . fair. But, I will come for you. It will happen."

I arrived home mid-day to find Dylan fresh out of a shower and shaving. I came behind him to fit my face right in the small of his back, right between the shoulder blades, put my arms around his body, and grazed my fingers right above his underwear line. I gave him kisses in that nook I fit perfectly in. He held my hands on his chest as he became relaxed with me wrapped around him.

*   *   *   *   *

I never dated a Latin man before. He was six-foot-one, had brown hair and brown eyes, with a bright white smile. He was always insecure about his background, but he always overcompensated with extra loving, kisses, good cooking.

"Hello." I held onto him. I smelled him I cried a bit. I asked for forgiveness in my head, but didn't have the guts to say it out loud. That day, we walked through Central Park. We drank hot chocolate in front of a fire. The next day, we made dinner and went to bed early. I overcompensated for my guilt, but he embraced it. I hope it worked. I woke up and watched him sleep, as I couldn't. Eventually, before the sun came up, I dozed off for a few moments.

Texts came in from Christopher during the week. He missed me; he wanted to come and see me. I would reply, "So, what are you going to do about it?" and then silence. He never came.

I suddenly felt a memory of myself and Christopher on the dancefloor. On the floor kissing, family, promises, kisses—everything, gone. All gone. If I wanted to move on, I had to let him go. I had to say my goodbye. But sometimes it was never enough. Every day, I would try a little harder until he was out of my head for good.

"Goodbye, Christopher."

I found myself, whenever having a dull moment with Dylan, drifting to dream about Christopher. I pictured the fantasy of being in DC. I tried to place what it felt like to kiss him. To touch his body. *What did he smell like again? I can't remember. Why am I lingering back? I must stay focused on Dylan.*

"Valerie. Hello, Ms. Valerie? Are you listening to me?"

"What? Oh, I am sorry. I was daydreaming about . . . so, I'm sorry, what? What were you saying again?"

"I was telling you about what happened at work today. I was in this budget meeting . . ."

"Dylan." I interrupted him, not knowing what he was saying to me. "Dylan, are we ever going to get married?"

"Valerie, mi amor, yes, of course! I want to marry you. Haven't we talked about this?"

"When?" He came up behind me and tried to comfort me.

"If I tell you, it won't be a surprise. Don't you want that?"

"No, I want to get married and stop playing house." I pushed him away and went into the bedroom and slammed the door. I was so mad. I was mad because I walked away from Christopher. I slammed the door because I was so mad that I hadn't heard from Christopher in over a year, and he promised he would come and get me. Promised me he wanted to spend time with me. Wanted a future with me. All I had was silence. So now all I wanted was to move on and start a life with someone who loved me, but he needed a push. I was creating my new future and pushing all my memories from this world, and past-worlds, away. I think today I had become reborn.

"Valerie, are you awake?"

"Nope," I said as I snuggled into the pillow further, I was tossed into Dylan's shoulder. I was fully aware that he was awake texting, running into the bathroom, and taking phone calls in Spanish. I really needed to learn the language. I forever thought, *This is it; he is on the phone with his mistress. She is probably young, beautiful, with big breasts, long, wavy, black hair. Of course, she would be Spanish. They would have everything in common. I can see him laughing with her as they made plans to take over my apartment while I am at work. My bank account that he would forge permission to gain access. They would laugh at me, how I was a fool to not see it happen. They would laugh and run into the sunset. I will sit here broke and alone.* Did I secretly want that as my escape? Or was I just jealous of what is going on in front of me?

"Who are you talking to?" I questioned.

"My family, just catching up with them. My brother is having some problems with his wife. I am sorry, I am speaking in Spanish, his English is not so good. I just don't want to wake you."

"Okay," I would say and ask nothing further. He always shut down anytime his family came up. I didn't understand why. I ignored this and moved on with my day. My fears would go away, as I had no choice but to believe him. I was becoming a crazy lady.

"Valerie, mi amor . . . " I hear in my ear as it is early morning. I am alive, but not awake. I haven't responded.

"Amor, Valerie."

"I am not awake."

"Valerie, please, I need you to wake up." My eyes are closed. I am not committed to being awake at this point. He is frantically moving about the room. I am fighting with my eyes to open and my body to move. I do not realize that he is packing a bag.

"Mi amor." He continues to kiss me and work on packing.

"My brother, Miguel, he is in the hospital, critical condition. I must go to Texas. I have to be there."

"What!" I jumped up. "No, what happened? What can I do? Am I coming with you?" I tried to grab him, but he was all over, running and packing. He was upset, avoiding me.

"STOP!" I screamed. He finally stopped, stared me down, and relaxed for a moment. He looked at me directly.

"I am not ready for you to come with me to Texas." It hurt like hell, but I FELT LIKE I DESERVED IT.

"Dylan, I want to be with you . . . forever."

"I do too." He kissed my forehead, zipped up his bag, grabbed his keys and walked out the door. I stood there as the door closed in front of me, and I didn't know what to do. I chased after him and caught him, just as the door to the elevator opened.

"I love you. Be safe," I said as we hugged tightly. He kissed me again.

"Thank you, Valerie. I will call you when I get there." The door closed. He was looking down at his headphones. Something was very off with him.

I didn't know what to do with myself except to pace back and forth through every room in my apartment. I listened to my headphones and only played songs that reminded me of Dylan, all the playlists he made for me, most of them all in Spanish, but I didn't care. They were soft and warm, just like him. I missed him; he had only been gone for two hours.

Facetime call:

"Hi, I'm on the plane. Just made this flight."

"Are you okay? I am so worried about you. I am so sorry about your brother. I really don't understand what is going on."

"I know, I know, I have kept you in the dark. My family is just a lot. I didn't want to bring you into it. My brother was on the farm. He came across a beehive that dropped and exploded all around him. He was stung several dozen times. They found him collapsed, and they rushed him to the hospital. He is having trouble with his wife. We talk all the time; it is just not good. They are a lot Valerie, a lot."

"Baby, why didn't you tell me? I want to be there for you. Let me come to Texas."

"Ahhh, I just. I just, I am not good at this." He was holding in tears. "I just need to get there; I don't know if I am ready for you to be involved in this. It is so messy. He as three kids and his wife. She is . . . she is not a good person. I don't trust her. I am afraid of you to meet them."

"Dylan, baby, I am sorry that you are so sad. I have no judgment on you or your family. If we are going to move forward, I have to meet them. Let me come down and be with you. Let me help you with this."

"I want to marry you, I promise. If I didn't have this on my plate, it would have already happened. Let me think about it? I do need you."

"Don't think. I want to come and be by your side. I can come out. I can move things around. I will come to see you."

"Okay, let's talk later. I must go, we are about to take off." The screen went blank. I sat on the chair in the dining room. I felt his emotional breakdown. Now that I took this moment to really understand Dylan, I realized we had not had that level of deep diving into each other's pains and burdens.

"How do I really feel about Dylan? Is he worthy?" I asked myself. I pulled up my favorite picture of us on my phone. His music was playing in my ears. The thought of him shedding a tear on the plane made me ready to go to Texas.

I checked flights. I moved meetings around. I prayed for this to be the right thing for us. For his brother to be okay. I became frantic and watched the clock, waiting for him to let me know he had a safe arrival. I paced all through the apartment. I went into the closet and smelled his clothes. I laid on our bed and hugged his pillow. I missed him.

I closed my eyes and Shelia came to memory. I remember her missing Tom, hugging his pillow when no one was looking. She had a worried look on her face as she waited for him to come home. She walked around the kitchen to waste time and forever check the driveway. Sometimes he came home. Sometimes he came with flowers and gave her a kiss. Sometimes he didn't come home.

Our house was always at peace when Tom was there. Shelia became giggly; she waited on him hand and foot. She dressed in beautiful colors and bright lipsticks. When Tom wasn't there, it was sweatpants and ponytails, vodka and cigarettes, fast food or cereal. When Tom was gone, the giggles were gone. The happy family life was gone. We all lived in a house together, alone. The dust built up into bunnies; the milk was left on the counter. Shelia entered into a coma in her room, hugging a pillow, watching aimless soap operas and drinking vodka. She was nothing without Tom.

Facetime call:

"Mi amor, hola."

"Hello, how are you?"

"I am good. I am at the hospital. Everything is okay, he is stable and resting. My mom and my sister are here with me."

"I am glad to hear. How are you? You hung up. You were so sad. I really want to be there with you and take care of you. Dylan, let me take care of you." He smiled and looked to the side. His Mom poked her head over and waved with a smile. We had only met via Facetime and long-distance hugs.

"See, Mama, someone wants to take care of me. What do you think?"

"I think you should let her." We all smiled.

"I am glad that you are with your family. I hope that everything will be okay with your brother. I miss you." I said the words I did not know that it were so emotional to me that I started to break down.

"Oh, mi amor, no, don't be sad, I just got here. I miss you too. All right, all right, I need you too." He looked away and held his hand on his chin as he paused, holding in emotions. "I need you.

Come down here to Texas. I want you to meet my family, my friends and help me get my brother back on his feet. I am ready."

"Dylan, that is the nicest thing you could have said to me. Now I am crying! Oh, Dylan, yes, thank you, I want to be with you."

"Good, so when can you come out?"

"I cleared my schedule, so I can come out tomorrow? I think a flight tonight is crazy."

"Yes. Perfect. I am beat. We are going to stay for a little bit, grab something to eat, then I am off to bed, so tomorrow sounds perfect. I will pick you up. Valerie, you are the best. I am going to make you so happy. I am the luckiest guy in the world."

"You sure are." We laughed and signed off for the night. I got up out of bed and went to go make a drink. I took out the glass, I got out the ice, and as I was looking at what poison I was going to choose, I had a gust of wind come at me that smelled like Shelia. I instantly thought of her throwing the glass against the wall at me, her anger, her ugliness. I thought of Dylan with his family sitting over his brother's hospital bed, with his mom and sister by his side. He needed me; I needed to be available for him. I threw the ice in the sink, put the glass back in the cabinet and heated some water for tea. I needed to be available for him, and my needs and wants became focused on Dylan. *I am ready for this.*

My flight was for 10:32 a.m. out of JFK, and in four hours and ten minutes, I would be with Dylan. I was nervous, like a first date, and excited that we would be together. It felt official. I couldn't wait to meet his family and learn about his life in Texas. He was so private and unwilling to share.

After take-off, I closed my eyes and realized I hadn't thought about Christopher in days, and I was okay with that. I wanted to reach out to him and throw it in his face that I was going to meet up with Dylan, going to meet his family, going to be his wife. I thought of many ways to do it, but then I thought about how much it didn't matter. I settled on updating my Facebook status that he is not a part of and may never see, but if I put it out there, maybe he would find me. Think about me. Wonder why I was in Texas and want to know all about it. Or maybe he wouldn't. He never saw the post.

I sat on a plane with my eyes closed, now sad and mourning a conversation that never was. A situation that never happened. What did I ever see in Christopher? I kept my eyes closed until I was asked for my choice of beverage and pretzels. I opened my eyes to a feather on my arm, from a jacket that was not mine. I sat on a plane over clouds and pastures. I sat on a plane full of people, alone. The higher up I was, the closer I felt to Madeline and Cal.

"Thank you," I said and giggled.

*　　*　　*　　*　　*

I turned the corner and walked toward the crowd waiting for our flight to get off. I saw two little ones with a sign, "Valerie, welcome to Texas" in bright colors and sparkles. I saw Dylan behind them. I ran straight to him, dropped my bag and jumped into his arms. He was as excited as I was. We both had tears and held on so tightly. We caused a scene, his niece and nephew giggled and held onto our legs. We kissed as he slid my body down to the ground. We stood there in silence as the crowd watched. Some cheered, some took pictures. All I could feel was his breathing on my face, the warmth of his lips pressed to my forehead.

"I am so glad you are here, Valerie, I am so glad," he said in a broken voice. I held him tighter.

"How is your brother?" I whispered to his face without opening my eyes.

He replied in a whisper, close to my ear as possible. "He died this morning. They don't know yet." I held him tighter and moved to kiss his forehead while he wiped away the tears and introduced me to the kids. He leaned down to their height and took them by their hands.

"Ms. Priscilla, Mr. John, this is my girlfriend Valerie. Can you say hello?" Immediately, Priscilla came to me and grabbed as high as she could which, in my heels, she came right below my waist and gave me a warm hug and would not let go, I almost lost my balance. John stood there and then came to my side and hugged me. They were adorable. I instantly fell in love. I looked up at Dylan.

He was so back in his Texas element with a baseball cap and a red, white and blue flannel open with a white tee shirt, jeans, and cowboy boots. This is the man I see in a button down every day; he was never so relaxed at home. I liked it. He was so adorable in his element. So relaxed, even though he was tense and upset.

He grabbed my hand and touched the kids to keep it moving as we head to the car. I made small talk with the kids. Priscilla insisted on holding my other hand.

"Ms. Priscilla, how old are you?"

"Four."

"Four? No way! You look much older than four."

"I do?"

"Oh yes, I bet you are very mature for your age."

"Oh . . . I like your blonde hair, you look like my Barbie doll." Dylan looked back and smiled.

"Priscilla, I only have Barbie dolls as girlfriends."

"Good idea," she replied in her adorable little girl voice. She was a chubby little girl with black hair that was messed up by her hands playing with it. Her tee shirt was tight; her little belly peaked out. She was so lovable and wanted hugs all the time. Who doesn't love a little girl with such love in her heart? We got into the car. She introduced me to her favorite stuffed animal, a little dog named Bingo. John was quiet and looked after Priscilla as if he was her keeper. He was six-years-old and at our first meet and greet, he was skeptical but loving. He had a weakness for Dylan, and since I was in the picture, he was kind to me. Dylan leaned in for a kiss as he always did when we got into the car. We put on our seatbelts and were on our way.

"So, my family lives on a farm that is my brother's, now that Matteo has passed on. There is a guest house next to my mom. I usually stay there. We haven't seen Lydia, their mother, since this morning. She disappeared. She does that a lot. We must wait for her to make plans and talk to these two. This is all very upsetting." I moved my hand to his neck to massage it as he drove, just to let him know that I cared. He held his hand on my knee and concentrated on the road. We pulled into gates that led to a sea of green. It felt like miles to get to the center where the houses were. Dylan's mom and sister sat on the porch, stood up, and waved as the truck pulled into their eyeshot.

"Abuela! Abuela! Uncle Dylan's girlfriend looks like Barbie, come and look!" Priscilla screamed as she ran out of the car. Dylan laughed as we were still in the car. He came over to me and gave me a kiss.

"Thank you for being here."

"I don't want to be anywhere else." We got out of the car and with open arms. I hugged Abuela, Frannie, and his sister Sofia.

"Ahhh, mi amor, Ms. Valerie, we finally meet in person. I am honored. I hear you are a Barbie Doll?" Dylan's mom said with a wink and a hug.

"I don't know, maybe Barbie is just a part-time gig. Thank you for welcoming me into your home."

"It is not our home; it is Matteo's home that we are lucky to live in. Come sit. Let me make you some tea."

"Mama, she wants a drink," Dylan told Frannie.

"No, no, no, tea is fine," I said.

"Oh, wait no . . . Dylan is right; you are a guest. This is a celebration of life. We drink. Tequila?"

I look at Dylan with a face, and of course, answer, "Tequila it is." We sat on the deck overlooking the farm. His mother, Frannie, told me stories of how Dylan's father, Matteo, bought the farm with Miguel, and they all moved in when Dylan was in high school. They were originally from Mexico and mostly grew up there in several parts. When they came to Texas, all of them were limited in their English, except for Dylan. He wanted to learn English when he was young, and he taught everyone else. He ran the business side of the farm and worked with customers, where Miguel and Papa did the labor.

"Dylan is our prodigy," she said proudly.

"If it wasn't for Dylan, the farm would not have been successful or expanded into stores in town. He was very good to us." I snuggled a little closer to Dylan as we sat on the outside couch.

"Stop, stop, stop," he said. She praised him further. He was so adorable at that moment. It was nice to see him with his family.

Priscilla came back from playing and sat next to me on the couch with Bingo. She laid her head on my side. She was so warm and adorable.

"Looks like you have a new friend," Dylan said.

"Pri, what are you doing? Did you make a new friend?" She snuggled into me a little closer. I put my arm around her.

"Yes," she replied.

"Okay, go play with John. Did you see where Olivia went too? Did we see her at all today?"

"She went to school, and then I sent her to a friend's house to play," Sofia replied.

"Okay, Pri go play with John, we need to talk as adults for a bit." Dylan was serious. I liked how he took order in the house at that moment. They listened attentively to him as they had such respect for him.

"All right, what is going on? Have we heard from Lydia? I think we need to be doing something. Someone has to talk to these kids."

"No, I haven't. She should go and make the arrangements and talk to the kids."

"Well, where is she? Is she coming back this time? I am not going to Mexico again and drag her by her hair to come back to him, this is ridiculous. If she is not found by 5:00 p.m., I am taking over, telling the kids and making the arrangements. I will not disrespect my brother or these kids. They need a loving home. I don't want them around her and her shady acts." As his anger on the topic rose, he stood up and stormed off into the guesthouse.

"Wait, wait, Dylan," they screamed, but did not go further than the porch. I lost my grip on him once he stood so abruptly and watched as he stormed off. I stood up from the push he gave me unintentionally as he stood up, gained my balance, and signaled that I would go find him with the reassurance of my hands in prayer. They placed their hands together and bowed with the same prayer back. I turned and could hear Sofia in the background, as she walked to Frannie and put her arm around her since the tears were coming.

"Oh, Mama. I hope that she can melt Dylan's broken heart. I do love her for him," Sofia said as she turned to Frannie.

"I do too," Frannie said. They hugged and cried for the loss of their dear Miguel.

I entered the guesthouse for the first time. The loud, screen door slammed behind me. I did not call out to Dylan, but walked around and found him up in the bedroom leaning into the dresser, facing the mirror and mouthing anger words in Spanish back at himself.

I entered the room and stood in the doorway, feeling out his anger and any other emotions he was having. I knew he needed me. He knew I was there. He didn't need to acknowledge it. I came up behind him and went in under his shirt, and moved my hands to his chest, placed my face into the perfect spot in the small of his back between the shoulder blades, and gave him kisses. I held him at just the right amount of firmness, giving him the comfort to sob for as long as he needed to.

"I don't understand why he married her. She is a cheating fool, a drug addict. I don't want those kids around her for another minute." He puffed and puffed as his anger continued to grow. Dylan turned himself around; my arms fell off his body. We settled into the sitting chair in the corner; I held him as I sat on his lap and let him talk and be upset for as long as he needed to, making sure he was relaxed and comforted.

After time and much of his venting in heat, I closed my eyes. We both eventually drifted into an unplanned nap in the late afternoon. There is nothing more comforting than an afternoon, unplanned nap. That was exactly what the moment called for.

"Dylan, Valerie?" The door opened with Sofia looking for us. Dylan woke up in a gasp and stood us both up; he wiped his face with his hand to wake himself up.

"Yup, what's up?"

"Okay, okay. Please hear me and don't get crazy."

"Now, I am getting crazy." The conversation slowly turned into Spanglish, then straight Spanish.

"Dylan, please calm down."

"Dylan se calmó, se trata de Lydia. La encontre"

"Dónde?"

"Sabes donde."

"Esa puta, está alta?"

"Dylan, relájate. Sí, la acosté en mi habitación para que los niños no la vean." As I watched the interaction, I understood that something was very wrong, I believed it had something to do with Lydia. Dylan walked around in a circle, creating a fist and ready to punch the wall which both Sofia and I held him back from doing. I held onto his shoulders and got him to sit down on the bed.

"I am telling them tonight; they are staying in here with me tonight. I don't want them around her; this is it. I am getting a lawyer and a court order to keep them away from her. Sofia, I can't." Sofia stood, looking directly at him, and did not argue. I looked at her and held onto him for support, not realizing I might have just been signed up to be the owner of three children in another state far, far away from home.

Dylan took off his hat and held it to his face to fight another round of tears coming in. I held his head to mine and pressed my lips to his cheek, close to his ear, and wrapped my arm around the other side. I just wanted to comfort him and was comfortable with all the decisions he was making for his family, for his brother's kids—for us.

"Okay, Sofia, come with me to the funeral home. Let's get this done."

"Okay, I will get my purse." Sofia left the guest house; I stood with Dylan.

"So, what happened?"

"She found Lydia in one of her "boyfriend's houses," drugged up, and she took her home. This has been years Valerie, years. Thank God, my Mama and Sofia are here to watch the kids. I want to take over custody of those kids and take them away from her." We walked outside to the truck and Sofia met us.

"Mama, we are going to make the arrangements. We will be back. The kids are with you."

"Okay," she shouted back. We made the arrangements, we went to the store, and had to buy a suit for a pair of brothers—one to watch his brother be buried in properly, and the other for the to be watched. It was as if the mirror effect should be enough. "I can't believe I am buying a suit to wear to my brother's funeral. I didn't think I needed to bring one."

"I am so sorry, Dylan," I said and grabbed him to hold and comfort. I brought a black dress, just in case. I somehow knew. I didn't even know it. We were hungry, as we did not have dinner, and emotionally drained from understanding Miguel's death. We walked into Mama's house as Frannie sat at the kitchen table with three little ones enjoying a game of "Go Fish."

Dylan went to kiss all of them on the top of their heads. He took a deep breath and asked everyone to meet him in the living room. They listened and grabbed onto every word he said. Dylan sat on the couch and held hands with Frannie and Sofia who sat right beside him. I sat on the other side of the couch and watched all three on the floor in front of them, tentatively waiting for an answer.

"Are you going to tell us where Papa is?" Olivia said with sadness in her heart.

"Yes, I am. Your dad went into the hospital when he got sick the other, day do you remember?" They shook their heads together and sat with their mouths open as he continued.

"Well, he was struck by a beehive. He got stung several times; then he went into a coma. They did everything they could, but he did not wake up. He will not be waking him up and coming home."

"Did he die?" John asked. Frannie and Sofia cried and looked away, as he held hands with both of them. Dylan, with tears in his eyes, turned to me. I gave him a nod.

Dylan replied, "Yes, your Papa went to be with the Lord this morning." John came running into him. Olivia went right behind him and was grabbed by Sofia.

Priscilla watched from the floor, and before she moved, she said, "Where is Mama?"

"She is taking one of her long naps," Sofia replied in an angry tone.

"Oh," she said, picked up Bingo and walked into my lap for a hug. Priscilla had no tears but watched them from her side, as she seemed to not understand the emotion. Her hug was warm as if she was giving me a hug, instead of me giving her a hug. I thought of when I lost Shelia and how I had no one to hug, no one to be there until Tom and Brenda came. I remember taking charge as instructed by my family. I can't remember the last time I saw my brother and sister; I didn't want to. I looked at Dylan across the couches and comforted Priscilla, rubbing her back; she could stay as long as she wanted. I needed it more than she did. I caught eyes with Dylan who smiled at the sight. After we all grieved for the night, Dylan stood up and came over to me and reached out his hand to bring me to standing.

"Okay, everyone," he said and wrapped his arms around my waist, so that we became one unit in front of the family.

"Tonight, I want you all to stay with me and Valerie. You will be with us for the funeral and thereafter, until we know what we are going to do. I don't know if your mama will be coming back. John, I want you to wear your suit, and be the man and watch over your sisters. Señoras, I want you to wear pretty dresses that you wear to church on Sunday. If you need to cry, then cry. If you need something, you come to one of us here. Okay?"

"Tío Dylan?"

"Yes, Pri."

"Do we have to move to New York?"

The room went silent. Dylan held me, I also looked in concernment for this was my life too. He looked around the room. I could tell by the layer of sweat gathered in his forehead, he did not think this through or even discuss with me. I wanted to be angry for him not making this life-changing proclamation without my consultation, but I also felt loved that it became a confirmation that he was making a bold decision for us and our future, and creating our family. I felt loved that he believed and was telling his family that he did not want me to meet, did not want me to understand. He overcame his fears and anxiety of these worlds colliding. He was making "me and you" into "us." I loved that moment.

We gathered the kids, found their pajamas and put them together in the second bedroom in the guest house. They all snuggled in, as Dylan and I tucked in both sides. Olivia pulled her hand out from under the sheets with her phone in hand, and flashed a picture of me as I came close enough.

"You are not my mama."

"I know that. I am not trying to be." She had anger in her eyes.

"I don't like you," she said with much courage and direction. Dylan stood at the other side of the bed as we had a stare down, and he surprisingly did not intercede. It reminded me of my first stare down with Ashley and the venom in her eyes. I think the room could feel it.

"Valerie, I like you." The stare down was broken by a loving four-year-old who thought I was Barbie. I moved my attention to the middle one in the bed, and leaned over for a kiss to Priscilla.

"Why thank you, Pri, I think I like you too." I kissed her, kissed John, and without hesitation, I gave Olivia a kiss on her forehead that had a purpose. She wouldn't admit it, she wouldn't say it, but she did smile for a second. For that second I caught, I embraced.

Dylan and I retired to the bedroom where I first found him that afternoon. I moved to the window to understand the weather of that night, and if the window should stay open or not. I held my hands on the opposite sides of the window sills closed my eyes and took in the air. Dylan came behind me, found his way under my shirt, and pushed his way across my back over to my stomach where his cold hands sat. He found his spot on the back of my neck, right at my hairline, and his wet lips kissed the little hairs that stood from the Texas breeze.

"I needed you today; you have no idea how much I needed you today. I love you, Valerie, for knowing what is best for me." I didn't reply with an answer as I didn't know what to say, but responded with kissing him from the side. We left the windows open and soaked in the air from the farm. The silence was so loud to me. I asked Dylan to sing me a song. We laid, face-to-face, in the darker than dark room. I couldn't see him and would have to place my hand on his chest to gauge his distance.

> Yo tengo una guitarra vieja
> Preñada con esta canción
> Amigos que nunca aconsejan
> Y un beso a mi disposición
> Lo que tengo es tan poco

Que vale un millón
Yo tengo el aire que respiro
Y el mar to'ito para mi
Amors viejos y suspiros
Y si alguien dice no, yo si
Yo poco que tengo es tan poco
Que es también pa' ti
Las huellas de tus pies descalzos
El humo de la cafetera
3 cuadros surrealistas falsos
Tu risa que trae primavera
Aun que el tiempo este fatal
Lo poco que tengo es tan poco
Pero es esencial
Tengo un aguacero para mi verano
Y una ola para surfear
Una sombra que me sigue a donde voy
Y 2 pies pa' caminar.

And before the song was over, he stopped and touched my face in the dark. Once he found it, he gave me a kiss as I held onto his wrist.

"I want to marry you, Valerie. I want us to have a life together, a family together. I want to properly ask you, Valerie. It is coming; it will be soon. I promise." He sealed his promise with another kiss.

I held onto his wrist, to make sure he wouldn't run away.

"Dylan, I will say yes when you ask me. But I need to be part of the plan for our life. What are we doing with all of this? It is a lot."

"I know, I need a plan, I know. I just jumped into it and didn't think it through. I just love those kids so much. I can't bear the thought without them in my life. I spent so much time on this farm and took care of them when Lydia was out with her boyfriends. Miguel was stuck here, overworking, miserable. So afraid to leave her because he was afraid she would take the kids and disappear back to Mexico. She is such a piece of shit. Miguel stayed here when she was around. They haven't been in the same house for years. It is horrible. I want these kids to have a proper upbringing and take over the farm in Miguel's honor or just do something with their life. I fear for their future. Olivia is so much like Lydia, it scares me. I can't bear the thought of her following in her footsteps. I will make a plan. I promise. I will talk it through with you. I promise."

"Good. Dylan?"

"Mi amor?"

"Thank you for inviting me into your life. Giving me a chance. I promise I won't disappoint you."

"I know you won't. Buenas noches, mi amor."

*　　*　　*　　*　　*

I heard footsteps coming toward us and into the bathroom. Once the door was back open, those little footsteps entered into our room. Before I knew it, those little feet climbed into the bed we are currently residing in, and came between us, without permission, to grab some morning snuggles. Dylan opened his eyes, but was not awake.

"Bingo, did you want to snuggle?" I asked. Dylan then had the visual come to his head, and he awake enough to realize what was going on. He placed his hand on her hair and stroked it slowly as his eyes closed back up. I moved back to accommodate the small being with a stuffed animal in tow. As I became comfortable and did enjoy the young being with us, another came in. This time it was John. He gravitated to Dylan's side of the bed. As my eyes closed again, Olivia would enter and find her way to my side, and after she crawled in unannounced and unapologetic, she closed her eyes and put her arm around me. And for that second, I broke a smile, and for that moment, I did not acknowledge it, nor did I let her know that I liked it. But I would take that second of time. I embraced it.

Can you hear me, Miguel? I asked in my head. The sun grew higher. The sounds of animals brewing around the farm grew louder. The world was waking up and so we had to as well.

"Just a few more minutes," I asked. A sudden tap came from the middle one, snuggled in between Dylan and me. I opened my eyes.

Pricilla handed me a feather she found on the bed and curled back into her spot and close her eyes.

Thank you, Miguel; I will do my best to represent you and take care of Dylan and the kids. I made my decision, my pact with Miguel, and I become the next Mrs. Zavala.

"Dylan!" The sound came just as the porch door slammed into its frame.

"Dylan!" The voice ran up the stairs and into the bedroom.

"Dylan!" Frannie was standing, catching her breath as she came into the room and sat on the edge of the bed. The porch door slammed again. Sofia also ran up the stairs and into the room and hung on the edge of the bed. Frannie handed Dylan a piece of paper folded up, and as he looked at it, he knew he didn't want to reach for it. He sat up, exposing his bare chest, and moved himself to reach for the paper and hesitantly opened it.

I watched his eyes flow from left to right reading the note; I didn't want to impose and reach over to read it, as I felt it was personal. He finished the letter and dropped it to his waist, and looked Frannie in the eye—with very angry eyes. He shook his head and looked at Sofia. She nodded and looked down. They both looked down. Dylan looked away with the note crinkled in his hands. He grabbed as many bodies as he could within his reach and held them tight. The kids did not notice or understand what was going on but waited to hear directly from Dylan. He looked at me. I sat with concerned eyes. I could hear their sighs from the corners on the bed. He signaled me to move in closer. I carefully moved Priscilla over to be next to Dylan in the bed. He handed me the note and placed his hand on my thigh with a tight squeeze.

> This is your fault that my Miguel is dead.
> You left us and didn't help with the farm, and look at what happened.
> It is your fault that we didn't work out and that our baby died before it was even born. Miguel saved me and gave me my children.
> It is your fault that my family is ruined.

Don't come back to find me, don't think you can
drag me back again.
You ruined my life, Dylan. Now my Miguel is dead.
You will never see me again; I hate you. I curse you.

—Lydia

I read it; I looked up. I read it again. *What does she mean their
baby died?* I looked up at Sofia. Frannie still looked down as they
were embarrassed about the whole situation.

"I never wanted you to know this side of the family," Dylan
mumbled under his breath. He held my thigh tighter. I suddenly
felt confused and not comfortable in a bed full of people that I was
forced to embrace.

"I know you have questions," he whispered into my ear. As upset
as I was, I handed him back the letter and decided to put my feelings aside, as I made a promise to be there for him in the moment. I
kissed Priscilla's forehead and summoned the kids to get up and get
themselves dressed as we had a funeral to attend. With Dylan's confirmation, they obliged and went back into their own home and got
themselves dressed. Sofia and Frannie also went back to their homes.
As I entered the shower, I wanted to cry, but I didn't. I pushed it
aside. *I am going to take care of a woman's kids who tried to have a
baby with my future husband. She doesn't even know me. Is she coming
back for the kids? What is going on? I feel so in the dark.* I finished my
shower. Dylan was waiting for me with an open towel which, as I
hesitated, I accepted his embrace.

"It's not what you think. I was young; we were kids. I was fourteen. She was my childhood girlfriend. It is a long story; I promise I
will tell you."

"Fourteen? Dylan, I am sick of promises, I need action. What
are we doing? Do you see the magnitude of this situation you asked
me to be a part of? I feel like you lied to me. Was she your girlfriend?
You didn't think to mention that?"

"Honestly, I forgot. I know it sounds stupid, but I put it out of
my head. She was so different then. I went to visit. We had sex. She

143

was my first. I was so naive and in love. I didn't know about protection. She grew angry when I went back."

"Dylan, I just . . . I just. I just need to not do this right now. We have a funeral to attend; I have a lot to soak in. We have a lot to think about of what is on our plate. We need to table this for tomorrow. We need to take care of what is at the moment and deal with this. Okay?"

"Si, si. Okay, we will table this." He still held me. I stood as a limp body as the affection of the moment was forced and unwelcome.

"Dylan!" I pushed him off me. He let go, jumped into the shower, and we both got dressed in the same room, alone. When I had a moment before Dylan was ready, I stepped outside and walked until no one could hear me, and called Tom.

"How are you doing? How is Dylan?"

"I want to leave. I am so upset. Dylan had a relationship with Miguel's wife, or dated her before Miguel got her pregnant. The baby didn't make it. She left, we have the kids, the funeral is in a few hours. I want to leave!" I said as I started to cry, speaking frantically, provoking a panic attack.

"Whoa, whoa. I need you to calm down. When was this affair? Sounds like a long time ago?"

"He said when he was fourteen." I continued my crying fit.

"That is a long time ago. He is in his thirties now. I think you need to be a bit forgiving. 'Judge and be judged.' You wouldn't want him to walk out on you when he needed you the most, now would you?"

"No, I know. I am just upset. I don't have a ring. He wants to take custody of these kids and me to be involved. It is just a lot. I am overwhelmed by all of this."

"Valerie, do you love him?"

"I do, but."

"But nothing. Let everything fall into place. It is overwhelming. Live in today and figure out tomorrow afterward. You have a funeral to attend. Right now, he needs you to be there with him, so be there with him. God will take care of you, just believe." I took a deep breath and got my tears under control. I needed those words of wisdom from Tom to stay on track.

"Okay, thank you. I needed that." I hung up the phone, cleared my tears, and went back to meet Dylan. He was nervous about me leaving, upset about his brother, wondering where I stood. We walked out to meet the family, and gathered together to walk to the funeral procession. As we gathered, I pulled my arm through his and reached up to kiss his cheek, and rested myself on his arm to create a solidarity. He obliged and kissed me back, and embraced me as he needed something to hold onto.

"Thank you, Valerie," he said as we all started to tear up for the road ahead.

We gathered at the site. I stood by Dylan as he did the same for the brother he admired so much. We sat and held hands as the ceremony went underway. Dylan got up and gave a eulogy for his brother, and it was the last time he spoke in his presence. He told a few jokes, stories of growing up in Mexico and moving to the promised land of Texas where their dream of building a farm occurred. He acknowledged the children, and vowed to do his best to watch over and take care of them. He spoke some in Spanish and some in English, and the end was a heartfelt goodbye to the only brother he had ever known and loved. With his hand on the casket, he dropped tears over him, gave it a kiss and said his final goodbye. When he came back to his seat, I welcomed him with open arms as he broke down over my shoulder.

I held Priscilla and Olivia's hands as we brought them to drop their roses into the casket and say goodbye to their father. Dylan held John's as he wanted to be so brave and the man of their trio. Sofia said goodbye with her family. Frannie fell to the ground in loud tears that Dylan and Sofia needed to hold her from falling into the hole. The sun shone upon us with whispers of shade from the trees moving about. Priscilla held Bingo, her thumb in her mouth, as she stared into the casket. I wondered if she understood what was happening at this moment, if she would remember it forever or have to be reminded. Olivia took pictures which as I felt was inappropriate. No one else felt concerned, so I let it be. We walked back as a family to the farm where we gathered with some local friends and relatives.

We mingled among the open yard between the houses, having conversations with people who came near and far and told stories they best remembered of Miguel. They questioned where Lydia was, but were not surprised that she was not present. Some had already assumed that she had been gone for years. John moped about the crowd, not knowing what to do with himself. I tried to find him to make sure he was feeling okay. I summoned his friends and cousins to take him to play, and off in the yard they ran to have a catch and chase each other around. Olivia took pictures and hid behind her camera, or was sometimes just on her phone. She wasn't much of a conversationalist. No one had a concern about it, but me.

"So, is your head spinning yet?" Sofia came behind me with a drink and a plate of food. "Come, you must eat something."

We found a place to hide for a few, off the side of the house where we could see the sun getting ready to set.

"I love this spot. At this time of day, I try to get a moment to sit here and feel the sun. It is quiet. No one else really knows about it, except now for you."

"Thank you for sharing. That is kind of you. I feel special, thank you." I concentrated on my food as I was famished from the day. My legs were tired. I needed this moment to decompress.

"Don't be mad at Dylan. Dylan has a heart of gold, with the impulse of a mad animal. He always means well, believe that."

"I do. This is all just a lot. I wish he let me in more before we came here. I wish I knew more to be able to soak it all in. I feel like he betrayed me just by not knowing. But he didn't. The past is the past. We must concentrate on the future. Now if I could only practice what I preach."

"If only we all did. Dylan dated Lydia when they were young, maybe nine or ten? She was beautiful. Nice girl. Matured way before the rest of the class. Dylan was in love with her, wanted her more than anything, followed her like a puppy dog. We moved to Texas to start this farm; it was hard for Dylan to come here. He begged to go back for her and Papa. Matteo gave in. ONCE.

"He went back. She told him she wanted to lose her virginity to him, and he just did it. She claimed she was pregnant, and Papa sent him back to be a man and take care of his new family he decided to impulsively create at fourteen. So, he did. He went back to Mexico, lived with them, rushed through school to try to graduate early. At five months, she had a sudden 'incident.' The baby died from a miscarriage. I, for one, don't believe there was ever a baby. She was enraged and blamed it all on him, and forced him to leave and come back here to Texas. He never talked to her again.

"Miguel, who looked out for Dylan, called her family and talked to them all. He tried to work it out as Dylan was heartbroken, and believed all of her ugly words. It was sad. He was depressed. Dylan laid in bed crying. He drowned himself in school and worked on the farm.

"We all worried about him and stayed together for him. It was a hard few years. He went to college, really helped build this farm. Through time, Lydia came back into our lives and set her target on Miguel. They kept their affair a secret to not hurt Dylan. One day, Miguel brought Lydia to the farm and made the announcement that they were getting married and having a baby. She did it to taunt Dylan, and it made him miserable. It worked, but he respected his brother. Through all of his hurt, he kept his feelings to himself. They moved to the farm and continued growing their family.

"By the time Priscilla was born, Miguel was living with Dylan in the guesthouse. Lydia was always off doing drugs, sleeping with other men, disappearing back to Mexico. It had been awful, but Miguel would not divorce her and said it was for the kids—which I do not think is right. Oh, men, they are stupid.

"Dylan helped raise those kids with Miguel. Although they had differences, especially over Lydia, they bonded as brothers and did it for the family. Just a few years ago, Dylan moved to New York as we pushed him to finally follow his dreams. And as he went for one dream the other came true; he met a beautiful woman who is strong enough to take care of him. He found you."

"He is a strong and loving man; I am the lucky one. I didn't have a good relationship with my brother or sister. I always wanted a loving family."

"Well, my dear, I think you have it. Look around at this farm, the people who came to cherish a life lost too quickly, kids that already have gravitated toward you. Dylan has a good heart; don't give up on him just yet."

"I wasn't planning on it. This is all just a lot to soak in. I appreciate your kind words and honesty."

"We appreciate you, Ms. Valerie. And soon we shall share the same last name." She embraced me. We clinked glasses and then went back for a refill. It was a long day.

The sun went down, the crowd dissipated. I found my way to Dylan as we took a seat on the couch on Frannie's porch. I placed my head on his shoulder, and put my feet up on the coffee table as Dylan was leaned back far enough to rest his head. There was a chill in the air; I needed to move in closer to avoid the endless goosebumps.

That night, we slept with the windows open, the dark so deep we could not see each other, and held tightly to not separate. The silence was so quiet, you could hear the wind talking to you. The sun started to rise; little bodies came into the bed, one by one. When the alarm went off, all five bodies woke up as one.

We spent the next few days in government offices, lawyer's offices, and records offices to gather if there was a will, a trust—to determine what would happen to the children, the business, and Miguel's fortune. We did everything we could to declare Lydia as an unfit mother, and gained temporary custody of the three. I made phone calls, sent emails, moved meetings as far out as I could to stay and help fix this situation. I cooked dinners with Frannie. We ate on the porch, I packed lunches, took the kids to school, sports, demanded homework was done and baths taken. Each night, and into each morning, we fell into the same rituals.

Dylan handled the estate and paperwork. His sister and mother were business as usual. He had hard decisions to make, and a life change for all of us lived in his thoughts. I didn't nag or demand answers as it—at this point—needed to come from him. I had already made the choice that I was in it with him, so I waited.

*   *   *   *   *

"Is this a nightmare?
Or the American dream?"
—New Jack Hustler (Nino's theme), Ice-T

We have now been in Texas, on the farm, for the past two weeks. The annual town barbecue is this weekend. The main street has been blocked off. The farm hosted, in the park, the music and barbecue pit. This was a big event in this suburb of Texas that brought everyone out for the weekend. I had no idea what to expect, but the kids were so upset from the most recent events and could not wait. Dylan said he had not done this in years. He used the excuse to pour himself into working the farm. He himself was excited to be there. As Dylan stood in Miguel's shoes, he took the job so seriously. I did what I could to support at home and take care of the kids.

The night before the big day, Dylan came back late. Everyone was already in bed. He was tired, sweaty and muddy from the preparation. I had cooked dinner that evening for the kids. I made their favorite chicken cutlets and homemade coleslaw. As I heard the truck pull up, I became the good wife and made a plate for him. We stood in the kitchen at the counter and talked quietly, sharing an end of evening beer.

"You look so tired. You worked so hard this week. I am sure tomorrow will be a big success."

"I hope so; I just want it to be perfect."

"It will be. I can feel it."

"Valerie, thank you for being here with me, doing so much with the kids and helping me. I am so grateful for you being here."

"I am happy to be here, but we have to make some decisions as, eventually, I will have to go back. I can only work remotely and part-time for so long."

"I know, I know, you have made big sacrifices for me."

"Dylan, I want to support you. I don't want to pressure you any more than you already are, but we need to make some decisions here. You have to let me in. I don't want this to linger. These kids believe that we are going to live like this. It is not fair for no one to know, or understand, what we are doing. We have temporary custody. WHAT IS OUR PLAN?" Dylan looked at me as he finished chewing, took another sip of beer, placed it on the counter and came over to me.

"Come with me." He took my hand and escorted me out to the barn as the kids slept in the guesthouse. It was dark. Dylan took a lamp to lead the way; I used my cellphone flashlight to assist. We went up to the top of the barn where there was a small area that used to be someone's rest area. We sat on some hay and looked out the window lit by the moonlight. He was sweaty and in his cowboy gear, hat backwards. We sat facing each other with his hands on my knees, that moved up to my mid-thigh and stayed put. You could see the whole farm from this view as if it were the top of the kingdom.

"I love this place; it was Miguel's dream. It became a huge part of my life. I want these kids to have a life here. I want to give it to them."

"What about your dreams, Dylan? What about starting your own family, our family? What about us? This is a lot, Dylan; you need to realize this affects all of us."

"I know. I know."

"Dylan, you keep saying the same thing. 'I know, I know, I promise, I promise.' I need some action, because I do love you, I do love these kids—but I have a business. I want to get married and have kids. I don't want to wait anymore. Dylan, I have dreams and plans. I do love you. But you are not letting me in. I feel like you are leading me on by just not doing anything. I should have put my foot down before all of this, as we have been playing house. I didn't press getting married because I was afraid of you leaving me. Maybe I thought I wasn't worthy since you didn't ask, but I am sitting here now, telling you that I love you, and want to marry you as I did before—and still no action!

Dylan, I am losing my patience. I think I have been honest and fair to you."

Out of anger, I tried to stand up; he held me down.

"No, don't get up. Yes, I have been occupied by my brother dying and taking on the kids, the farm. Yes, I did make you promises, but I didn't hesitate to lead you on. You are so perfect, and fancy. I grew up on a farm. I am afraid of you not loving me, because I am not enough for you. I didn't want to bring you here and see this life, because I thought you would run. I would die without you, so I hesitated.

"Valerie, you are more to me and have proven, the second you got on the plane here, that you love me unconditionally. I want to honor you properly. I think about it every day and want it to be perfect. I have a created a ring for you and want to give it to you the way I have planned; it is coming. I promise, I promise.

"I told my job in New York today that I am leaving. I know I didn't tell you. I was going to do it all together, put it all on the line. I want to move here, and work on the farm, and take on full custody of the kids. I want you to be my wife and start a family with me here in Texas. I know you need to travel, but I have been watching you. You are working, enjoying the kids, and you seem so relaxed here. I want the happy, relaxed Valerie; not the nervous, overworked, and preoccupied Valerie that I had the last few weeks before we came here."

"Dylan, I . . . I . . ."

"Don't say anything; I don't want you to answer. I want you to spend the weekend here. Come to the barbecue and soak it all in. Enjoy the fun with the kids, and really want to be here. Not just for me, but because you want this life with us and build on it." He put his finger to my lips to prevent the words he did not expect and might change everything. I decided to stay silent. I moved over to him, and as we kissed, we faced the window and let the moon shine on us until we started to doze off and went back to the guesthouse. As we approached our bedroom, we could see a little body in the middle sleeping, and awakened as we entered.

"Where did you go? I was worried?" a sleepy Priscilla said as she rubbed her eyes and held Bingo tightly.

"Oh, Pri, we were just outside, *ven, ven, vamos a la camos.*" Dylan said as he tried to pick her up and bring her back into her room.

"No, Dylan, I want to stay here with you and Valerie." She pushed her way back into the pillow and made herself comfortable.

We looked at each other, both tired, and laughed a little as we could use the distraction from our conversation. He signaled to me if it was okay, and I shrugged and nodded that it was. We changed our clothes and moved in around Pri, and I was able to still face Dylan as she snuggled into him and kept our arms over each other. It was a great night's sleep.

The sun came up. The routine continued with one less to crawl in and find space, as she already had one. Olivia clicked her phone and took pictures. Her friend request came on Instagram; she displayed her love and affection for everyone that she could not in words to us. I now understood her camera addiction.

"Who's ready for the barbecue?" Dylan screamed in his sleepy, morning voice.

"Yeah!" The screams came, they started to jump on the bed and around the room. We headed over early. The girls insisted on showing me around, as John worked to help Dylan with Frannie and Sofia. We threw sandbags to knock down tin cans, and gained a few more stuffed animals. We got our faces painted and ate cotton candy. We danced with the band and ran from booth to booth as the girls introduced me to everyone they knew. It was fun. Before we knew it, we entered into the early evening. Dylan came around to find us taking a break. He came up from behind us. We cheered as we carried our winning prizes to a safe haven.

"I am so beat!"

"I believe it! Wow, this is fun!" I said to him out of honesty and having a genuinely good time with the kids. He kissed me to mark the moment as an unforgettable memory.

"Let's go to the hammocks; I need a rest."

"I think we do too." He grabbed a few beers and waters from behind a booth. We headed over to some haystacks and trees.

We all sat on the haystacks, and sat back as Dylan wiped the sweat off his head with his flannel. He was so tired but enjoyed this annual event his family created so many years ago. His joy—their joy—gave me joy. The beer felt like water that tingled into my legs.

Dylan signaled me to the hammock. We curled up, my arms overhead, his arm around my waist holding the other hand above.

My leg crossed over his, with his face in my neck. He slowly drifted off into a pleasant afternoon nap. I also drifted off for a few moments and could hear the clicking of a camera above us. Olivia was in the tree taking photos. As concerned I was with her climbing up there, I wanted that moment captured on film. Our nap was broken short from Priscilla deciding she wanted to climb into the hammock, and with much determination, she got herself up there with help from John who also crawled in. Olivia, after a few photos, came down and into the hammock and snapped selfies. It was a family moment.

The sunset we soaked in the last minutes, the music played in the background. The warmth of the family in this tight hammock, with my legs crushed and sides pushed in, was the moment I could never imagine a family could be. I closed my eyes and pictured Todd holding me as a baby, and giving me love when I thought I had lost it. I could see his eyes of joy, his smile of happiness. This could not compare—this was better. Dylan kicked them all out and grabbed me for another kiss as he looked me in his eyes. All I could say back was, "Yes." He didn't need to respond.

"Let's go dance!"

"Yeah, yeah!" We got off the hammock and headed over to the dancefloor. Dylan grabbed another round of beers, grabbed Sofia and Frannie to join us. The lights were laced within the trees; the crowd was having fun, the music was vibrant, you could do nothing else but smile.

"Tio Dylan?" Priscilla tugged on Dylan's shirt as we danced. She could not compete with our height. "Tio Dylan?"

"Si, si, Pri!" He lifted her up as his thought was that she wanted to be at our level instead of feeling like a mouse. We danced around. She still tried to get his attention. Olivia and John danced around with Frannie and Sofia, but kept coming back to us.

"Tio Dylan!"

"Si, Mija!"

"Are you going to marry Valerie?" she expressed loud enough for me to hear. I twirled around as to pretend I didn't.

"I don't know! Do you think she will say yes?"

"Yes."

"Then if you think so, I will."

"Okay, then Olivia and I will make you a ring."

"I can't wait! Make it beautiful."

"OKAY!" She wiggled out of his arms. We laughed, but could not talk. The music was loud. There was nothing to say. She ran to Olivia and whispered into her ear. They clapped and jumped, and went running around to their stuff, and started planning their jewelry creation from their variety of string.

We drank beers, we ate hot dogs, we danced the night away. When we went home, full of prize collections, everyone was exhausted and wanted to go straight to bed, but were too excited to sleep. I went to see the girls who jumped on the bed, John who played DJ for them, and eventually retired to the bed. The girls stayed up plotting in the bed next to him. Dylan called me into our room that he filled with candles. That night, we locked the door kept the windows open, danced slowly to Dylan singing in my ear. And that night, as tired as we were, we did not sleep or let anyone in early the next morning.

That morning, I went to my phone and pulled up my email, read my Facebook page, then checked Instagram. Olivia had posted all the pictures from the day before, all the love and fun we shared. It was such gratification to me. I saved to my phone the picture on the hammock, and made it my screen saver. I felt so safe in his arms; I loved how she spoke through a camera.

I went back to NY to reorganize myself and prepare to be in Texas full-time. I arrived back to the farm and to Dylan with an angry face. He was screaming at the kids as they hid upstairs. This is not how I left this household. I dropped my bags in the living room, as I was about to take off my jacket, he demanded that I bring the bags straight upstairs and not leave them there.

"Excuse me?" I said as I could not believe he was speaking to me in this manner. He slammed his hands on the counter and looked down in disappointment, in himself. I was not moving.

"It has been a hard few days without you," he said, still looking down.

"Dylan, I hate you!" the scream came from above. It was Olivia.

"What is going on?" I was about to run upstairs and not listen for an answer.

"Wait," he said as he grabbed my arm. "Just wait."

"How am I walking into this? What is going on?"

"Come and sit." We moved into the living room. He was heated and angry. I had seen him angry, but not at this level for this long.

"Dylan . . . " He held my hands and kept his face down as he couldn't find the words.

"She is back and got an order to get her kids and take them to Mexico. She told Olivia and John that I am evil and made her leave, and not be there for the funeral. How am I brainwashing them? How I killed their father . . . and . . ."

"Okay, stop."

I grabbed him and hugged him as he began to cry.

"Where is she now?"

"She is back in Mexico. She has some sort of order that she can bring them there. I contacted the lawyer who says they should go, but we could get them back. I don't want them to go. But now they believe her and are lashing out. My patience is low. We have three days to get them there. I don't want to take them. What do I do?"

"I don't like this. We will fight to get them back. We will. Let me talk to them. Let's make this situation right and not ugly." He nodded and got himself together. I asked him to stay down in the kitchen until I signaled for him. I went upstairs and opened the door. They were on defense and had torn up the room out of anger.

"Hi, guys, no hello?"

"Valerie!" Pri screamed and ran to hug me.

"Don't talk to her, she is the enemy." Olivia pulled her ponytail back to the other side of the room. They stood, John closest to me, Olivia holding Pri back on the wall by the window.

"Enemy? Of what? What happened when I was gone?"

"My mom says you are evil and will try to hurt us." I gave a shocked face and pulled out my cross underneath my scarf.

"Would someone so evil wear a cross? When was the last time I hurt you?" She didn't have an answer.

"I love you, guys; I would not hurt you. Dylan would not hurt you."

"Why did you leave us?"

"I can tell you why I left you and came back. Maybe you should think about why your mom left again and again. I'm sorry. Where is she now? I left to put my business in order so I can live here with you all and Dylan. We can start our life together with all of you."

"See, I told you, I told you! They are going to get married, I told you!" Priscilla jumped and pointed at Olivia's face. I hoped it broke her down. Olivia stared me down. I didn't give up. I won this game before.

"Do you really think that me and Dylan are evil? That is crazy; we love you all! Your father would want you to be with us."

"Dylan killed my Father!"

"What? Prove it? What did he do? He was with me in New York when your father was struck by a beehive? How could he make him get stung by hundreds of bees from that far away? A little absurd, don't you think? Who is giving you this 'fake news?'" I said as I gave my sign language for quotes.

"Mama," John said as he had tears running down his face. "I believe you, Valerie, please don't leave us." He ran to hold onto me. Now we stood as a dividing line across the room. There was a moment of silence.

"I believe you, Valerie!" as Priscilla broke from Olivia and ran over to me. It was now three against one. She was trembling and confused. Dylan was creeping himself up the stairs to hear what was going.

"Olivia, why don't you want us to be a family? You don't have to give up on your mother or father, but I don't think your mother can take care of you right now. Let us take care of you, let us be there for you. Don't tell me you haven't been having fun with all of us together?"

"I'm having fun, Valerie!" Pri answered and broke the tension. Dylan felt safe to come up into the room and stand behind us.

"Olivia, your mother is scared and is not being fair. She is not fit to be your mother, but she demands you go back to Mexico and, according to the law, we must take you guys. Valerie and I will do everything we can to get you back here if you want us to, I promise." We stood in confidence to her. I will admit my stomach was on the floor, afraid of her reaction.

She looked at the ground and to her phone for some pictures. After her personal meditation, she nodded her head, and came across the enemy line to us. The relief was unanimous. That night, we started the morning ritual before bed as we didn't want to part with them or lose the moment. I closed my eyes in the dark of the night, the windows open with the Texas air pushing its way through the room. I closed my eyes and saw Madeline kiss Cal, as he came home from work, Shelia comes down the stairs as she was called, and they all sat at the table for dinner. Madeline looked back at me as the rest of the table held hands with closed eyes, and she smiled and me and whispered "Thank you." That night was peaceful.

*   *   *   *   *

"Children waiting for the day they feel good
Happy birthday, happy birthday
And to feel the way that every child should
Sit and listen, sit and listen"
—Mad World, Michael Andrews, Featuring
Gary Jules (*Donnie Darko, Riverdale*)

The next day, we packed bags, snacks, fired-up electronics, got into the truck and headed down to Mexico. The ride was going to be about seven hours, but due to the time of day, and Dylan knowing it would probably take a few hours to get to the border, we decided to camp out overnight at a local Holiday Inn in southern Texas, right before the border. Dylan took us to a local Tex-Mex place where we could sit outside. There was a playground for all of them. After we ate, they ran over to the swings as we watched from our picnic table.

"Are you going to be okay with this?" I asked Dylan.

"I don't want to think about it. I just want this to be over with as quickly as possible, and get them back home."

"Do you think they understand what is happening?"

"Nope. I just hope they are there short enough that she doesn't brainwash them, especially Olivia."

"I agree." I sat in his arms and watched the kids play as the sun set. I did not tell Dylan that I was scared to go over the border, and that we might never see these kids again—that this could be dangerous. I was scared. I believed in Dylan. He seemed to be at peace with it. The sun went down; it was time to go. We set back to the hotel where we shared adjoining rooms.

"Okay, PJ's for everybody," I said to the crowd.

"Tio Dylan?" Priscilla beckoned over Dylan as she waited for the bathroom to clear out to brush her teeth. "Uncle Dylan, Olivia and I made you a ring for you to give to Valerie. Can you give it to her before we leave tomorrow?" She pulled the red-string ring woven into a waffle pattern.

"Oh, this is beautiful! You ladies made this?" As he whispered back to her, Priscilla and Olivia gathered together. He went over to close the door to our room so I could not hear, even though they were speaking in Spanish.

"*Tan encantador, quiero darle un anillo tan mal, cómo lo sabes?*"

"*Así que mañana?*" *¿Puedes?*"

"*Hmmm, esa es una buena idea, pero quiero esperar hasta que vuelvas a nosotros y todos se lo damos juntos.*" *¿Qué te parece?*"

"*Si usted piensa que es lo correcto para hacer, entonces está bien. Dijo decepcionado.*"

"*no te decepciones, te diré qué.*" *Mañana, cuando lleguemos a México nos reuniremos y se lo daremos juntos, pero viene de ti, ¿de acuerdo? ¿Qué te parece?*"

"Yeah!" they said in excitement.

"Okay, then put it away safely in the bag, and let it be a secret, okay? Now get to bed." Dylan went into the bathroom to freshen up.

"Who wants a bedtime story?" I cried out.

"Dylan said he was going to tell us a story tonight," John said, very upset that he might miss out on something if I opened up a book.

"I did not know; we shall wait then." They played on their phones and iPad as we awaited Dylan to exit the bathroom.

"Story it is," he said when he got out, very excited, which was the opposite of feelings I had. I was so nervous about the next day. He told an elaborate story, in Spanish, of monsters and villains as he made a vivid interpretation where we all screamed, laughed and ran around the room from him chasing us. He ended with a lullaby; then they headed into their beds. We shut the lights and closed the door, just enough to see shadows and hear giggles. After about forty minutes, Dylan went into the room and asked them to be quiet and go to bed. It didn't work. Ten minutes later, it all continued. He went into his wallet, turned on the light and put them all in their beds.

"Okay, here is $20 worth of singles. I am going to put them on my dresser, and the next noise I hear, a dollar comes off the pile. Whatever is left in the morning, you all can share. How does that sound?" They all nodded and closed their eyes. To my dismay, it worked. The only giggles for the rest of the night came from us. I feared the morning and was awake the majority of the night as I caressed Dylan to keep him asleep; but as I could feel him, he was awake too. He was just better at pretending than I was. The morning came, and one by one, they came into the room, into the bed. We sat in a somber silence as this was the last moment we would have together until we could get them back.

"Everyone, listen to me," Dylan said. We all gave our attention to him.

"Okay, this is going to be hard, but today you will go to stay with your mother. As you know, your mother and I do not get along. She has said things about me that are not true. She is going to try to convince you that I am bad, I think she called me 'evil.' I am not evil. Valerie is not evil. We are here to love you and want to be a family with you. Do you want that?"

"Yes," Priscilla said. They nodded their heads.

"Okay, come in for a group hug then." We hugged on the bed. Olivia took selfies as we used Dylan's long arm to take a picture with us all looking up. Olivia posted it and labeled it "La Familia forever" in black and white.

*   *   *   *   *

We got to the border and waited in line that looked hours long. Dylan reached out to Lydia to let her know we were waiting. We got closer and could see her waiting as she approached the truck from the walkway. We all had our passports out. The kids had them in their hands. She was with three men that Dylan said were her brothers. The kids started to scream, "Mama, Mama!" and waved. They ambushed the car and grabbed the kids out of the backseat. As I attempted to get out because they were already gone, the door was slammed back at me and a man leaned in with a gun pointed at my chest. I sat back and did not look at him. Dylan went to do the same. He was also approached by a man, whom he seemed to know, with a gun to his chest. There were no guards around. We were told not to make a sound. Lydia grabbed the kids and their passports, left their things in the car, and told them not to say a word. I watched her run to the walkway and cross them over until I could not see them anymore. The men slowly eased up on us.

"Pedro, why are you doing this, we came in peace with the kids. We now have to go over the border. Can we at least say goodbye to them? Please, we are trying to do the right thing here."

"If you can find us. Don't make a scene, don't do anything stupid, don't talk to police. You know what happens when you talk, right Dylan?" Dylan blinked as if to answer the question. They put their guns away, pretended to say happy goodbyes and walked away backward, until they too became a blur.

"Dylan, what the FUCK just happened? We need to grab someone; we need to."

"Stop it!" He grabbed me with force. In the Mexican/Texas heat, we dripped an abnormal amount of sweat.

"You don't know what they are capable of."

"Who are they?"

"They are Lydia's family. They are in the corrupt part of a cartel and can get away with almost anything."

"Dylan, why didn't you tell me? Why didn't we come without police protection? Why are we doing this Dylan? I can't believe you again left me in the dark on this."

"It is for your protection. If we got the police involved, we would all be killed. You think my brother getting stung to death and dying was an accident? He is terrified of bees and allergic—no coincidence. They did this him. They are all evil. There was no beehive on the farm. I helped him build it! He tried to serve her with divorce papers. We had been talking at night for weeks about it. I thought he was safe. We had lawyers. We had protection. Now, this. Frannie and Sofia won't admit it, in fear. I care so much about those kids." Dylan was emotional. We held hands and talked under our breath.

The line became shorter. Still, we continued to drip sweat and try our hardest not to lose our emotions. It was hours before we made it across. It felt like three days.

We got to the booth. The officers looked us in our eyes as they examined our passports. My mascara was all over my face, shirt soaked. My hair up in a messy bun. Dylan did his nervous hand through his hair, but we continued to hold hands and pretended to have no reaction. After a search through the car and a check of paper-work again, they let us through. We pulled over as we needed to stop for the restroom, fuel, and food.

"What is our game plan, Dylan?" I said as I didn't feel I should have to ask. I wanted to run. I wanted to call the police. Call Tom—anyone. I wanted to scream for help. But they didn't notice the back-packs or that it was odd that we had three kids backpacks and no kids.

"They are in on it," Dylan said.

"What? Who?"

"What you are thinking." It relieved me to not say it out loud at that moment." "We are going to finish our food, then I am going to walk you back to the border. You are going to get a car back to the hotel. I am going to go find them at the house and try to reason with them."

"Dylan, that is crazy. You can't go alone. I am not leaving you or going back without you."

"Valerie, I love those kids. I can't give up on them. Not now."

"I thought you loved me."

"I DO LOVE YOU! I could not bear the thought of you getting hurt through all of this; it is too much. You must go back."

"So, you plan on getting hurt? Do you hear yourself? What are you thinking is going to happen? You remember the story you just told me about your brother? You." I went to stand up, he grabbed my hand and pushed me against the wall with his hand over my mouth.

"Valerie, shhhhh, shut up. You have no idea who is listening to us. It is final. You are going back to Texas and to the hotel. Enough." I pushed his hand off my face and shoved him off me.

"Fuck you, Dylan, I am not going back without you. I love those kids too. If you go without me, we are done. I will go and get my own lawyer and make sure you are all unfit, and get custody of those kids myself. Are you serious, right now? Do you know what I am capable of?" He came over and held my hands in the hope I would not escape.

"Valerie, Valerie . . . hold on; please hold on, stay right here. Stop talking, please. Uno momento." He ran to the car parked right next to where we sat. He went in the back and rummaged through bags, and found something in the front pocket of Priscilla's bag.

"Got it." He closed the door and came over to me. He went down on one knee as close to me as he possibly could.

"Priscilla and Olivia wanted me to ask you to marry me. Marry us today before we got over the border. They wanted to ask you, for me and for them, to have us all be a family. They made you this ring and wanted to give it to you. I want to give you this ring as a promise to you, to them, to our family. I want to marry you. I want to live on the farm and raise them with you. I want to have babies of our own, with you. Valerie, I plan on coming back in one piece, and if I can, with them. Valerie, will you marry me?" He knelt with is head in my lap and no tears. No hesitation. No fear that I may say something other than yes.

I could have died that day, or I could've start the rest of my life. I held my mouth open. No words could come out. A truck flew by us so close, we reacted and jumped. It was a truck of chickens that quacked and squabbled and threw white feathers in the air that covered our car, our table; pieces landed on us.

"Dylan, I want nothing more than to be your wife, start a family with you, the kids—our own kids. I have moved my business to be here and can be everything we both need to make this happen. But, I will only accept this ring if we are now a team, and we go and get them together."

"Valerie, this is dangerous. I understand your bold, fearless ambition. I can't let you come with me. I love you too much." We stood head to head, heart to heart, hand in hands. I had to make a decision.

"Dylan, I made a promise to you. I did what I said I would do. I tried my best to be a man of my word. I am not backing down, so if you don't let me go with you, then right now, I will say goodbye." I gave him the ring back and went to the car, grabbed my bag and walked vigorously to the border and as tears ran down my face, I couldn't look back.

"Valerie, Valerie!" he screamed and ran after me. He tackled me from behind. We fell.

"Are you crazy?" he screamed

"Apparently," I said.

"You are one bad-ass bitch."

"This is the revelation of the moment?"

"No, the revelation was when you called yourself a man just now." We giggled. "All right, all right. You come with me today, now and forever."

"Promise?"

"Promise." And he put the ring on my finger. We kissed on a dirt road in another country, and went on a ride or die voyage. We drove on a highway that turned into off-the-beat dirt roads, dark with no streetlights. Dylan assured me he knew where we were. He made lefts and rights. I would never be able to get myself out of here, even if I tried. We could see a fire in the distance. He said, "Holy shit, that is the house." He sped up to get to it, but it was still a distance away. We got closer and closer. When we came to where he believed the house was, a fire blazed in the background. He pulled up to the house with the lights off. As he put his car in park, the lights went on and a few men in guns—some in uniform, some not—checked their guns. Car lights went on around us.

Pedro came to the door and opened it for Dylan. Someone else came to open my door and dragged me out. I held my hands up. We were dragged into the center of the lights. Pedro smacked Dylan across the face with the back of his gun.

I screamed, "No!" I also was smacked across the face with just the back of a hand, and kicked in the stomach as I fell to the ground next to Dylan. The men stood over us. Lydia came out and stood over us, smoking a cigarette in one hand and holding a gun in the other, as we agonized in pain. She was dreadful, like the woman from *Orange is the new Black,* with the crazy hair and bad unibrow. She had a baseball bat and stood over us, angry. Pedro held down Dylan; someone else held me down with a foot to my neck.

"So, Lydia, which one are you going to do first?"

"Hmm, Dylan because he fucking killed my baby and my husband." She whacked him in his legs and in his side, then turned to me without notice and whacked my sides and my stomach. I turned over, she got me from behind. Pedro grabbed Dylan and gave him a few punches and kicked him. Then he kicked us both and chased us up and back to the car. I looked up as I was being dragged, and I could hear the kids screaming for us from the window, with the fire blazing behind the house. I waved my hand with the ring. I hoped they could see it from where they stood. They threw us back into the car and told us to drive to the border with an escort, which was two Mexican police cars that rode beside us.

"You tell anyone about this, I will come to kill you like I killed Miguel and Matteo. I will kill each kid starting with John. I will make it look like you did it, Dylan, let you rot in jail and then come to kill you. Or should I make your Barbie doll over here pay for the crimes? How do you think it should go down? And pretty, kiss your idea of having kids away, as I think we took care of that tonight." Pedro turned away from the car after he made sure I caught his eyes. He walked back into the circle and took a sip of a large bottle of a dark liquor.

"Say goodbye! Say goodbye to your fake family!" Pedro yelled to the kids with his hands open to the sky. We gave kisses to them in the sky, as much as we could lift our arms without pain. Dylan held my hand. We drove off at a brisk pace of the fake police car escort. For the entire ride to the border, we drove in silence, hand in hand together.

I took my extra shirt on the floor and wiped away the blood off Dylan's forehead as he drove. It was dark. All you could hear was the roar of the cars escorting us to the border. He bled. I kept the pressure on his wounds to hope he wasn't going to lose too much blood. The border approached and the same men that let us through let us back in without documentation necessary. We drove to the hotel. They let us to a room without a check-in. The maid who serviced our room brought towels and buckets of hot water. She also was a nurse and helped sew up some of Dylan's wounds. This was apparently not the first time this had happened here. She checked me and I needed no stitches, but she gave us a strong Tylenol and placed us into bed with water bottles and some snacks. We laid there together in pieces, but together.

"Dylan, I was pregnant, but I don't know anymore." We cried in bed together, hugging and bleeding and in pain. He took his weak hand still trembling from all of the shock and pain. He got his hand to my stomach, below my belly button, and rested his shaking hand there for a moment until he could build the strength to move it down into my underwear and to feel his way inside me, slowly moving his finger in as far as he could and pulled it out slowly back to look at it with one open eye.

"You're not bleeding. Does it hurt?"

"Yes," I said in a whining voice, I was in so much pain and agony, it was too hard to respond.

"You can't go to the hospital here; we have to go back to Mexico."

"No, Dylan, no, we are not going back." Both of us were too weak to fight, too weak to be mad, too weak to continue to ask questions. We shed tears and moans. Through time, we closed our eyes and slept together in blood, sweat and tears.

I woke up several times from strong pains in my stomach and begged the baby to be okay; I checked Dylan's stitches that still slowly dripped blood. "Dylan, we have to go to the hospital."

"I know. We need to take care of that baby."

"Dylan, you are bleeding you need attention."

"We have to get over the border."

"Why? That is crazy."

"No, it's not. How are you going to explain what happened to you? How are we going to not have suspicion around us? Do you need that? Think of your business, just think. Over the border, they don't care. They know the corruption. They will understand. Trust me; we go over the border."

He got up. I helped him get to the bathroom and put on some clothes. We gathered a bag with passports and some cash. He talked to the maid, our current nurse, and he asked to get us a ride as close to the border as possible so we could walk over. She got us the hotel van who took us. We gathered the bag and held each other to the other side. He was weak and held onto me for strength that I didn't have—but I found it each step of the way. My pains got deeper and I had to stop from point to point until they passed. We stood in line, kept our hats low over our sunglasses and faces. We looked down.

"Bro, you okay?" Some random young man came over to Dylan as they watched us from behind. Dylan signaled with his hand.

"I'm good, thanks." I was going to another country to get healthcare that I had insurance for in my own country. I got beat up for loving this man and his nieces and nephews. I was walking with a man that I had been asked to believe and trust in. I was walking in faith with him.

We got through customs. No questions were asked other than to take off our sunglasses. My pains grew deeper. Dylan looked down. He saw blood running through my jeans.

"No, no, Valerie." I started to feel weak and needed to sit down. It was starting to happen; I was going to lose the baby. Dylan put my arm around his shoulder, he lifted me, ripping the stitches done by fishing wire by our maid in Texas, but who was a nurse in Mexico.

"Dylan, your stitches . . . I'm too heavy."

"You are going to bleed to death; the medical center is not too far. I have to get you there."

I continued to fade. I drifted in and out as I could feel daggers in my lower abdomen. Dylan now had my blood all over his arms and his shirt, along with his own scars. We got to the medical center, and as we walked in, we looked like we just walked out of a burning car.

"Please, help my wife!" And as he screamed, the room looked at us in shock and horror. The patients waiting sighed, the front desk screamed at the back with urgency in Spanish. Doctors came running to us; a gurney came with a crew of scrubbed up men, and women ran straight to us as Dylan was about to drop me. I was thrown onto the gurney, a woman with scissors came up to me and cut my jeans off of me, right there in the waiting room for everyone to see. They moved us to the blocked off hallway and continued to clean us, and probed us to find out where we needed attention first.

"Dylan!" I tried to scream, but it came out as a loud whisper.

"Sit back, sit back," the woman said. I couldn't find Dylan within my view. Someone came up with a needle and stabbed my vein inside my left inner arm. I felt the strong prick; I felt a sensation, then my arm felt cold. I could see the hallway in the distance. It was white, then turned gray, then became blurry. A wash of black came over me. Then I could hear Dylan and I concentrated on his voice.

"Ella está teniendo un aborto espontáneo." Por favor, cuidar de ella, por favor, ella es mi todo."

"Okay, okay, sir. She is in good care; we will take care of her. Please, sit down, we have to attend to your wound. Your stitches came open; they are infected. Where did you have this done?"

"Lucinda, you know Lucinda at the hotel in Texas."

'Si, Si. Okay, sit back, this is going to hurt." He poked Dylan with a needle to numb the pain and cleaned the wound, took out the old stitches and re-stitched the open wound. They gave him an IV drip for the infection and one for his dehydration. I could hear his moans of pain in the other room. I concentrated on his voice as I felt fuzzy. And soon, I blacked out.

I was jerked by a pain and a feeling of my body coming back alive. I awoke to black as I was not ready to open my eyes. As I opened my eyes, it was grey. It was fuzzy. I shut them again. I could smell my surroundings. It was stale, like cheap bleach and led paint. I attempted, moments later, to open my eyes again. It was too hard. I went back to concentrating on the smells, and now focused on the sounds. I could hear the light buzzing above me, the ceiling fan in the hallway buzzing around. The speaker was announcing codes in Spanish and then in English. I could smell the bleach, the paint, the sound of sneakers squeaking on the tile floor as doctors and nurses walked along the hallway from room to room. Then I could smell a musk that ran through the room from the ceiling fan. I knew right away it was Dylan. I tuned into my other senses; I could feel his limp hand holding mine. I gave as much of a squeeze to it as I could.

"Mi amor, you are awake!" He was excited and had some life back in his voice. I still could not fully open my eyes, and the light that shined was still too bright for me. I turned my head toward him and tried to open my eyes again. He sat in the recliner next to the bed, in a fresh white tee shirt, fresh bandages on his face and an IV drip. His bruises seemed clean, and his hair was combed back perfectly as he didn't have the strength to do his nervous, anxiety-ridden brush throw with his hand.

"Come and lay with me," I said and inched my way as much to the left as I could, holding onto the metal bar. I put my face on the bar as it was cold, and I needed to feel the relief of it. It was sticky; I didn't care.

"Come and lay with me!" I demanded from him.

"I don't think we can both fit?"

"Dylan!"

"Si, Si." He did his best to stand up, held onto the drip, and leaned backward into the bed in slow motion as he was still in pain and his stitches were raw. He leaned back, and soon, his head hit the pillow. The bed felt like a metal slab with a terrycloth towel as a mattress. It was uncomfortable, but we couldn't really feel anything at this point. Dylan held onto his IV pole until he got situated in the bed and felt steady enough to let it go. He put his hand on my lower stomach with caution as we lay in this tight space with our backs to the hard surface. I grabbed his fingers and held onto them, and drifted back to sleep. I was broken. I was sad. I was no longer alone. There was no one else I would rather spend this moment with other than Dylan.

*   *   *   *   *

And I find it kinda funny,
I find it kinda sad.
The dreams in which I'm dying are the best I've ever had.
—Michael Andrews Featuring Gary Jules
"Mad World" (*Donnie Darko, Riverdale*)

The next day, we awoke to a nurse prodding and poking at us, and before I knew it, we were free from drips and had both received new bandages.

"Okay, you are going to bleed for the next few days, so here are a few pads. You will probably need to change about every two hours.

"Senyor, make sure she takes Tylenol every few hours, and you also take one every few hours. Watch your wounds and change the dressing on them. You can wear these clothes. The ones you came in are ruined." She threw blue scrub, drawstring pants to both of us and new white tee shirts.

"Senyor, here is your bill." I looked over at the piece of paper she handed him as I ran down the list, and at the bottom read $47,485.

"Are you fucking kidding me?" I said, and Dylan shushed me.

"How do we pay for this?"

Dylan looked up at the nurse and said, "I have ten thousand dollars in cash; I have a truck that is worth about $28,000. I can drive it to the border. Will you accept that?"

"Si," she replied. We picked ourselves up like wounded soldiers, put back on our hats and sunglasses, and walked arm and arm back to the border.

"You have done this before," I said to Dylan as we made it back into Texas.

"I have done it for Papa, I have done it for Miguel, and now . . . I do it for you."

"I want to know why."

"No, you don't. And I am not going to tell you. Just let it go, Valerie, let it go."

We got back to the hotel, drove to the border, and exchanged the truck for our unborn child that now was somewhere in a red, hazardous waste bag somewhere in a trash can—somewhere without its parents, in a foreign country, without us.

"I love you, Peanut," I said as I looked at Mexico and shed a tear. Dylan brought me in as we wore matching outfits like we escaped from an insane asylum together. In some ways, I believed that we did.

"Okay, let's go home. Let's leave this all behind us." We got our things, rented a car and went back to Texas and left that memory behind.

"Dylan, I am broken."

"I know . . . I am too." I took a picture of us holding hands so that the cloth ring the girls made for me was visible, and posted it on Instagram.

"Maybe Olivia will see it?"

We got likes, we got more likes, but nothing from Olivia. I checked for days until that memory too faded away. She posted nothing further, but her account was not deactivated. I checked every day for her. I prayed and hoped that she would reach out to us and find us. We wanted them back.

"Come with me." Dylan signaled to me one morning as the sun came up. We walked out into the farm, past all the horses, past the cows, to where the trees started to clear a path to the woods. He took me to a spot where you could watch the perfect sunrise, and he planted a bed of roses.

"I planted these for Peanut, and for you. Valerie, I know I have asked a lot of you, and you stood by me through all of it. I love you, Valerie, and I want you to be my wife. I want to try again to have another baby, and I want to have it with you. Again, will you marry me?" Dylan got down on one knee in front of the roses and presented me with a simple band, as I requested, and placed it on my finger. I knelt in front of him and placed my hands behind his ears, and we both looked into each other's eyes.

"I already said yes. I'm not turning back now." And the commitment was made.

We continued to mourn the loss of the kids. One day, the story was about John and when Dylan played catch with him before dinner. We remembered Olivia and her snapshots, and pointed out moments perfect for capturing. We mimicked a snapshot with our hands when we were without phones, and I worked on perfecting the "Valerie and Dylan" selfie. I posted to Instagram in desperation, in desperation of the kids finding their way back. In broadcasting to the world that Dylan now belonged to me. We made inappropriate comments to interrupt each other and remember Priscilla, and that is when we broke down. As we could see her face—so innocent, so adorable, so lovable holding Bingo and her belly sticking out of her shirt—the tears did not stop. The pain, the memory of our losses, of Peanut. We were drawn closer and closer in these moments, until one day they became too old, too fragile to hold.

At these conversations, I find myself picturing Shelia, pregnant with me, not sure of what happened between herself and Tom. I pictured her calls to Cal, where Cal would hang up on her angry and disappointed that she had a child out of wedlock and out of desperation. I could feel her tears. Her pain. Her anger and how she channeled it back out to Todd and Ashley. I was starting to understand her. And during these moments, I became closer to Shelia than I ever knew.

* * * * *

Spring. We decided on a spring wedding. It was far enough away and close enough at the same time. Sofia and Frannie got excited by the news, and did all the planning for the farm to hold the extravaganza. I had no interest in the planning. The wanting to be a part of it. I just wanted to get married in a white dress, with my husband to be, in front of God. With the ones we loved, that is all that mattered.

I didn't have a mother. I did, but I didn't. Then she died. I could manifest Tom and Brenda, then Kellie fell off. Ashley and Todd were nothing to me but an anxiety attack. I went back to nothing. I sat in the barn with my red feather and my picture, worn and tattered, of Cal and Madeline, and wished they were here with me. I talked to them.

"Madeline, Cal, can you walk me down the aisle? Do you like Dylan, Frannie, Sofia? Did you meet the kids? Can you bring them back to me?" I was asking for clarification from people who were not present, not here right now, and two people that were so part of my heart, even if I never knew them. I was asking questions about things I needed to have the answers for, instead of asking for permission from somewhere else.

No one should need permission to be in love—no one. I felt alone and frail. I wanted to run, but then I saw Dylan out in the field and how much he cared about the farm, his family, and me. He was good for me. Deep down, I loved him. But was he worthy of me?

I left the barn that afternoon and walked into Frannie, on the porch of her house, looking for me to pass by at some point that day. She flagged me down as I wanted to run into the house, hide under the covers, and cry in my disappointment of where Dylan stood in my heart. After all we had been through, he had power over me that I didn't see or know about. I should have run. I lost my baby—our baby—because I was beaten. We gave up our truck for healthcare in another country to carry a secret. Their secret. Now it was my new secret.

"Hi, Frannie!" I said as I waved and walked toward her.

"Come for a walk with me," she said as she met me halfway and linked arms with me.

"How is the beautiful Bride-to-be doing?"

"I am good. Yeah, I'm good."

"Convincing . . . listen, I know you have questions. Dylan won't give you answers, you are confused. I can't believe you haven't run away just yet. He loves you, he really loves you, and only wants the best for you." She pushed back her salt and pepper hair up in a bun, and small strands fell as we walked through the farm.

"Um, yeah, I do have questions. I think I am afraid to know. Dylan said I shouldn't know. What does that mean? Yeah, I do feel crazy marrying a man after what we went through, but . . . umm, but . . . I am somehow bound to him; I just can't explain it."

"There is not always a way to describe out loud how you love someone. But if you didn't love him, you wouldn't be here. So, yes, there are stories. There are questions, and yes there are things you don't need to know.

"Lydia and Dylan were young lovers, and we moved here to Texas to start this farm and follow a dream. That dream came with a price tag. Lydia was beautiful and innocent, but her family was another story. Papa borrowed money from them to buy this farm, they worked out a payment plan, and Papa paid back every cent, maybe even more. That wasn't enough for those greedy fucks, and they wanted to come and have a piece of the ownership once they saw how profitable it had become.

"Now they had an agreement. Off the books, no paper. Now I loved my husband, Matteo, but he made a deal with the devil. He knew what he got himself into. He believed once he paid off the debt, it would be over. It's never over. Matteo decided to fight them, because that is what hot-blooded Latino men do. He went to battle with them, and they beat Matteo up pretty badly. He went to the hospital in Mexico, but they didn't give him the proper care. He came home and was internally bleeding; we didn't know about it. Eventually, he died.

"Right before this happened, Dylan went back to Mexico. He knew nothing of the corruption, or the arrangements made. It didn't help us, but we kept our children in the dark at this time. Matteo wouldn't talk to Dylan, and despised his betrayal, and sent him to live in Mexico and 'be a man.' Lydia loved Dylan. She was traumatized by the miscarriage (although we don't believe she had one) and really believed her family. He was willing to stand by her, but the abuse from her family was horrible. Dylan, as you know, wears his heart on his sleeve and would take it, because he loved her.

"This family is crazy. I believe they made her 'miscarry' that baby, and they convinced her that he did it. She went downhill from there with drugs, alcohol, and then she went into prostitution. It was ugly. The fight over the farm disappeared after time, but when they were broke and needed money, the conversation came back. Miguel decided he was going to settle the score and Lydia seduced him. She suddenly becomes pregnant, and he married her. I think you know the rest from here.

"So, the past is the past, the rivalry may never end, and we have to accept that the kids are with her, and just pray they are well taken care of."

"I believe they will come back. I want them back. I feel them in my heart and fell in love with them."

"Ahh, an optimist; okay, you believe and believe, but don't come to me when you are disappointed. Listen, start your own family. Live here in peace. Don't let him go back for more. He loves you, and after this, I believe it can end here." I had so much to say. I felt so many things. I should have run. I should have run but I am trapped now.

"Okay, I will"

And my inner voice screamed aloud, "LIAR! LIAR! RUN!" I told it to shush and appeased Frannie.

*　　*　　*　　*　　*

Tom and Brenda came the night before, and on this casual wedding day, Tom wore jeans with holes and his favorite sports jacket. Dylan stayed in Frannie's house on the days that led up to the wedding, as we didn't want to see each other on that special day.

"Okay, this is it! Ready?" Brenda said in her happy, "trying to be my mom stand-in" way as possible.

"Okay," I said as she caught me wiping away a tear.

"Oh, tears of joy and jitters, so exciting!"

"Yeah?"

"What's wrong? This isn't nerves, is it?"

"No. Yes? I don't know. Am I doing the right thing? Am I crazy? Have you ever been married before?"

"Oh, honey. You are doing the right thing. Don't worry about that."

She took me to the window where we could see Dylan standing, waiting for me.

"See, look at him. He is so nervous; he can't stand still. Don't be nervous. He looks at you as his favorite daydream. I think you have nothing to worry about. Yes, I have been married before. It was wonderful. I was nervous, just like you are. But the second I walked

175

down that aisle, and locked eyes with him, I knew it was right. I just knew. I don't regret a thing. You won't either."

"So, what happened?" I asked concerned. I never knew she was married before.

"Oh, honey. Story for another time. He died, then I met your dad. I was blessed with two wonderful relationships. Now stop these tears; let's go get your man!" We nodded and hugged in the moment as Tom waited at the bottom of the stairs.

"Thank you for sharing," I said. I locked arms with Brenda and Tom, and we walked to the beat of the music played by a local band. As each step went by, I was somber and could hear my head beating.

The beating in my head was louder and louder; I looked up toward Dylan as he was shedding tears. The pounding was so loud in my head, I shed tears also that were masked. Everyone believed it was out of joy, when they were really tears of fear and maybe a little anger.

My hands left Tom's, as he kissed my cheek, and gave them over to Dylan. I could feel his cold, clammy hands that stuck to mine and the pounding went away; the pain went away. I looked into his eyes as he smiled back at me with his face wet with tears. He was so kind and endearing at that moment, I couldn't help myself and the feeling that came to me like lightining.

"Dylan . . . I love you."

"I love you too." We said our vows, we ate a three-course meal, we cut cake, and we danced under the stars. And as the night was over and guests were packing up to leave, I looked out across the dance floor into the long farm tables, and I could see a feather being swept up by the hired help. I felt the anticipation of watching it being swept, and wanting to save it. I nudged to get out of his hold; he just made it tighter. He distracted me by the conversation, and as I took one second off the feather, it was gone. I broke loose and ran to it, and it was gone, lost in a pile of garbage and streamers. It was gone, and I couldn't save it.

"Valerie, are you okay?" Dylan stood a few feet away from me with his hands folded across him, and his voice was of high concern. I was crying; I was so upset. I was an emotional mess from the day. Losing the feather was like saying goodbye to something—but what?

"I'm good, sorry, just a lot today. It's all good." I turned to him and moved into his chest to find comfort. We danced to Dylan's voice whispering in my ear.

*   *   *   *   *

We had been trying to get pregnant for months now, and nothing. Each month, our frustration grew as my cycle started, and Dylan pouted for the next five days. I felt as if I failed him. Dylan wanted us to start IVF, but I refused. I didn't want my body injected with chemicals and hormones. The bigger house was very empty. We were eager to fill it. Even in our forties, we still wanted to try to have a few children, but we also wanted the kids to come back. So each night, when Dylan came back from a day on the farm, we would try and try. And each night, I would pray it would work.

"Please, Lord, give us a child. Bring the kids back. I am ready for our happy home to be filled." One night, a car pulled up into the farm after dinner, after our lovemaking sessions, and after a joint shower. We heard someone pull up to the house. The car was black, and neither one of us knew who it was. Pedro and Lydia walked out of the car as we came outside, and from the other houses, Sofia and Frannie came walking up to the car as well. Frannie brought her shotgun.

"We come in peace, Frannie." Pedro held his arms up as Lydia opened the back door and out came John and Priscilla.

"You can have them back," Lydia said, "but Olivia stays." I wanted to ask why, but I couldn't as Dylan put his hand over my face when I opened my mouth.

"What is the trick here? You can't drop them off, and then come back for them and steal them from underneath us again."

"No, I won't," Lydia said in defeat. She said goodbye to the kids who were not enthused nor upset by their departure. They came over to us and stood at our sides.

"Olivia wants to stay and take care of Lydia as she will go through chemo. Lydia has cancer," Pedro said. As sad as it was, no one reacted.

"She only has a few months to live. We don't want trouble, but the kids talk about you every day. Lydia doesn't want them to see her sick; she can no longer care for them. This is it. No more, we end our feud tonight."

"Pedro, we end it all tonight. No more."

"No more," Pedro agreed. They shook on it, and Lydia looked me in the eyes and waved goodbye as I took her children from here, and she would go home to die a slow death. I asked the kids to go upstairs, and as they pulled backward out of the farm, I ran to the car, and Pedro stopped. I came to Lydia's window, reached in and gave her a hug.

"I will take good care of them for you. Thank you."

She cried, and they continued back to Mexico. That was the last time they showed their faces again.

I got the beds ready for John and Pri. They were tired and kind of not understanding what was going on at that moment. It had been a few years since we last saw them. They outgrew all of their clothes we had kept in their drawers. They slept in what they had on. John was so tall; you could see the maturity on his face. Dylan went to sit with him as I went to sit with Pri.

"Are you my mommy now?" I wasn't sure how to answer that question so soon as I still didn't have it all processed.

"You have a momma. I can't change that. But as your mom is not here, I will do my best to stand in. How does that sound?" I said as I took Bingo and gave him a snuggle. I sat on the bed next to her and was ready to tuck her in.

"Yes!" she said with a smile, with her cheerleader hands in the air. "Can we go back to school now?"

"You haven't been in school?"

"No."

Holy crap, I can't believe this; oh man, we have work to do.

"Yes, my love, you will go back to school as soon as we can get you registered. Good night, mi amor." And as I kissed her forehead, headed for the door to shut the light, as I turned my back, she reached out in her new, grown-up voice.

"Good night, Momma Valerie," and my heart melted. I went in to watch over Dylan and John as they were in a deep conversation. My presence interrupted them, and Dylan clammed up. I walked over to the other side of the bed and sat next to John, and tried to push his long hair out of his eyes as he fussed.

"Glad that you are here, John."

"Thank you," he said as he looked down. I glanced at Dylan who signaled to let it go. I gave him a kiss on the forehead and wished him a good night's sleep. We went into our bedroom. Shortly after, Dylan said good night to both, came into the bedroom, and shut the door.

We woke up to a little body crawling into our bed, working her way into our sleeping bond. She held Bingo, and from the last time she laid with us, she was a little taller and thicker. She found her spot on Dylan's leg and drifted back into sleep. Dylan and I opened one eye to each other, and with a chuckle, he moved his hand off of my shoulder and onto hers.

We enrolled them in school, sports, and a lifestyle back in their Texas home. We went shopping for new clothes and went to doctors, dentists, and redecorated their rooms. After a few weeks, life became normal again, and we had a set routine.

Dylan and I still missed Olivia and Peanut, but we believed and prayed that Olivia would eventually come back to us; and eventually, we would have a new Peanut in our family.

Weeks went by, and our routine became normal again. Dylan worked on the farm. I took care of the kids and household as I also ran my business from the sidelines. I went to drop off John at baseball practice, and picked up Pri from a playdate. My phone went off.

First, it rang, then it would hang up. Then a txt came through; then it rang again. I was driving and didn't answer as it wasn't Dylan's ringtone or anyone else's I recognized right away.

"Who is Colby?" Pri asked from the backseat, as she leaned in and watched the incoming call on the dashboard screen.

"Colby? I don't know . . . hmm, I think someone from my job. I will call him back later." I took a minute and held my hand to my chest to hope that the beating would not be loud for her to hear. She was so receptive to my feelings.

"Let's sing a song Pri, what do you suggest?"

I turned on the radio, and she shouted "This song!" We sang to the lyrics on the radio.

"Let it go! Let it GOOOO!" I turned it up loud so she could not hear my heart beating. We returned to the farm, and I sent her into the shower, and ran down into the woods to check my texts.

V, are you there?

I need to talk to you.

I need you to call me. It is important. It's about Christopher.

No time to think, no time to waste, no time to react. Dialing, dialing, *ring, ring* . . .

"Valerie, I need you, it is Christopher. He had a stroke at work, collapsed and hit his head. He is in the hospital, in and out of it. He is screaming for you . . ."

Silence . . .

"Valerie, are you there?"

"Yes, yes, I am here. I, I, I . . . I will be on the soonest flight I can get out."

"Valerie, you know he is so difficult. He always thinks about you."

"I know, see you soon."

I closed my phone, went back into the house, and helped Pri from her shower. I cooked dinner for the family, and at 6:30 p.m., like every evening, we sat as a family to eat. I made the family favorite of chicken cutlets and fresh coleslaw.

"So, how was everyone's day?" Dylan asked.

"I had practice and hit a ball out of the park!"

"Nice, John, you are going to be a pro for sure, I can feel it!"

"Valerie got a call from Colby," Pri said, excited that she could contribute to the conversation. I wanted to cringe, but instead, I put on a smile.

"Ooh, Colby, mystery man. Tell me more," Dylan said back as he dangled his fork in the air. She giggled and held Bingo as some slaw sat on her lip from her last bite. She kept her smile as Dylan went to wipe it off her mouth. I changed the topic.

"Dylan, how was your day?"

"Ah, it was good, a regular day on the farm. We did get a new client a few towns away today. Very excited. Can I ask you for some office help this week?"

"Dylan, I have to go out of town for a client. I have to go to DC for a few days. They are my best client and never call me, except for today. I hope that you understand."

"No, don't go!" Pri screamed. "I want to come," she added.

"No, no, you can't come, you must go to school. It's Tuesday! I will be back in no time," I said to her and wiped her hair out of her face. Then I had to look Dylan straight in the eye.

"I just found out. Sofia and Frannie said they could watch the kids. I can help you when I get back." He looked at me as he chewed his food and didn't respond right away. I was nervous and felt as if my face was burning up, red of heat and guilt all piled up. It was showing.

"You seem so nervous? Of course, if you have to go, then you have to go. Did you think I would stop you? Mi amor, you have your own business, I know you have to leave from time to time. You just haven't in a long while is all." He looked down into his plate, which traditionally meant, disapproval.

"I know it has been some time. I just want to get in front of them. If they are asking for me, it must be important." I looked right at him, but he continued to look into his chicken.

The table was finished, the kids cleared the dishes, and Dylan sat with his beer and checked his phone. I went over to him and tried to kiss him, but he seemed uninterested. I felt as if he knew I was going to see Christopher. I went upstairs to check flights and got my bag together for the early morning departure. I wanted to leave before the kids woke up to avoid the guilty goodbye.

"It is just a trip," I said to myself in my head, but it didn't make it feel any better.

"So, DC, so fast. What's the rush?" Dylan said as he came upstairs and stood in the doorframe.

"I know, I am sorry. I think I am just eager and miss being in front of my clients again. I just maybe feel like I miss a little bit of a city? Does that make sense? I will be right back, I promise." I gave him a smile of assurance, and he let his guard down.

"I know, I kidnapped you to this farm," he said with a laugh. "I don't want you to feel trapped."

"Dylan, it has been a lot. I want to be here with you and the kids, and work on having our own kids; I just need to do this for a bit of sanity and to help my business." He came behind me and lifted my hair, as I sat in front of the mirror taking off my makeup for the evening. He gave the best cranial massages, and I think he was hoping it would make me stay. Somehow, maybe we both knew this trip was more than just a few days of escape.

"Yes, of course." He kissed my neck, carried me to bed and the night ended.

*   *   *   *   *

"But if their hearts were dying that fast,
They'd have done the same as you
And I'd have done the same as you."
—Cath, Death Cab for Cutie

I napped on the plane with my head against the window. I dreamed about Madeline. She was watching the man across the street out the window, and then, one day, she got the courage to walk across the street in her favorite black dress with the white collar, and a red belt that made her waist look thin. She clenched onto her pearls and smiled as she waved and tried to get this man's attention.

"Helloooo!" she said in a high-pitched nervous voice.

"Helloooo!" she said again, as he was obviously not listening, and he could not hear over the lawnmower. She sucked in her stomach and smoothed out her dress, she held her bunt cake up high, and eventually he took notice and shut off the lawn mower, and stood in awe.

"Hello, I didn't hear you through the lawn mower."

"Oh, I understand. I saw you working so hard. I just took this out of the oven and thought you might want a break?" She waved it in front of his nose.

"Why, that is awfully nice of you, will you join me for a slice? I can make some coffee."

She nodded, and as they went inside, she made sure she checked if her hair tied up in perfect curls were still intact, and continued to clench onto her pearls.

They went inside, and politely she said, "Oh, please sit, you have been working hard. If you don't mind, I can find my way around your kitchen. May I?" He nodded and sat down at the head of the four-person table that was covered with a floral tablecloth covered by plastic. She fiddled around the kitchen and put on a pot of coffee. He didn't assist much as to where things were kept; she seemed to already know. Madeline found two plates and placed a slice of bunt cake on each, and as the coffee was served she sat with him at the table to the right of him, and they enjoyed their afternoon coffee and tea.

"I so love this time of year when everything turns green and is fresh? Don't you agree?"

"Yes, Madeline, I agree. This is a mighty good bunt cake, thank you for thinking of me." He placed his hand on her hand as they both smiled and sipped their hot coffee. He gave her a wink and finished his slice.

"What are we doing here, Madeline?" he asked her as he leaned in close enough to touch her lips. It was more than enough space to smell the perfume that Cal bought her.

"What do you mean? We are having cake and coffee. What is wrong with that?" She went to take another sip, and when she closed her eyes to lift her head to the cup, he firmly grabbed her free hand again.

"Madeline! Cal comes home in a few weeks. What are you going to tell him? What are you going to do? I can't stand to be without you. Madeline, I am falling in love with you." She looked away, and when her tears started, she stood up and walked into the living room. He sighed and sat back in the chair, afraid to know the answer, as the body language was the message that it was over.

"I just need some time; can you give me some time? He is coming back from the war, I mean, we need some time."

"No, actually, you don't. If you don't love me, Madeline, if you won't leave him to be with me, Madeline, then that is it. This is it; it's over."

"I do want to be with you, I do . . ."

I was startled by someone shaking me. It was the person in the middle seat.

"Hey, sorry to startle you. I think you were having a nightmare, and we are landing in a few minutes."

"Oh, okay, thanks." I wanted to punch seat B in the face. What did Madeline choose? Wait, I know who she chose. She stayed with Cal.

Cal! I could scream in my head, but then what would I say next? I got off the plane and was greeted by Colby and Erika who drove me to the hospital.

"So, how is he?"

Colby and Erika looked at each other as I sat in the back seat of the Range Rover, and as they collected themselves, Erika answered.

"He is better, calmed down today, just out of it."

We drove in silence the rest of the forty-minute trip from Regan International. We entered the hospital and went straight to his room. It felt like an FBI mission as we walked, all taking the same step forward and the same look on our faces with the actual belief that I was here. We walked into his room, and he was sleeping. They stood in the lobby of the floor to give us some time. I looked him over and held onto the bar at the side of the bed. The cold bar that reminded me of losing my baby in Mexico. It brought back all the pain in my gut, or was it the pain of the damage I was doing in this hospital room at this minute? That pain was much worse. I went to hold his hand and leaned in to touch his hair that no longer was combed proportionally to hide his receding hairline. As I leaned in, my hair fell from out of behind my ears and touched his face, and it prompted him to open his eyes.

"You came," he said in a grumbling whisper, and his eyes opened and closed.

"Shhhhhhh, yes, I am here. Keep resting; I am not going anywhere." With his blind eyes, he looked for my hand, and I grabbed onto him as I found a chair on the far side of the room next to the window, and perched there for the next few hours. He was so peaceful and so vulnerable.

Whatever happened between us? Why didn't we ever happen? I questioned myself.

Why? I was in love with Dylan. The switch went back and forth in my head. Colby and Erika came in and out, pacing the room and floors, not knowing what to do with themselves. I sat by his side and continued to touch his hair and moved down his arms and legs to keep the circulation flowing as gently as possible. Nurses came in and checked vitals, and ask me if I was his wife or girlfriend, and all I could respond with was, "No."

As the day became night, Colby came over and insisted that I go to get something to eat.

"Why don't you take a break? He is stable and sleeping. Come grab something to eat with me." Colby was trying to pry me away from the perch I created.

"I will stay here."

"Please, Valerie, it has been a long day, go with Colby," Erika insisted. Their concerned looks got to me as I was growing tired.

"Okay," I responded and went downstairs to the cafeteria with Colby. We sat in the large room that was almost empty, except for some workers on break, and we shared sandwiches and salad. I could hardly eat anything.

"I am so glad that you came. I know he appreciates it. He really needs you, but is too stubborn to tell you that."

"Colby, what does that do for me? I couldn't wait anymore; I just couldn't. I have a family now. Dylan and I are starting a family, and we adopted his brother's kids. I had to move on."

"I know, but you are here. Why did you come? Don't tell me that you don't still wonder. Have feelings? Maybe, just maybe . . ."

"Maybe what? Should I just leave my family? Come to DC and wait to be ignored? Wait for him to what?"

"Okay, I get it. He is my twin brother. I know him. He is an ass, but he has such feelings for you. Just know that as you are here, you came here of your own free will. All I did was ask." We stared at each other. As I wanted to eat my salad, I no longer could and threw my fork into the plate. I looked away in shame, just as Madeline did. I stood up and took steps away from the table. He was right, he was so right; and I was so scared to give up what I had for something I always wanted to be safe. But I wasn't safe.

I was almost killed. My baby was killed, and that, in turn, almost killed me. Am I living in danger? Is the feud over? I don't know, but I wanted to know what I was missing, and the "what if." WHAT IF I still wanted Christopher?

We went back upstairs, and as we came off the elevator, we could hear screaming.

"NO, NO, NO, where is she? Where!" The buzzers went off, and before we could figure out where it came from, Erika came out looking for someone, anyone; and she found me.

"Please, he is calling for you, he is ripping everything out of his arms, help!" Erika grabbed my arm, nurses went running into the room, and they were able to hold him down and sedate him as we stood at the back of the room and watched.

"Valerie." Christopher tried to reach for me, but the restraints were in place. And as the sedative set in, he faded to black into the pillow and was shortly out. When the excitement was over, he was back to a normal heartbeat. Everyone was exhausted by the episode.

"I am going to stay here tonight," I said with confidence to Colby and Erika.

"No, you don't have to."

"I know I don't have to. I want to," I said to Colby without blinking. I needed to know why I was here, because I wasn't going to leave without knowing. The nurse brought me blankets and a pillow. I got myself comfortable into the chair next to Christopher, and as I watched the monitor, as his heartbeat stayed normal, he was snoring at a consistent pace. It felt safe to grab my phone.

Hello. Miss you so much. Heading to bed. I will call you in the morning, xoxoxo. Dream about me.

Miss you, Mi Amor, hurry back ♥

I hung up my phone and could feel them all. *What am I doing here?* I closed my eyes and tried to find Madeline again; I could see her coming down the stairs and buttoning her dress as her curls from her perfect hairdo now lay on her shoulders. She left out of the front door and, with no apology, she walked back into her house in that early morning. She slammed the door and cried as she held her hands to the back to see if she could still feel him. I could feel her pain. I could understand her decision. Before long, I could see Cal walking up the front walkway with a green duffle bag and in perfect uniform. She came out screaming and crying to greet him. He picked her up and swung her around.

Eight months and three weeks later, she gave birth to a child. They named her Shelia. When they brought Shelia home, the man across the street came out from his garden and watched them walk up the walkway into the house. He nodded to Cal and said, "Congratulations."

"Thank you!" Cal said back, Madeline looked down. Three days later, he moved with no forwarding address. Madeline and Cal never saw him again. Since then, she resented Shelia from that day forward.

I felt a squeeze on my hand. I jumped, almost scared that it was Dylan and that he had caught me. It was Christopher as he had awoken. He could not move.

"How did you find me?" Christopher could feel that I was awake. He was at peace with what the situation was.

"How do you think?"

"Colby?"

"Yes." There was a silence. He tried to swallow, but his throat was so raw.

"Do you need some water?"

"Yes, please." I got up to gather him a glass with a straw, and brought it to his lips until he was content with his sip. The nurse heard the voices and came in to check in on him.

"Doing much better, Mr. Sullivan, much better."

"I have my lucky charm with me, that is why," he replied. He was calm and collected. The color was coming back in his face; his obnoxious personality was back. He was on the road to recovery.

"Can we take these restraints off now? He clearly is better; I just think it is so uncomfortable for him to rest." I wasn't really asking for permission, but was being polite as I was already starting to take them off.

"Yes, I think it is safe to do so. Quite the scare this evening, Mr. Sullivan, we are not going to do this again, are we?" she asked. I gave him a stare that told him to just cooperate.

"I am good, just want to be free in the bed and get comfortable." She smiled at him. We worked together to take off all the restraints. He soothed his wrists as they became free. She brought him some Jell-O to nourish him, and to help his throat from its raspy, chalkboard scratching sound it gave off. I fed it to him slowly like he was a child in a highchair.

"Valerie, why are you here?" he asked in a humble, honest voice I never heard before. I smacked my lips together, not sure if I was holding back from talking, or from crying; or just unsure what would come out first.

"I don't know." I blurted out, holding the tears in.

"Why, Valerie? I want to be with you. I want to spend my life with you."

"Really, Christopher? Now? Right now? Because this is a really hard thing for you to ask me right now. I waited for you and waited for you. I called you; you gave me nothing. So now? Now you want me? As you came close to death, I came running like a fool and now you want to be with me?" He chuckled a bit and grabbed my arm as I started to walk away.

"You are adorable when you are a man." I was not amused.

"Fair, I agree, fair enough. I suck, I will admit it. I am difficult; I am sure that Colby could attest to that. I wasn't fair to you, because I never felt the way I feel about you with anyone else. I don't know how to deal with that."

"Christopher, I have had you in my head since before I could remember. Do you think I don't know what that feels like? You ran away from me instead of drawing me closer."

"I was afraid; afraid that you wouldn't feel the same for me the way I feel for you. I'm not as strong as you are." *I am so sick of hearing that.*

"My wife left me because I screamed for you at night, it created a distance between us. She took the kids. I hardly see them. I deserve it. I am nothing without you; I hope that you can understand that. Be with me. Let's run away together. Come with me."

"Christopher, I have a family. I made a commitment. I can't run away from that. I am breaking such a trust with him, such a trust. You can't ask me to come with you; you just can't."

"Then why are you still here?"

"I don't know." He moved himself in the bed far to the right, and held onto the metal bar, and touched it with his face for the cold to hit his skin and get into his bones.

"Come and lay next to me. Please just come and lay next to me. I need you." He made enough room. I curled into the open spot in the tight hospital bed and crawled into him. He held my arms, and we laid back to back in this uncomfortable bed. I closed my eyes and could picture Dylan, remembering the pain and the upset. I inched closer to Christopher, but the memory of Dylan was too strong. I was physically there, but mentally in Texas, thinking of Dylan.

Dylan, please forgive me, please forgive me, I said in my head. The sunlight came quicker than I was ready for, and our favorite nurse, who pretended to not notice us in the bed together, woke us up before shift change so we would not be scolded for violating hospital rules. Christopher's vitals were taken. She was pleased.

"Mr. Sullivan, you had big improvements throughout the night. She really must be your lucky charm," she said and winked at us. "If you keep this up, you may be able to go home soon. Maybe even tomorrow."

"That is great news! Thank you! Thank you!" we both exclaimed. Our smiles of joy were so big it just enhanced the moment. His breakfast came with bland egg whites and broth, with bland white toast. He was well enough to feed himself, and obnoxious enough to complain about the taste the whole way. As he was bitching, Colby and Erika walked in.

"Oh, you are feeling better, nice," Colby said.

"Yeah, I had a good night. They told me I might be able to go home tomorrow," Christopher said with a mouth full of food, chomping.

"Valerie, how did you sleep?" Erika asked as she came over to me.

"I am good, slept well."

"You are lying; she was up the whole night. She didn't sleep at all," Christopher said, taking away the attention off me then bringing it back to him.

"Listen, Colby give, her my keys and make sure she goes to my house and takes a nap. She is exhausted." Colby listened to his orders and handed me his keys.

"I'll take you over," Erika said. "I need to check on your dog anyway."

"Settled. Don't sit here and stare at me. Go and rest."

"Okay," I said. Erika and I walked out and went to his house. It was a townhouse in the district of DC that was surrounded in gardens and splendor. Inside was decorated like a bachelor pad. Dark wood and leather chairs. His antiques stood him apart from being in his later forties from the thirty-something crowd. It had a distinct smell of fine scotch and stale cigars. If you got into the sheets, you could smell his deep sweat smell from the last time he slept here. His fridge was empty. A few Goose Island beers, heavy cream for his coffee, and a few take-out, duck sauce containers.

"Not much to eat here. Go and rest. I'll check on you in a few hours?" Erika said in a kind and motherly voice.

"Great, thank you so much. I am beat." I really just wanted her to leave so I could snoop around the house. She left. I sat in the kitchen to soak in the surroundings and committed them to memory, to feel if I belonged here or not.

"I forgot to call Dylan. Shit!" I dialed him right away.

"Mi amor, how are you? I have been thinking about you. Just dropped the kids off at school. How is the trip going? Are your clients good?"

"Yeah, it's going well. All is good. I will be home soon, I promise."

"When?" He was serious about his request. I was so tired and confused, I couldn't lie or make something up.

"Dylan, my friends that live out here, I reached out to catch up, and my friend is in the hospital. He is okay, coming home tomorrow. I just would feel better to stay and make sure that he can settle back into his house." I was asking for permission, even though I was going to stay no matter what. Not sure if this was foolish on my part to open this box, but my fibbing skills were deterred at the moment. This was either my scapegoat or my best act ever.

"Oh no, that is horrible! You should stay with your friend. Let me know how he is. Do I know of this . . . this . . . What is his name?"

"I told you about them. You know my DC friends? Colby and Christopher? I have known them for years."

"No, I don't remember them. Were they at the wedding and I just didn't meet them?"

"No, nope they didn't come to the wedding. You know, just only so many people to invite, you know?"

"Oh, okay. Keep me posted; you are a good friend. We will miss you. Remember you are out on loan."

"Loan, hmm."

"You know I am kidding. I miss you, Mi amor, hurry home."

"I will." We hung up the phone, and I went into Christopher's bedroom, took off all of my clothes and got under the covers in Christopher's bed. The sheets were cold; the pillow was mushy. I closed my eyes and could feel him sleeping in this spot, night after night. Tossing and turning, dreaming about me in DC, me dreaming about him in Texas. Both under the same night sky, thoughts and feelings together—but the difference was he was here in DC. Dreaming about me, wishing I was here. He was here all alone.

I was in Texas. In a warm bed, next to a warm body. Kids were sleeping in the other room. My life was content. My life was with Dylan. *Why am I here? I should leave and go home.*

Make a decision, make a decision, make a decision, I said in my head; no answer. I kept the water on cold in the shower as I wanted to feel something and numb the feelings I shouldn't have been feeling. I could hear Erika calling for me as she entered back into the apartment.

"Valerie, are you here, Val?"

"In here, Erika!" I ended my shower. I went out in a towel to find her.

"Oh, okay, take your time. Do you want to go back?" She asked as if it was a chance to run.

"Yeah, I will go back. How is he doing?"

"Good, he is going to be able to come home tomorrow!"

"Nice, that is great news. I am so glad."

"Val? I hate to pry, but . . . so what does that mean for you? Are you going to go back to Texas?"

"Erika, I have no idea why I am here, but I came. I can't stay. I have a husband and kids. I can't leave everything to come here, I mean, that is crazy. Would you leave Colby for someone?"

"I guess you are right, but your chemistry is amazing. I know he is so difficult, but when you really get to know him, he is such a kind, loving person. I wish I could make you stay, but you are right. I couldn't leave Colby for someone else, even if I felt what I see between what you guys have. I don't blame you, I just wish for his sake. He just hasn't been the same since he heard you got married. I guess he always thought you would wait for him."

"Erika, I gave him many chances."

"I know. I am sorry, I will leave it be. But Valerie, if I must say one thing, one last thing."

"Yes, of course, Erika, what is it?" She came up to me and gave me a hug. When she pulled away, she said, "Follow your heart."

We went back to the hospital and back to the good news of Christopher's clean bill to head home the next day. We ate burgers and fries, as Christopher still kept to bland food. The night came, Colby and Erika left. Christopher made room for me, and with his laptop, we watched silly movies to pass the time. He touched my knee, and playfully I smacked it off.

"You know I love you," he said during one of the movies. I wouldn't look at him. "I really love you Valerie, whatever you decide to do, I will always love you."

"You know what I have to do; it's not fair for you to ask me to stay," I responded.

"I know."

My phone rang early in the morning. I was able to catch it without waking Christopher. I went into the bathroom and answered Dylan's Facetime. It was Pri.

(Facetime Call)

"Valerie! I miss you!"

"Pri, *mi amor*, I miss you. How are you?"

"Why are you whispering? When are you coming home?"

Dylan grabbed the phone from her, giggling as he told her to go get dressed.

"Oh, Valerie, she kills me. How are you?"

"I am good, so glad to see you, but I wish I could touch you."

"So, come home."

"I will. My friend is going home today so I am going to try and get a flight out tonight."

"I am so happy to hear that, Valerie, I was starting to get worried. I thought I lost you. I miss you."

He was humble. I could see his insecurity through the Facetime call. I was so unfair to him.

"Don't be mad when I wake you up tonight."

"Oh, I welcome it, mi amor."

"Okay, see you tonight, kisses to everyone."

I hung up the phone and looked myself in the mirror, and in the dark room with the only light through the crack in the door. I looked into the mirror and saw Shelia; then I saw Madeline. I took a hard, angry look at both of them as I was so disappointed in myself. I felt like it was their fault, and I was so upset with both of them. I went to grab for pearls that I wasn't wearing, fixed my lips that were bare, and as I re-positioned my ponytail, I spat at the image in the mirror and walked out the door. Christopher was awake and talking to the nurse.

"Mr. Sullivan, the doctor will be in soon and ready to sign the papers to release you. Is Valerie taking you home?" He looked at me. I nodded.

"Yes, she is."

"Great, then it is safe for you to gather your things. He will be in shortly." She left the room, and he looked disappointed by the happy news.

"Why do you have a face on? You are going home, that is great news!"

"So, you have chosen?"

"What?"

"You have chosen. I heard you on the phone."

"Christopher, I can't just drop everything. I just can't. We already talked about this, and . . ."

The doctor walked in as he knocked on the door.

"Mr. Sullivan, so you are ready to go home, I hear?" He reached out his hand for Christopher to shake it and he gave out his. The doctor took some listens to his heart and asked for deep breaths. He read a few charts and called in the nurse to take off the tubes and monitors. He signed some papers and handed me instructions on his medications to pick up, and how often he should take them along with what they were to cure. I nodded but didn't hear a thing. All I thought about was the anxiety I had to drop him off and get myself back on a plane.

"Thank you so much, Doctor, you are wonderful. We are so grateful, thank you," I said, holding the papers in my hands, and reaching out to shake at the same time.

"You are welcome, Mrs. Sullivan. Take good care of him. See you, buddy, on your next visit." He walked out the door. I couldn't correct him, as we needed to leave this fantasy at this hospital in this room in DC.

"Okay, Mr. Sullivan, I will have someone take you down." She closed the door, and I helped him put on his clothes. When I was buttoning up his shirt he drew me into him; I was procrastinating on each button.

"Thank you so much." He kissed me. It was painful as I resisted. He forced it upon me. He never had to try so hard with another woman before.

"You have already chosen," he said as he took a step backward and tucked his shirt into his jeans. There was a knock on the door, and a man with a wheelchair entered the room.

"Mr. Sullivan?"

"Yeah, that's me," Christopher answered as he turned his back and sniffled away his running nose. I hid in the bathroom and looked at the mirror with my spit still dripping its way down to the bottom of the frame where it spread out and settle. I screamed a silent scream; I slammed a silent slam to the base of the sink, and I cried a tearless cry. I couldn't look at myself. I was so upset. This hurt more than walking into Mexico in the heat, bleeding. Having a miscarriage. The death of Shelia. The burning of my attic; altogether, this pain was more than all of that.

"Are you ready, ma'am?" the orderly asked as they were ready to go. I got myself together and walked out of the room.

"Do you have your things?"

"Yes." He held a plastic bag with a bunch of his things on his lap. He looked pathetic and old; he couldn't look at me. We took the elevator in silence, the Uber to his apartment in silence, and the walk into the townhouse in silence. He dropped the keys on the kitchen counter. I helped him take off his jacket, at which he had an angry resistance.

"I don't want your help. I don't want you to be here, so just get your stuff and leave."

He wouldn't turn around and kept his back to me, and held onto the kitchen chair for support as he wasn't strong enough.

"I can't live without you; I just can't. I wish you could understand that."

His emotions showed in his body language as he was convulsing and hunched over on the chair, that he eventually turned around and sat in it, bringing his hands to his face and sobbed.

"I don't understand! You were in my heart before I ever opened my eyes. I met you, and I mourned you, and your cold shoulder. You ruined my life for years and years. I hit rock bottom; I had to leave my job because I couldn't handle it. You have no idea what it means to live without you. Those feelings are so dangerous. You hurt me so much; I can't turn back from that," I screamed at Christopher.

"I'm sorry."

"It is bigger than 'I'm sorry,' Christopher. BIGGER!" I said with my range of tears and sweat.

"I know it is too late. I will wait for you; I will wait even if it is for another lifetime. I will wait for you."

"That is so unfair."

"No, I am unfair. I was afraid of rejection from you, and now I live in my fears. Just go."

I was so angry, I picked up my bag and headed down the stairs. I got to the last step and sat there. I remember the feeling of meeting him and sitting with him at the bar that first night, the chemistry and draw. I remember my first memories of being on the dance-floor, and laying there with him in another lifetime. Another world. I remember.

I turned around and ran up the stairs, ran into his arms on the chair and kissed him as hard as I could until he kissed me back. I ripped his clothes off, he ripped off mine, and as I sat in this man's lap right—after he walked out of the hospital from a minor stroke and head injury—we put that aside, and he carried me into the bedroom, and we closed the door.

We opened our eyes one after the other, with one eye in the pillow, and the other right at each other. I touched behind his ear, and he pulled in to kiss my wrist.

"Christopher, you are always in my heart."

"I know. I will wait for you; I will wait a lifetime for you."

"I know."

* * * * *

I don't want to hear
I don't want to know.
Please don't say forgive me.

—Sorry, Madonna

We were back as a family. After a few weeks, we were back into our routine. My trip to DC was in the past. Dylan and I stood on the porch one evening; he hugged me from behind, watching the sunset. He kissed my neck. He moved his hands down to my stomach, found his place, and embraced me harder.

"Valerie, I noticed that you haven't had your period. Am I off track?"

"Nope."

"Oh, so is it next week?"

"Nope."

"Did you have it and I missed it?"

"Nope."

"No? Are you okay?"

"Yes."

"So, wait, when is it? I am confused; I lost track of time."

"Dylan!"

"Yes."

"Pay attention."

"I am! You said I didn't miss it. So, do I have the dates wrong?"

"Dylan! I'm pregnant!" He turned me around to him.

"Wait, what? Are you serious? I can't take a joke like this."

"I am serious; we are having a baby!"

"Oh, mi amor! Ohh I am so happy!" He picked me up, and we screamed in endless joy.

* * * * *

Eight months and three weeks later, I gave birth to a girl. We named her Marisol. She was our perfect angel. The pieces were coming together; we only needed Olivia to come back to us and make us complete. For now, we were very content and grateful for what God had given us. Frannie came to visit us that evening and brought the kids.

"Pri and John, here is your new sister, Marisol," Dylan said as he escorted them into the room. Their faces were bright as the sun and they clapped.

"Can I hold her?" John asked me.

"Of course, you can!" Dylan propped John in a chair and placed her into his arms. Frannie sat on the edge of the bed and took pictures.

"Pri, do you want to give Valerie our present?"

She nodded her head as Frannie asked her. She grabbed the gift bag and gave it to me, as she also jumped onto the bed. I opened up the card first.

"With much love from Frannie, Sofia, John, Pri, and Bingo. May this bring your newest addition love and happiness for years to come."

"Bingo?" I looked at Pri and tickled her to make her laugh. "Thank you so much."

"Open it! Frannie sewed it, I helped," Pri said. Dylan came over to look. I opened a perfect baby blanket that was stitched together from Dylan's baby clothes, and a piece of Pri and John's baby blanket. It was beautiful and made with love.

"Did you notice it?" Pri asked me.

"Oh yes, I can see the part of your blanket right here! That is so sweet, Pri, Marisol will love it and cherish it forever. What a great sister you are!"

"No, Valerie, no! You didn't see it. Look!" And as she pointed to a square on the far-left center, right off the edge was a blanket piece that was pink satin with a lace border. I didn't get it . . . until I got it. It was from my baby blanket that I had dismissed up in the attic of the house I lived in with Shelia. Tom had saved it and gave it to Pri. I felt it, and the pain was there. The feelings came back. It was hard to go back to that place again. I remember Ashley. I remember Todd. I remember our first interactions of love, hate, and confusion. I didn't want them to steal this moment from me. I didn't want to give these memories to Marisol. Dylan saw that I was getting upset and, yes, the hormones did not help.

"Valerie, look on the other side," Dylan said to me as he came in to console me. I turned it around, and embroidered was a red feather. Dylan gave me a kiss on my forehead as I sobbed without apology. I grabbed Frannie's hand as she too was crying.

"Thank you so much." I tried to get out. I had everything I needed at that moment. Dylan took Marisol from John and wrapped her in the new blanket. Frannie took John and Pri to the park. We sat together and admired the new life in our arms. I had made the right choice. I was in the right place. I was not going to lose this moment; it belonged to us.

*   *   *   *   *

Dylan spent time with John each day as he was getting older, and middle school was going to become a thing of the past for him very soon. We recognized that he had a love for baseball, and Dylan also loved the sport, but never had the chance to play in high school.

"He has serious potential," Dylan would say.

Each night, they concentrated on his swing, his stance at bat, his strategy for running bases, how to catch the perfect out. John joined the school team, and also a travel team. Our lives every day, all year round, revolved around baseball. If it wasn't games, it was clinics, or just simply Dylan coaching John from the back of the farm. Pri became the best batgirl and helped catch fly balls, put the bats back next to the home plate, and held John's helmet. She was his best cheerleader. John grew to be tall and slender. His workouts matched his eating patterns, strong and frequent.

Pri was growing up slower than John. Her learning disabilities didn't disappear as she grew older. It's what was cute to us, but a nuisance to the rest of the world. We got her help, but her time in Mexico, and away from proper care and schooling, hindered her learning growth. She loved the farm, tending to the animals, and giving them loving care. As a preteen, she still held onto Bingo wherever she went. The other kids ridiculed her; she did not see it. I would get upset.

Frannie would say to me as she got on the bus, "Stop your crying, she holds no pain. Look at how she is smiling. She knows no difference but love. Don't give her the ability to see that it hurts." I kept my sunglasses on, so she couldn't see my red face. We waved and smiled as the bus carted her off to school. She would always have a safe haven and place at the farm; that is where she wanted to be.

Marisol grew up so quickly. Before I knew it, she was walking and talking. She had brown hair and hazel eyes. Her lips were not as thin as mine. She was tall and lanky; it must be from her father. She was curious, cautious, and handled being loved much better than I ever did. She knew how to charm hearts and get what she wanted. If anything, she wanted such attention from Dylan. It was hysterical to watch him fall for her tricks every time. When he melted for her, I giggled. He would throw something at me, it was adorable.

*   *   *   *   *

The barbecue came each year, and Marisol was at an age that she was able to enjoy it. I invited Tom and Brenda, as they had never been to one before. It was an experience for all of them to also enjoy. We walked around with Pri as our tour guide. She introduced them to everyone, even if they already knew them. John was now old enough to go off on his own and no longer have to tend to his younger sister, and was starting to be embarrassed by Pri; it was normal for him at that age.

Thankfully, again, as Frannie would say, "She doesn't know any better, just relax and let it be." Tom and Brenda were very unamused by the annual barbecue. When I first came, the nostalgia was all within Dylan in his element. This was not California; this was Texas barbecue, cowboy boots, and ribs. I still never fully adapted as Tom pointed out my Hermes belt within the crowd of people.

"Shut it, Tom," I said, and we laughed.

Each and every year, I looked forward to walking around and watching the kids in excitement. For me, I was just a politician for the farm and Dylan. I looked forward to him being tired and coming out for a break as the sun started to set. I insisted we retreat to the hammocks. This year, it was Marisol's nap time, and all the more excuse for us all to cuddle up together and enjoy the sunset.

"You smell like pig."

"Thanks, that feels good." We laughed, but out of exhaustion, we closed our eyes and enjoyed a few moments within our own heads, and in each other's company. Tom came over with Pri, and she wanted to rock the hammock "gently."

"When was the last time you guys took some time away together?" Tom asked as he leaned into the hammock himself.

"Never," we said in unison.

"You guys need to get away. It will ruin you." We didn't answer, because it was true. It was ruining us. Dylan had the farm and baseball, daily with John; I kept busy with the girls, my own business, the house and building the farm's business. We just brought on a new store in town to make it more accessible for the town to get to us, along with an online store. We had a baby, expanded, and before we knew it, Marisol was in Pre-K and we forgot about ourselves.

"So, what do you suggest we do, Tom?" Dylan asked as we swung in the hammock, taking our nap but still talking.

"Disney. Hear me out."

"Dylan and I, Marisol in the hammock in our lap. Pri swinging us. Tom hanging over us. Brenda watching from the side. Dylan and I never opening our eyes. Both said a unanimous

"No."

"Haha! I knew you would say that! Hear me OUT! Don't you kids listen?"

Again, a unanimous, "No." Brenda chimed in.

"It's not as bad as it sounds, just listen to him."

"Brenda, Tom, you are awesome. I just . . . we are just overwhelmed now, and have you met Valerie? She is (no offense honey) no Disney queen, if you know what I am talking about." It was well known that I was not a Disney fan, nor could I relate to the Disney characters. I was never a child. I could never give in to fantasy or the fun of a cartoon. I was envious of Marisol and Pri as they both could embrace these things.

John came by at this moment and also replied, "I am not going to Disney."

"Okay, okay, I get it, you are not a Disney family. Valerie, I apologize I never took you. Wait! No, I did take you and your friends one year to Disney Land!"

"And . . . " I replied without moving, opening my eyes, or giving a movement. Dylan held me tighter.

"Right, you hated it, and left me with your friends," Tom said in disappointment, and Dylan pulled me closer as he held in laughter. Then Brenda came back.

"HOLD ON, just listen; we put a lot of thought into this, just listen!" At this time, Frannie and Sofia came over to the hammock. Dylan and I at this point in our lives learned to half sleep, half stay awake and half listen. We could officially work for the CIA.

"Pri, John, can you go and get us some lemonade?" Brenda looked to Frannie for approval. She pointed to where they could go to make it happen. And they ran with pleasure.

"Valerie, you are my only daughter, my only flesh. I am so excited and celebrate life with yourself, Dylan, John, Pri, Marisol, Frannie, and Sofia. Frannie, Sofia, Brenda, and I are worried about you and Dylan. We want you to be happy. We have all made mistakes, some serious mistakes; we don't want to see you two make them as well. Let's all go as a family. We will take care of the kids. You guys have your own room and spend quality time together, join us with the kids as you feel you want to. What do you think?"

Dylan squeezed my arm as he wanted me to answer, which meant he wanted me to politely bow out and say, "Thanks, but no thanks," but Tom made sense. We were losing each other; we were falling into a slump and dying. We needed this.

"I think it is awesome, when do we leave?"

Dylan gave me a kick; I punched him back, again, both of us too tired to open our eyes.

"We don't even have enough energy to open our eyes, how can you disagree?" Dylan went limp.

"Book it, Tom!" I said and dozed off in the hammock and the fall of the Texas sun. Dylan lifted his head to see a reaction from the crowd, but most knew enough to walk away and book it—he was outnumbered.

"Dylan, are we going to Disney? Bingo wants to know," Pri said as she didn't get her cue to leave with the crowd, and had no sense of personal space, so she waited until one of us reacted.

"Pri, do you want to go to Disney?"

"Yes," she replied. He did not move his head from within my neck, nor open his eyes.

"Pri, how badly, do you want to go?" Dylan asked again.

"So bad!" she said with excitement.

"Like how bad?" He kept egging.

"Dylan, bad, so bad!"

"Yeah? Who is your favorite Disney character?"

"Elsa from Frozen!" Then she started to sing and twirl around. "Let it go, Let it GOOOOOO!"

"Thanks, Dylan, this is great. Thanks, Tom, love you, mean it, call me," I shouted but still did not open my eyes.

"All right, I got the hint, so how about we go at the beginning of December?" Tom asked. He was not giving up.

"Perfect!" I said and lifted my arm with a thumbs up. Tom walked away taking Pri with him. Dylan and I had a few moments of silence together. Dylan looked up to see if anyone was still around.

"Disney? You hate Disney."

"Yup."

"So why did you agree to this?" We moved in closer. I grabbed his hand and held it to the sky as I brought out my phone for a selfie, which we still took as often as possible, posting to Instagram and hoping that Olivia was watching.

"Because we need it. When was the last time we were alone together?"

"How about right now? We are alone now?"

"Dylan! Seriously? Open your eyes and look at us!" He opened his eyes and forgot that Marisol was sleeping between us. It was so natural he didn't even notice.

"Good point."

"Yes, I am not a fan of Disney, but we have all these people to take the kids. Does Tom do anything low budget? We will have our own time and space; we can relax as the kids are with us, but not. It's a win, win. I think we need this. We don't even talk anymore, Dylan. We are falling apart."

"We are falling apart? You think so?"

"Dylan, when was the last conversation we had that wasn't kid-related? When was the last time you joined me in the shower? Had dinner alone?"

"Si, Si, well, that is true. Hmm, okay, I am in."

*   *   *   *   *

We sat at breakfast; I wanted to make it super special.

"Morning, Marisol. Morning, Pri. Morning, John . . . pancakes with chocolate chips or blueberries?"

"Strawberries!" Pri screamed. Everyone was a yes thereafter.

"Pri, I don't think I have strawberries . . . DYLAN! Do we still have strawberries?"

Silence. Oddly, he was still asleep.

"Pri, do you know if we still do? Can you go pick them?"

"I know where they are; I'll go," John said and left the breakfast table.

"DYLAN?" I screamed again; it was way past his time to be awake. He was still fast asleep.

"DYLLLLLL!" I went upstairs, while Pri and John searched for fresh strawberries. Marisol sat at the island, searching for her orange juice. Dylan was still in bed, out cold and snoring with his face in the pillow. He never slept like this. I went over to him and hugged him gently.

"Dyl?" I continued to rub his back as he didn't immediately respond.

"Dyl." I kept whispering in his ear. After a few tries, he jolted and looked at me with glazed eyes.

"Hi," he responded, then went back into the pillow.

"D, do you need coffee? What happened to you? I didn't even know that you came to bed last night? Were you in the barn drinking? Okay, I don't care. Are we going to tell the kids today? Remember? I kind of need you? Hello?"

"Right . . . Disney, the trip we don't want, the trip to be alone together because you avoid me, don't want to be with me, got it."

"Dylan . . . stop it. We need time alone together. The kids need this. We, as a family, need this. Tom loves to do elaborate gifts; it is just his thing. Didn't we agree on this? What is wrong? Is it the hangover?"

"NOOOO," he screamed into the pillow.

"Then what is it?"

"Ugggggghhhhh." I got up from the pillow, walked down the stairs, slamming my heels so hard they were bruised as I reached the kitchen.

I slammed my heels around the kitchen hoping it would wake Dylan up a bit. Pri and John came back with fresh strawberries which we cleaned and cut up to add to the fresh batter of pancakes. The griddle was hot and made a sizzling noise that matched the bacon also on the stove. I made coffee for Dylan, hoping that the smell would bring him down. It did. The messy hair, wrinkled tee shirt, flannel pajama bottoms came down the stairs. He kissed foreheads around the kitchen island, except for mine. I placed the fresh pancakes, bacon, toast, and sausage on the table with fresh orange juice, and they started to eat. Dylan helped Marisol put a plate together.

"So, who wants to go to Disney World?" Dylan exclaimed to the island.

"Yeah! I do, I do, I do!" Pri stood up and jumped around, then Marisol followed.

"I do! I do!" John was not amused, or just didn't hear it correctly; I went over to him to ask again.

"John, you want to go to Disney World?" I asked him as the screams and dancing going on around the kitchen. He took a few moments to think about it and looked at his uniform.

"Am I going to miss baseball?" he asked out of concern.

"Don't worry, buddy; we are going to leave after your game. We will be back just in time for your games next weekend. So, what do you think?" Dylan said to him as he shoved pancakes down his throat.

"Yeees!" John gave his signature arm pull in, and got up to join the dancing around the kitchen.

"Great," Dylan said and got up to go back upstairs. Something was not right with him; I followed him back up the stairs to find out what was wrong. He was already back on his stomach with his face planted into the pillow, not the way he slept at all. I went over to him and rubbed his back, but he flicked me away.

"Go away," he said into the pillow.

"No, what is wrong? Why are you so angry? What happened? Is it about Disney? Why did you say that I avoid you and don't like you? That is absurd, Dylan really. Where is this coming from? Can you talk to me please?"

"Who is he?" he asked still talking through the pillow.

"Who is the man you dream about? Who is this Christopher?"

"Christopher?"

"So now you are silent, nice move, Valerie."

Dylan came out from behind the pillow and looked me in the face.

"SO, WHO IS HE?" he demanded of me.

"Christopher, the only person I can think of, is my friend in DC. I told you about him. Why are you asking about him now? I haven't seen or spoken to him in years."

"Valerie, who is he to you? Because I can't take another night of you talking about him. So, start talking, Valerie."

"Dylan, I didn't know that I was talking in my sleep at all. How long have I been doing that?"

"You always talked in your sleep. Most of the time, it didn't make sense. But for the past ten years, he comes in and out of your sleep. The other night, you must have had some sexual fantasy about him, because you screamed for him and told him how much you liked it. Yeah, and by the way, Valerie, when was the last time we were together like that? Why haven't we been together in months? Why do I have to hear about him?" He was so angry. I was so to blame.

I didn't know how much Christopher was in my mind, even after I got rid of him in my every day routine, but there is always something that drew me back. I could flash through my Christopher history, the life before, the picture in my head, the first encounter, the meet-up, taking care of him in the hospital. The desire to want to wake up next to him every day of our lives. It never really went away. I didn't think it ever would. I told a lie; I told another lie. Now I was about to enter into another one. I sat down on the bed and leaned into Dylan as he was so flushed with anger.

"I really didn't know that I was screaming for him in my sleep last night, or past nights. I honestly didn't. I don't remember dreaming about him (lie), I don't even think about him (lie). I met him before I met you (true). I always felt like I knew him (true). We had a connection; then he disappeared from my life. I just took it that he didn't feel the same (true). Then I met you. I fell in love with you (true). Yes, I did question what could be with him, but it's too late (lie). I am in love with you, Dylan. After all that we have been through, if you think that is not true, not real, I would be so upset. I never want to lose you (true). Dylan, it was just a dream, just a dream (true/false)." I was able to lay across him without him running for the hills. The red in his face went down. He was able to hold my arms without an angry grip.

"It may be just a dream, but it hurts. Why didn't you tell me about him before?"

"Why didn't you tell me about Lydia? I did tell you about him, but why did you need to know more? I had all my feelings wrong; I thought I was crazy. It is old; I don't know why he is in my head. I don't even know that he is there."

"I didn't tell you about Lydia because of the same thing. All right, Valerie, we are even."

"Even? What does that mean?"

"We both didn't tell each other about our past loves; I guess that is even."

"Dylan, there are always going to be things from our past that will come up. It will just be that way. I think I have been pretty forgiving. Remember Mexico?"

"Si, si. I am sorry. I am still upset. Just give me some time. I need to sleep off this hangover." He turned back around, putting his face back into the pillow. I laid on his back.

"Are you still coming to Disney?"

"I am still going to Disney. Please just let me sleep for a bit." I left him alone.

John played in a doubleheader that day. We went as a family to watch. Dylan took John early to talk with the coaches. I followed up with the girls once the game began. Dylan always wanted to play baseball. Maybe he even dreamed of playing professional baseball. He lived through John on some of the childhood he missed. Dylan sat up by their lineup and talked to the coaches the whole time. Sometimes, he needed to be reminded that he was not the coach; at this point, they were all in a respectable understanding.

John went between playing first base and pitching, but after this year, he decided first base would be the favored position. I somehow believed Dylan convinced him of this. Dylan seemed louder than usual at the games today. He was loud and jumping around, instead of focused and strongly determined on John. He was calling out to the empire, screaming at the other team—it was very disruptive. The coach came to talk to him and to quiet him down, but no matter what, he didn't look up at us.

Nine innings became eighteen innings; four base hits for John. Six overall homeruns for game One. A loss in game two which made a very sad teenager and an angry stepdad. When the game was over, John held his head down in disappointment as he was afraid to face Dylan.

They smacked fake high-fives with the other team. John worked his way to me for a hug, instead of an unsympathetic disappointment from Dylan. Today, Dylan was not predictable, but John always wanted his approval.

"John, you did awesome. Great game, love," I said to him as he came in for a hug, I believe to hide away from Dylan's disapproval.

"We lost," John said in the hug.

"There will always be a loss, John. What matters is how you played. You played awesome!" I said in return.

"John! You are the best!" Pri said right after me, and rushed in for an unwanted hug.

"Whatever . . . " he said as he still held his head down and walked to the car. I felt his upset. His anger. His disappointment, disapproval. Then he walked himself to the car, and locked himself in with his seatbelt and melting face. I had to do my part as a step-mother to say hello and thank you to the coaches, find out what he needed to work on to get into the best college, or overstep college and straight to major leagues, farm-team, etc. Dylan walked the opposite way, running his nervous energy fingers through his hair as he took off his baseball cap, got into his car, and drove away. The dust from the dirt lingered in the air, and as we all had a door open to get in our car, we watched his dramatic exit. And all of us, without saying it, wondered where he was headed.

"John, you played great today!" I reassured him.

"But we lost."

"You lost one game. Relax, you can't win every game."

"I suck."

"No, you don't at all! I talk to your coaches often. We all believe you have a serious future in baseball, if you want it. Is that something you want?"

"I don't know. Maybe?"

"No pressure at all. We need to start thinking about college soon, so think about what you want. I believe in you, John!" I looked at him as he sulked in the front seat. He tried to smile but was still disappointed. "What is wrong, John. Is it really just the game?"

"I don't know; I just feel like Dylan is mad at me."

"What? That is crazy. Why would you think that? NO, he is not mad at you, please take that out of your mind. He always wants what is best for you."

"Why did he just leave? He doesn't even want to talk to me. He is so mad."

"No! No, no. It is not you at all, I promise. Dylan is fine; if he is mad at anyone, he is mad at me. Please don't think it has anything to do with you; it doesn't."

"You never fight. Why is he mad?" Pri said as she kept her head out the window and felt the breeze as we moved.

"Yeah, you never fight," Marisol also stated.

"Yes, we do," I said, but they were right. We never really fought. Anytime we did, we always made up by making each other laugh, or we found a compromise. We had always been blessed with that.

"It's true, you never really fight, even when you have a reason to," John said.

"When I have a reason to? I don't like to fight. Wasted energy. When would I have a reason to?"

"Because of our mom, for starters. I know you know about Olivia."

'What about Olivia? Is there something I don't know?"

"I thought you did."

"John, what is it?"

"I will tell you later."

We pulled into the farm. Dylan's car wasn't there. Everyone jumped out of the car and into the house. John waited for me as I hesitated to understand what was going on. We walked around the house for John to drop off his equipment in the garage.

"So, John, do you want to tell me something?"

"Well, I feel bad. I really thought that you knew."

"Knew what? John, I am not sure what it is. Is Olivia in danger that I am not aware of? Have you spoken to her?"

"No, I haven't. I haven't spoken to any of them. I don't want to. It's just that . . . uhmmm . . ."

"John, I am nervous. I don't want to pressure you, but what is going on?"

We sat down on the edge of the walkway to the garage, and John was rubbing his hands on his thighs as he was so nervous to tell me about Olivia.

"John, I won't be mad, I am just worried at this point. I want to be able to help with this, but I can't if I don't know what you are talking about."

"You can't help. I don't know that she is in danger. It's just that, that . . . Miguel is not Olivia's Father. Dylan is. I really thought that you knew, and now . . . now I don't want you to be mad at him because I told you. I shouldn't have said anything, I am sorry."

He got up and ran away into the house and into his room as I could hear the door slam from outside. I looked around, and still no Dylan.

"Who wants Chinese food?" I screamed as I entered the house. Doors upstairs opened, the girls came running down. John was reluctant to follow.

"Come on, John. We are going out for Chinese food."

He came to the top of the stairs and asked, "Can we do Hibachi instead?" I looked around; everyone nodded okay.

"Sure!"

"Awesome, I just need to get ready." He ran into his room with excitement; I didn't know that food was the current way to his heart.

The girls went to watch TV to pass the time. I decided to skip out to the back of the farm, to the rose patch that Dylan planted for me in memory of Peanut. The weather was starting to change. The sky became a grey. Clouds were rushing through the sky; I felt the earth trying to tell me something. I decided to go to the rose path and do something that was long overdue. I went to the rose patch, and I prayed.

"Lord, I know I haven't talked to you in a long time. I need to fix that. I need you, God. I need to feel you with me. I want to ask for forgiveness for my affair with Christopher, for loving him. For keeping him a secret. I pray for Dylan who is holding a secret; is it true about Olivia? I know he misses her dearly. I miss her too. God, I am not perfect. We are not perfect. Help guide me, help us get through this. I just want to do what is right and just. I don't want to live in lies. Thank you, Lord, thank you. Amen."

I sat and touched the flowers and thought of a what life would be like with Christopher. I wouldn't have to live on a farm. We would live in DC in a fancy townhouse. I would be able to wear my fancy clothes and jewelry, and we would have fancy places to go to. Christopher would grab me from behind and twirl me around and around. I could smell him. I could feel him hugging me, and as I prayed for him to go away from my mind, he came in stronger and stronger. I made a commitment to Dylan, and as I made a commitment and a promise, I would stick to it. As I thought more about my life now, I loved being here. I loved Dylan, even if I was so angry with him. I wouldn't change this for anything. Maybe my prayers were answered before being asked.

"Another life," I said to myself as tears came to surface. "Another life, my Christopher."

I tried to let him go. Again, the pain was stronger and deeper as I loved him so much. I fell to the ground. I went back into the house. I sat in between the girls on the couch; John came running down, dressed up and even wearing Dylan's cologne.

213

"Why, John, you are looking good. I didn't know you liked Hibachi so much."

He blushed.

"He likes the girl that is the hostess, oohhhhh, Clarissa, ohhhhh." Pri mocked him.

"Shut up, no I don't."

I smiled at him, and he blushed again.

"Hibachi it is."

Going for Hibachi, Dylan, will you meet us?

No response.

We entered the restaurant, and John led the way as he flirted in his nervous, young adult way with Clarissa. It was adorable and put him in a good mood, which I needed right now. We sat around the hibachi station, and John positioned himself where he could see Clarissa from his angle. We watched the master chef do his tricks and serve us; the girls always loved to come here. I continued to check my phone, and there was still no response from Dylan. When we left, I encouraged John to ask Clarissa out on a date as the girls and I went to the car. I searched the street to see if we could find Dylan's car. Where could he be? John came out with a smile.

"She said yes!"

We all cheered as we got into the car. The sky became darker from before the grey clouds became black, as the night time was coming in and a storm was brewing.

"See, John; today is a good day."

"It is, thank you." He smiled. We put our conversation about Olivia in the back of our minds.

The night sky was fierce. I continued to check my phone to see if Dylan responded, and looked out the window for him. He loved to drive away to clear his head from time to time, but he never stayed out this long. The sound of thunder approaching was heard in the distance. Before long, a drop to the window became thousands. I stood in the bay window in the living room and watched for Dylan.

"Can we watch the storm on the porch?" John asked in excitement. As scary as a storm was, it was an electrical excitement.

"Only until the lightning comes closer." We sat on the covered porch and watched the rain pouring out of the sky. The thunder rolled in closer. I taught them the Poltergeist scene.

"One one-thousand, two one-thousand, three one-thousand." And then the thunder came. Marisol loved this game.

"One, One-thousand, two—"

And the crash of thunder. A flash from afar felt blinding. I scattered the kids to run inside. The storm was low. After fifteen minutes we lost power. I continued to run to the window and check for Dylan as I packed for our trip in the morning. No Dylan.

> Dylan, I am worried, please let me know that you are okay.

And no response.

I sent the kids to bed. The storm was moving west and the grumbling of the sky, the blinding lightning, followed like unwanted guests in the night. It still rained, and eventually, it faded off and followed behind the noise.

I could feel Cal and Madeline running into their house from the rainstorm, laughing and hugging. They stripped their clothes and made love on the kitchen table. They were young, before Shelia, and maybe the night Shelia entered into their lives; but at that moment, they were happy and in love. No one else mattered.

"It is going to be okay," a voice said.

"Thank you, Jesus," I replied.

Dylan pulled up to the house and came up the stairs. He came behind me, smelling of Heineken and smoke. He put his head on my shoulder, his hands around my waist, and kissed my neck.

"Can you just hold me? I know I don't deserve it, but I just want you to hold me."

I turned into him, stripped him of his smelly clothes, and as he laid on his side, I found my spot in the small of his back between his shoulder blades, and wrapped my hand on his chest as he held it and drifted off into sleep. I stayed awake, afraid that if I closed my eyes, I would dream of Christopher.

*   *   *   *   *

We arrived in Orlando and everyone was excited as we found Tom and Brenda at the hotel. Although John and Pri were teenagers, they were still excited to be here. They had never been. Marisol was in awe. Pri would be her partner in crime for this adventure. We set out to hit the popular rides, and to get to as many as possible we could that day.

"I think the purpose of this trip was for the two of you to spend some time alone," Tom said with a concerned, parental look on his face.

"I was a bit petrified. We had so many elephants in our relationship we needed to address.

"No, you are right. We are here to spend some time together. I have made dinner reservations for us. We should go back and get dressed," Dylan said as he and Tom seemed to have pre-planned this together.

"What do we need to dress for? I don't think I brought a dress." I pictured myself before I moved with Dylan to Texas, and how I was dressed up every night for dinner. I gave so much away to charities. I had dresses I could not part with in my apartment in New York. I brought jeans, shorts, bathing suits—but nothing fancy. I was now depressed about how my life had changed. Upset that I now missed my previous life. I missed . . .

"I bought a dress for you," Dylan whispered in my ear, as he brushed my hair back onto my neck.

"You did? Okay." I didn't understand how he had a dress for me. Both Dylan and Tom smiled at each other as they had something pre-planned. I was nervous about what it was about.

"Get lost, you two; and Valerie, please enjoy yourself," Tom said. I nodded back. With Dylan's arm around my neck and holding my hand, we drifted off back to the hotel.

"Close your eyes," Dylan said as he held his hand over them, in case I didn't listen to his command. We entered the room, and Dylan guided the way to our bedroom in our suite. When his hand released, on the bed lay a beautiful, red dress with spaghetti straps, and a flowing a line to the knee. It was beautiful.

"I know it is cheesy, but I saw it and thought of you. I know you miss dressing up, and we don't go to fancy restaurants anymore. We don't do a lot together, anymore. I miss you; I miss us." He kept his arms wrapped around my neck as we both admired his beautiful sentiment.

"This is lovely, thank you. So where are you taking me so fancy to wear such an eloquent dress?"

"Aha, I hope I can impress you. You will see. Now let's open some champagne." The bubbly was popped, we clinked glasses on the deck, and watched the sunset. Dylan was wrapped around me and was affectionate. I was shut off. Something wasn't right; I didn't want to be here with him. I felt alone and uncomfortable with the man I married and was raising three kids with. I didn't know who he was anymore. I didn't know who I was anymore. I was falling out of love with Dylan. I didn't know how to stop it. I was hoping that he wouldn't notice, so I sipped champagne until the bottle was done, and then I went back in for more. I kissed him back which led from our deck to the bedroom. I smiled back, reciprocated the pleasure, and every time I closed my eyes, I held in tears and wished for it to be over as quickly as possible.

He picked Il Mulino's, a favorite restaurant we frequented when we lived in New York. I took Dylan there a few times when we were dating; he did put some thought into this evening. I wore the dress he picked out for me; I looked good on his arm. I felt like a prisoner with the man I told friends and family that I loved, for better or for worse, forever. I was trapped.

We drank more champagne that turned into wine, that turned into more after-dinner drinks. Our conversation was mostly Dylan talking and me with my fake smile. I can't remember the last time we sat face to face; I almost forgot what he looked like. His eyes had become saggy, his wrinkles grew around them. His hair was thinning and became gray. His hands were worn and torn from working on the farm; it was hard to believe this man used to wear a nice shirt and tie, and go to an office every day. Who had he become? Dylan wore flannels and work boots to work. I sat in front of a screen and talked to people through a computer. I wore tee shirts and jeans. After time, the fancy Gucci outfits, Hermes belts, gold jewelry, all sat in drawers that were never opened.

"I miss wearing high heels every day. I miss a good martini. I miss going to an office every day and wearing sparkling earrings. I miss New York. I miss who we used to be before we got here. Are you mad at that?" He sat back in his chair and looked at me as he held onto his after-dinner scotch.

"No, I am not. This is a different life. We went through a lot together. I am glad that you are with me in Texas, I wouldn't want it any other way."

"I am getting bored."

"Am I boring you?"

"Yes."

"Oh, Valerie, we are busy people and need to find our way back to each other. We jumped into a lot, had a great loss, and we need to bring back some of the romance. I am partly to blame." We left the restaurant and walked back to our hotel. On our way, the sprinklers went off on a patch of grass that was a garden-gated off. I took off my shoes and ran through it.

"Valerie! What are you doing?" Dylan was screaming from the sidelines. I twirled around and wanted to wash away my memories of our past. The bad times, the good times, the times we never had. I wanted to drown in these sprinklers and was glad that it wasn't a pool, because if it was, I was sitting on the bottom waiting for my world to fade to black.

I wanted a new life. I didn't know what that meant. I didn't know where it was; I didn't know who I wanted it with. I didn't want to be here anymore. I stood in the sprinkler and soaked in the power of its spray, and closed my eyes. Dylan took off his shoes and jacket and came to save me.

"Valerie, you are drunk. Let's go back." I looked him in the eyes as he was holding me, and trying to get me out of the sprinklers.

"I don't know you anymore, Dylan; I don't know if I ever really knew you." Dylan, now also drenched in the sprinklers, brought me closer to him and held his forehead to mine, closed his eyes and he took in a deep breath.

"Will you ever love me the way you loved Lydia?"

He looked at me and kissed me, as the sprinklers tried to get in our way.

"I love you more than I ever loved Lydia. It was always you, even when I didn't know you. It was always you. But when you scream someone else's name when I am lying next to you, it hurts Valerie, it really hurts.

"Who is this guy that is in your heart? Who is this Christopher that is in your head? Who is this Christopher that has my beautiful wife's attention? I want to be in your heart, the way you are in mine. Tell me, Valerie, how do I get into your heart?" He said this to me as we stood together in this garden, soaking wet, vulnerable. All the time we had been together, it was saying out loud what I had feared for so long—the lie of Christopher and what sits within me.

"I always believed that I knew him in a previous life. Then I met him. It was a dream. Then he disappeared from me. Then he needed me, and it was so special. Then there was you. He didn't want me. And now he is nothing, nothing to me. I just don't know. Sometimes, I hate you because I hate him. Because I hate myself. I don't know why he was in my life. Why he isn't in my life. Why I am with you."

"Valerie, why didn't you ever tell me any of this?"

"Why didn't you tell me about Lydia?"

"I, I, I guess for the same reasons."

"And Olivia? I know that Olivia is your daughter. Why didn't you ever tell me?"

"I don't know either."

We went back to the hotel room and went to bed. My mascara was down my face; my dress was ruined. The game field was even. I didn't know where we could go from here.

"I do love you, Dylan, I do. You do have my heart, even when you don't think so."

"Mi amor, come to me." He signaled to me. I crawled into his chest. I fell asleep.

*   *   *   *   *

We spent the next few days enjoying Disney together, and hooked up with the kids, Tom and Brenda from time to time. Dylan and I took time to get to know each other again, laugh again, and remember why we came together. He needed me; I needed him. We could see this now. This trip was a blessing to our marriage and to our home. We came off of Thunder Mountain laughing, and headed to find cotton candy.

"Valerie, I have your phone, I think I heard a text. Let me get it for you."

"I am not expecting to hear from anyone; I have to go to the restroom. Read it and let me know if it is important." I went to the restroom and came out to Dylan's face stark white, and looking unsure of what he wanted to say.

"Oh no, did Disney run out of cotton candy?" I said as he looked away and then back at me. His nervous hand ran through his hair, and he had the serious anxiety of holding his bottom lip together. He took his hand away from his mouth and onto my shoulder.

"Valerie, let's sit down." He took me over to the bench not far away.

"What is wrong?" I said,

"Okay, Valerie. Hmmm, I don't know how to say this. I checked your phone. I think you should know, hmmm, well, it's from Chase."

"Chase? My brother in law, Chase?"

"Yes, that Chase. Valerie, I don't know how to tell you this."

"Dylan, what is it? Do they need money? What could it be, seriously? I don't have a relationship with either one of them anymore; I don't care what it is, so just tell me," I said, not knowing what to expect or to feel.

"Ashley died," Dylan said abruptly as he cut off my rant. A moment of dead silence—the person who I fought with the most, the person that was my mother's favorite, who destroyed my childhood, was gone. I hadn't spoken to her in years; I don't think we had much of a conversation since Shelia died. Since our last time together in the house, we grew up together alone. He handed me my phone to see the message.

> Valerie, I want to let you know that Ashley died last night on the couch after she had a seizure in her sleep. She went peacefully; the funeral is Friday in Colorado. Hope that you can make it. She would want you to be here.

I stepped away from Dylan into the crowd, where I stood in amazement for the moment. I didn't have a mother; Tom was with my children across the park; I no longer had a sister that I didn't want. I felt alone all over again. I saw faces in the crowd and thought it was Shelia, or Madeline, or Cal. I could almost reach out to them, but resisted. Dylan came up behind me.

"I am so sorry, Valerie. Let's make arrangements to go. You should be there."

"Okay," I responded, and in shock, I followed him back to our room.

We made arrangements, gathered Tom and the kids to tell them the news. On Friday morning, we all left Disney and headed to Colorado. I closed my eyes on the plane and thought about Chase.

"I am on my way," I said to him in my head.

"I know," he replied. I kept my eyes closed and leaned on Dylan's shoulder. Madeline was in my mind, cooking dinner and watching out the window for Cal to come home. No one lived across the street anymore, no other man was on her mind but Cal. The table was set.

Soon enough, Cal came up the driveway. She was smiling, waiting for her daily kiss that she dreamed of all day long. She fixed her apron and blouse, checked her lipstick in the reflection of the appliances, and as he waltzed in the door, he kissed her. She was whole again.

"Girls, dinner!" she screamed upstairs, and down came Shelia and behind her, Ashley. They sat at the table, held hands for prayer, and shared dinner together.

*　　*　　*　　*　　*

We arrived at Chase and Ashley's home where the funeral was being held, in their field in the back of their house. It was a lovely canopy that was built for their wedding. Her coffin was at its center. The flowers were all colors of a pale rainbow. Chairs faced the front, and people went up to say kind words about Ashley. She had friends who loved her. Chase loved her. Neighbors that came out to pay respects. Todd and his family arrived after the ceremony had started, and we sat across the lawn from them.

"Are you going to get up and say something?" Dylan whispered into my ear.

"No," I replied back. And he held my hand.

"When I lost my brother, we weren't on the best of terms. I spoke at his funeral, even though it was short and sweet. I am glad that I did it. It helped me let go. I'm not telling you what to do, Valerie, but I am telling you how I felt," Dylan again whispered in my ear.

I sat on the aisle of the left side, facing the coffin. When her neighbor finished talking, I let go of Dylan's hand and went up to face the crowd. I looked at Chase, then to Tom, and fixated on Dylan who smiled back at me. He was my rock. I could see that now. He made me a better person; he gave me the family I wanted. He gave me love when I needed it. I could see that now.

"I didn't get along with my sister. I am sure most of you don't know that I exist. I remember playing soccer, one of the most important games of my fourth-grade career. No one in my family came. It hurt. It hurt a lot. I won that game. When it was over, Ashley was there waiting for me. Maybe she saw the game, maybe she didn't, but I didn't know until this moment that she was there because she needed me.

"We both hurt in different ways, and we needed each other to heal the pain. Instead, we fought. The fights were vicious and ugly, and then we never had a relationship after I left to live with my father in California. I was mad at her for being a nasty bitch, for being my mother's pet, for destroying our childhood home that almost killed all of us. I was mad that she stole my best friend who became her husband. I was mad at her for many things. But today, I am going to say goodbye to the ugly memories, and the ugly times and the feelings I had about our past relationship.

"Today, I am going to start a new relationship with Ashley, because today is the day she needs me. She needs forgiveness to move on into her new world; her new life, to watch over us with love and kindness.

"Ashley, I hope that you can find heaven and bring joy into your heart to share with us. As I am up here, I also want to thank my husband for being a rock to me when I needed one, being here with me. I do love you with all my heart." I went back into my seat shaking a bit, as I was not prepared for that. Tom held out his hand to me. That felt warm and calming. I sat next to Dylan who, as he put his arm around me, whispered into my ear, "I needed that. Thank you, Valerie. I love you too."

The ceremony was over. People lingered until late evening, drinking, eating. At some point music came on, and dancing occurred. People shared stories of Ashley that made me not recognize her. Chase and Ashley still lived a hippy lifestyle. The grownup version was now clean, clothes made of hemp, eating healthily, and bathing at least three times a week.

The drugs became a childhood phase. They did enjoy some pot brownies from time to time. They ran a local grocery store that was organic, and grew lots of vegetables in their yard. Chase and Dylan bonded over farming techniques. She had friends that went to yoga with her, cooked at each other's homes and hiked on the weekends. They had a relationship with her. I never knew her. The night got old, and people went back on with their lives. The kids and Dylan went upstairs to bed. I stayed with Chase to help clean up. After the dishes and glasses were cleaned, we ended up on the kitchen floor and shared a bottle of wine.

"I am sorry, Chase," I said, handing him the bottle to take the next sip.

"She was a whirlwind, Valerie; she was a whirlwind," he said and sipped from the bottle before passing it back to me.

"What does that mean?" I asked, after so much wine. I didn't care anymore. Did I really want to know what that meant?

"She was a lot. She was lost. She was angry. Before I knew it, I was under her spell. I asked myself all the time how I got involved with her when I was so deeply strong with someone else. And when I say someone else, I mean you. I picked the wrong sister, because I wasn't strong enough to tell you that I wasn't strong enough to be with you. I hate myself for pushing you away." Chase looked away in shame.

"I always wondered what happened when I left and how she got to you. Now I no longer want to know."

"Valerie, I thought about you all the time. I wanted to be with you, I missed you. Then the drugs came in, she seduced me and brainwashed me that you were a horrible person. Through the years it went away. She became a wonderful, sweet-as-pie wife. Then the mean streaks came out. It was horrible. The drinking never stopped, the throwing of things—but then it went away. I became afraid of her. Afraid she would hurt herself. Maybe all her anger got the best of her. Maybe it ate her inside.

"I made the wrong choice, Valerie, and I know I must live with that. I am going to miss her. I am not going to miss her. Does that make any sense?"

"It does, it does. She needed you, that is why you chose her. Chase, you needed to be with her to be needed. I was strong. I didn't want to be, but I was. There was someone else for me. I see that now. Ashley needed you. Lydia needed Miguel. Cal needed Madeline. Shelia needed Tom. Tom needed Brenda. Dylan needs me. It is all the circle of life," I said and drank more wine to take away the pain.

"Am I supposed to know who all of these people are? Because I don't, I really don't know anything about your family." We laughed.

"Yeah, neither do I. Chase, you can't turn back. Just move forward, fall in love again, and start over and put this behind you. You can still start over."

"I lost you, Valerie," Chase said as he was disappointed in himself.

"You didn't lose me; I am still in your life. I can still hear you even when I am not around. Go find your next love; she is out there." Chase was still handsome with his salt and pepper hair, his pot belly and, now, adult-hippie-turned-retro style. We walked up the stairs together. He walked into his bedroom to sleep in the bed he shared with his wife, alone. I went into bed with Dylan and the kids on the floor around us.

*　　*　　*　　*　　*

We woke up and packed our things to head back to Texas. We said our goodbyes, and I caught a feather waving in the wind as we exited; it was, for sure, Ashley.

"Chase, Chase!" I called to him as he went far back into the house.

"This is from Ashley; it's from our growing up. I want you to have it and keep it with you. Be well." I gave him a kiss on his cheek and ran off to catch up with the family.

We arrived at the airport. Everyone was tired and cranky from the highs and lows of this trip. We said goodbye to Tom and Brenda. I headed with the girls into the restroom before we boarded our flight. As I left my stall, I went to wash my hands and called out to Pri and Marisol.

"I am over here, Valerie," Pri answered back.

"Marisol? Where are you, Marisol?" I called out and no answer.

"Pri, do you know where she went?"

"No, sorry, she went into the stall, and I didn't see her."

She answered now believing she had done something wrong. We checked under all the stalls and didn't see her. I ran outside, and across the corridor. She stood talking to a man that I could see from behind. I was frantic and went running as Dylan also came out of the restroom and ran to her as well.

"Marisol! Marisol!" She pointed and waved to me, and as I came close enough, the man she spoke to turned around. It was Christopher.

"Well, hello," Christopher said as he recognized me right away.

"Hello," I said back.

Dylan picked up Marisol who was confused, and now calm that she had found us.

"So, this little lady came out of this bathroom, looked around and walked into the other bathroom. I presume she was looking for you and got confused. My daughter who is right there, found her calling out to mom and tried to help find you. We just wanted to stay with her until you were found, and here you are.

"Valerie, your daughter is beautiful. I always knew you would be a wonderful mother," Christopher said to me as he stood up to be at my height. I stood in amazement that he was standing in front of me.

"Thank you," I said in reply. He reached out to touch my hand. I reached back; we locked eyes. It was hard to not feel the tension in the corridor.

"Wait, Valerie, do you guys know each other?" Dylan asked as he came closer to us. I quickly looked down and looked away. My whole family stood there confused.

"Dylan, this is Christopher; Christopher, Dylan. This is my daughter Marisol, our stepchildren Pri and John." Christopher held out his hand to Dylan, and as Dylan gave me an ugly look, he shook it.

"This is my daughter, Madison."

"Hello, Madison," I said and shook her hand.

"I took her skiing for the weekend, so we are just heading back to DC now," he said, Dylan had an angry face on and gave him a very disapproving look.

"Nice to see you, Christopher." I ended our encounter as I could feel Dylan steaming up and ready to punch him.

"Nice to meet your beautiful family, especially this one." He gave Marisol a pinch to her cheek, and she giggled. "Nice to meet you, Dylan, you are a lucky man to have such a lovely lady as your wife. I wasn't strong enough to see that, once upon a time. Please cherish her and take care of her." They shook hands again. Dylan's desire to punch him was strong, but now he was deterred by the comment.

"I always do," Dylan said confidently and threatening at the same time. We walked our separate paths, Christopher walked backward. I continued to look back until he became a dot in my vision. I was always saying goodbye to someone I didn't want to let go of in an airport.

The flight home was full of tension. Dylan wanted to scream at me, at Christopher, at anyone. I was tense from the encounter and believed that it was possibly the last time I would ever see Christopher again. *His eyes, oh his eyes.* As beautiful as they were, they had sadness in them, and now I could feel it. *He was broken, he was hurt, He needed me*, I said over and over in my head

I have to say goodbye to you, again. I'll see you in another life, I promise, I said to Christopher in my head and tried not to shed tears in front of Dylan.

Dylan faced the window. I could see his lips tremble, and the anger in his hand gestures. He did his nervous hand brush through his hair. He was adamant that he didn't want to look at me. I held the tears until I couldn't anymore. I got up out of my seat, and ran to the bathroom to let it out. Why did I love him so much? Wasn't he a part of my life? Why did I see him again? Why? I was so angry; this was so painful.

That night, we got home, exhaustion rested in everyone. The kids went to bed early. Dylan and I followed right behind them. I was scared to be alone with him. Dylan got right to the point.

"So, that's Christopher?"

"Yes," I replied.

"I can tell you are not over him, the way you looked at him. Don't tell me you're not meeting up with him at one of these 'work trips' you take. I can tell you have been seeing him. I can't believe you lied to me."

"Dylan, I am not meeting up with him! I, no, I told you I went to see him when he was sick. It was a quick trip, that is all. Dylan, I haven't seen him in years; I promise you that."

"I don't believe you. Not after I saw you with him today."

"Dylan, I am not seeing him. I am not with him. I want to be with you, I only want you. He is the past, Dylan."

"How do I believe that? How? The tension . . . you call him in your sleep. Seriously, Valerie."

"Dylan, I don't want him, I want you."

He got up and stomped around the room until he eventually got up, took a pillow and went downstairs to sleep. After a few hours, I was still wide awake. We should never go to bed angry. I went down to find him asleep on the far away couch, with his head buried into the back cushions. I went to sit by him and played with his hair, that I sometimes did when he was asleep. He was comforted by my touch, and since he was unconscious, he forgot that he was still mad at me. I whispered in his ear, "I choose you, Dylan, I choose this life with you, Dylan." I gave him a kiss on the forehead and grabbed his body where his hands embraced mine, got comfortable and fell asleep.

"I choose you," Dylan returned as I snored away and dreamt about nothing but being in his arms.

*   *   *   *   *

"There's a breech in your security."
"Corrupt", Karrisa Nole (Johnathan Peters Sound Factory Edit)

It was time for John to make the big decision of where to go to college. John chose Florida State where he was able to obtain a baseball scholarship. He had worked so hard to get good grades and was dedicated to baseball. We were so proud of him. That graduation was so special for him, as he earned it.

John was quiet, kept to himself, so we planned a small party for him as he didn't want to have a big fuss around him. I went to the supermarket to pick up some last-minute items for the party, when I noticed a few of the moms from Marisol's class look at their phone, and were looking at each other in shock. I dismissed it and went about the aisles trying to concentrate on my list.

I heard, "Is that really Dylan Zavala? Wow, I thought he was in a happy marriage. Oh well, I guess not. He still so cute." They were talking about my husband. Immediately, I went back and came to where they gathered in the center of aisle five with their carts as barriers. As they didn't see me coming, they stood in shock as I approached. They scattered.

"What about my husband? Yes, he is happily married," I sternly said to them. One brave soul stopped in her tracks and turned around.

"Valerie, I am sorry that you heard that. I am sorry that things aren't going well for you and Dylan. I shouldn't be gossiping." She tried to escape with that.

"What is it that you seem to know? Because there is no problem with my marriage," I said again sternly.

"Valerie, I don't want to be the one. Maybe you should ask him. I'm sorry." She tried to walk away.

"Show me the picture, at least show me the picture," I said. She hesitated but showed it to me. There it was. I am sure, by now, it was all over Instagram. Dylan was with one of the young single Moms from Marisol's class.

"Thank you for being honest with me," I said and left the store without a thing in my cart. I went straight to her house and sat outside. She was in the living room playing with her son and noticed me. I got out of the car and waited at the end of the driveway; she came outside.

"Valerie, did Marisol and Logan have a playdate today that I am not remembering?"

"Stay away from my husband," I said up close and in her face, with my finger pointed in her chest.

"Valerie, I don't know . . ."

"Cut it. I saw the pictures that are floating around town. Just cut the lies, stay away from my daughter, and stay away from my husband." I walked back to my car and drove home. Dylan and I were not in the best situation. I went to the farm to find him, and went straight up to him as he was in the field talking to some workers. I was aggressive in my walk. When I found him, I grabbed him and kissed him intensely.

He stopped me, laughing. "Valerie, wow, what is this all about? Wow."

"Come, let's do this." I grabbed his hand and started to walk with him toward the house.

"Wait, right now?"

"Yes."

"I like it when you are feisty, let's go into the barn. Everyone is leaving for the day." We went into the barn, and in a vacant stable, I forced myself onto Dylan. He came back just as forceful.

"Wow, Valerie, we haven't done that in a while. I miss it. I miss you."

"Nope, we haven't, just wanted you to remember what it feels like."

"I never stopped," he said sadly. I couldn't look at him. I picked up to leave and get back to prepping for the party.

"Wait, sit with me for a bit, I want to touch you."

"We have to get ready for the party," I said and put the rest of my clothes on, and left him there alone in the stable.

"Valerie!" he screamed to me and laid back into some hay out of frustration and grunts.

John wore his new school colors and baseball cap, as he was so excited to start right away. His friends came by, Tom and Brenda came into town, and some neighbors were there. Frannie and Sofia joined us. Pri was always my best helper.

Clarissa came to the party in a beautiful pink dress that was a little tight for her, but she wanted to impress him, and she didn't want him to forget her while he was away at school and traveling the country for baseball. She was nervous and tugged the dress down. She tried to hold her top up from falling out. She didn't have to try so hard to get John's attention. He couldn't stop staring even if she was in sweats. If she only knew the power she had over him.

"Pick your chin up, John," Frannie said to him and smacked the bottom of his chin. John blushed in embarrassment. I felt the same way Clarissa did. I wore a tight dress and was nervous that my man was going to leave me for another woman. I didn't have to flaunt as Dylan kept his hands on me most of the evening. We were ready to blow out candles and cut the cake. Dylan insisted on giving a speech. He took me over to John, and had the girls gather around us. He held onto my waist, and Clarissa held onto John's.

"John, I am so privileged to be able to raise you into the fine, young gentleman that you are. Valerie and I enjoyed watching you grow up and take your talents to the next level. You used your smarts and skills to get this amazing opportunity to college. Valerie and I love you very much, and can't wait to watch you become a star. Cheers to you from all of us." We raised our glasses, and John blew out his candles. Clarissa pulled John in for a kiss.

"Thank you, Dylan and Valerie, for taking us in, raising us. I would not have any of this if it wasn't for the both of you," John said as the strong, shy, confident man he was becoming. That night, John and Clarissa stayed in the guest house. We pretended not to notice. Dylan's phone went off a few times at the end of the party. I noticed him checking it as we were cleaning up. He looked up and at me, and look back at his phone. I looked at him and walked upstairs into the bedroom. He followed. I took off my dress; it fell to the ground, and just as it hit the floor, Dylan flew into the room and slammed the door behind him.

"Valerie."

"Yes," I said as I looked into his eyes.

"Okay, first stop using sex to seduce me, nice move by the way. I know that you know."

"What is it that I know exactly, Dylan?" He pulled me onto the bed and held my wrist over my head with an angry force that hurt. He knew it.

"Stop the bullshit, Valerie; I know you found out about my affair with Logan's mom, Teresa."

"Yes, I just found out. Thank you, it was lovely to hear from Marisol's classmate's moms in the supermarket. Thank you for letting me be the last to know." I tried to struggle out of his hold and with nothing to say, he let go.

"What happened, Dylan? If you were so unhappy, why didn't you just leave?" I asked with my back to his on the side of the bed.

"You are the one unhappy. You stopped looking at me. You don't even want to talk to me," Dylan said angrily.

"Is this still the Christopher thing? Because that is a dead avenue. You have all the evidence that does not lead me to him."

"I don't know, Valerie, but you make me feel like I am not good enough for you, so I found it somewhere else."

"Dylan, am I supposed to jump you every day? I mean, I need a little romance too. We had this conversation years ago. Why are we still here?"

"Because we didn't change. We didn't make an effort. I fell out of love with you," Dylan said to me. He got up and packed a bag, left the house and went straight to Teresa. It hurt. He was right; we went back to our ways. He lied to me. I went to bed alone. Dylan went into the arms of another woman. I was afraid I might never sleep in the same bed with him again.

I cried myself to sleep. I was miserable. I never thought I could feel good again. After all my tears and vodka, Marisol came and crawled into bed with me. Shortly after, so did Pri. I was not alone. I was loved. This was just a season.

*　　*　　*　　*　　*

John left for school, Marisol went to sleep-away camp, and Pri was spending time with caring for the animals and keeping Frannie company. Dylan came to the farm to work, and then went back to Teresa. He nodded hello if he saw me, but he never came over. Before long, it became winter break, and John came home from college.

"So where is Dylan? Why isn't he here?" John said. We did our best to keep it quiet from the kids.

"John, Dylan and I are separated. He lives, I believe, with his girlfriend," I said as I sipped tea and looked out the bay window into the field.

"Wait, what? Dylan has a girlfriend? Since when? This is crazy." He was right; it was crazy.

"Apparently, it has been going on for a long time. I found out right before you left for school. I didn't want you to know. I didn't want you to worry about it. He spends time during the day with Pri; she doesn't really see it. He sees Marisol when she leaves and comes home from school; she doesn't really notice. Then you are at school, so no needed to bother you. Pay attention to your studies, and kick some ass on that ballfield! Don't worry about this." John came in to give me a hug. I needed it.

I was sober and somber through this whole ordeal, and prayed every day at the rose patch Dylan planted for Peanut. Although I felt God with me, I needed the physical hug that was as close to a replica of Dylan that I could get. For now, it was the best I could ask for.

"I miss him, John, I do. I guess I can't give him what he needs anymore." John hugged me tighter. I let out my tears. Now, when I closed my eyes, I could see him with her. I never want to sleep again.

Clarissa came over to meet up with John, and we had a quiet dinner together. They went out to try and find some old friends. I went into my empty bedroom where Marisol came in and cuddled with me. I stayed awake and caress her hair and listen to her sleep.

"Clarissa, Dylan left Valerie and is with some chick Teresa," John said to Clarissa in the car.

"Yeah, I know about it. It's all around town, but you know that Teresa left him, right? I thought that he came home, or at least stayed in the guesthouse."

"Wait, you knew about this?"

"Yeah, Valerie asked me to please not say anything to you about it. She wanted you to concentrate on school. She really just wants the best for you. I agreed. I wanted to wait to tell you. I hope you're not mad at me?"

"No, no, I'm not mad. I am just upset about it. So where is he living? He doesn't live here?"

"I know a few guys that hang out at the pool hall that are single. Maybe he goes there?"

"Oh, I know the one. Yeah, he goes there sometimes. Clarissa, do you mind if we go there? I need to see him. He is not answering any of my texts. I am kind of worried."

"Of course, anything for you," she said and brushed her fingers through his hair as he picked up the speed to get to the pool hall.

"There he is." Clarissa spotted him as they pulled in. He was walking in from having a cigarette. John and Clarissa followed him in.

"Dylan," John said to him as Dylan was shocked to see him there. Dylan had been drinking and didn't have many words.

"John, my boy, you are home. I got your messages, sorry. I was going to get you tomorrow, you know," Dylan said in a slurred speech.

"Dylan, where are you living? Why aren't you with Valerie?" John asked. Clarissa stood behind him.

"Oh, Valerie. She hates me. Then I was shackin' up with Teresa, and she kicked me out. So, I suck, can't live with them, can't live without them. Drinks? You guys need drinks, right, Clarissa?" Dylan was hardly standing and leaning in on his pool stick.

"Dylan, I was just with her, and she told me how much she loves you. Come home with me. You can't drive. I don't even know where you are staying."

"In my car, I sleep in my car," Dylan said.

"Dylan, come home with me."

"No, no, Valerie hates me. She hates me."

"Dylan, listen to me. She doesn't hate you. Now, come home."

John took away his beer and pool stick, and pushed him out the door and into the car. He sat in the front and Clarissa snugged up to the front seat, as close as she could from the middle backseat.

"She does love you, she told me herself," Clarissa said. Dylan laughed to himself.

They arrived back at the house; it was now after midnight. I could hear the door open, and the scatter of feet and mumbles. I checked to see if Marisol woke up, I walked to the top of the stairs to see if it was John.

"John?" I whispered aloud.

John looked up, as did Clarissa, carrying in a very drunk Dylan.

"Dylan?" I said in disbelief.

"Yeah, I found him, Valerie. He was living in his car; I couldn't let him. He wants to talk to you." John said, as he gave Dylan a nudge. They whispered and poked at him to talk to me.

"Valerie, I cheated on you. I made a big mistake. But you hate me. I'm drunk. I need you. But you don't want me, so I am going to leave." Dylan took himself outside and went toward the guesthouse. I sat on the top step and watched him get himself in the door, and turn on the lights on the first floor.

"Okay, he is inside. Can you go check if he is alive and get him at least onto the couch?" I asked of John. John went over and did just as I asked. Clarissa came to sit with me on the step.

"He misses you, Valerie," she said and placed her head on my shoulder. He sure did have a funny way of showing it. John came back to pick up Clarissa, and they went to sleep in the guesthouse with Dylan. I went back to bed and caressed Marisol's hair. She was never interrupted by the noise.

The next morning, I went down to make breakfast, and Dylan came in just as the coffee was ready. He sat down at the island. I poured him a cup. He smelled like cigarettes and Heineken; it remind me of my days of destruction when we first came to Texas. Marisol came down the stairs and hugged Dylan a good morning, as she was excited to see him within the four walls of our home.

"Daddy's home!" she screamed as she sat down next to him to snuggle as close as she could. I made them both scrambled eggs with bacon, and went upstairs to change as they ate. Dylan finished quickly as he wanted to get me alone before the day started.

"Finish your breakfast and get dressed, I have to go talk to Mommy."

She nodded. Dylan came up to find me in the shower. He bravely pulled back the curtain. I gave him a glance as I lathered up the shampoo in my hair. I lifted my head backward to rinse off. He just stood there.

"I still think you are beautiful, Valerie. I missed you. I made a big mistake, a very big mistake. I just freaked out and really thought you gave up on me. I just want to let you know I want to be in your life again, if you will take me." Dylan stood there as I rinsed out my hair and my body, then I turned off the water. He stood there with his arm holding him up against the wall.

"Can you move so I can get a towel?" I said as he just stood in my way.

"Sorry, sorry, Valerie, I was just admired by your beauty. Here, let me get you a towel." He grabbed one off the wall. I stood in front of the sink; he came behind me to wrap the towel around me, and to find his spot in between my shoulder blades, where I used to perched myself in him on the mornings when we first got married.

"Dylan, I just got out of the shower, and no offense, but you smell like cigarettes and Heineken. I don't want to smell that all day."

"Si, mi amor," He stepped back, kicked off his boots, stripped off his clothes, and took a shower behind me. I brushed my teeth, combed out my hair, and before I was finished, he jumped out of the shower. I took off my towel and threw it at him as I walked into the bedroom.

"Don't get my floors wet and slippery," I said. He sighed in disappointment.

Dylan moved back into the guesthouse. John went back to school. Each morning, he came in for breakfast and coffee. We had a casual conversation. I was cold toward him. He continued to try. He picked roses from the garden and brought them over. He continued to tell me that I was beautiful, and he'd send me sex texts as if we were young kids dating. It was nice, but I could only picture him with her when I closed my eyes—and it hurt. Time passed, but he didn't stop trying. He had my car cleaned, set up picnic lunches in the rose patch, and invited me to candlelit dinners in fancy restaurants in Texas.

"Come on, Valerie, come to dinner with me. You told me that you miss dressing up and wearing heels. I am listening Valerie, please come to dinner with me." His invite came with another set of rose and kisses on my hand, as he placed a beautiful bracelet on my wrist, decorated with charms to reminded me of all our memories. He wore his hair slicked back, a button-down shirt and dressed up jeans. He wore his cologne again that brought back memories of the good times, the times when we woke up gazing into each other's eyes smiling, making love at all times of the day. When we belonged to each other and couldn't live without each other. When his power over me was so strong, I couldn't resist him.

"I will come to dinner with you," I said as I was growing weak, and his charm was working on me.

"Really? Oh, yes! Valerie, you are going to be so happy, I know you won't regret this. I will pick you up at 7:30. Dress fancy!" he said as he ran away singing and laughing. Pri came over as she was watching from her porch.

"I am glad you are going. What are you going to wear?"

"I don't know. Help me decide?"

She agreed. We went to pick something out. I was a bit nervous like it was the first date with a man I had a crush on. As I got ready that evening, I thought of Shelia and Ashley getting ready the first time Ashley went on a date with Chase. Shelia brushed Ashley's hair in the mirror and gave her red lipstick to wear. Ashley was nervous as she really wanted to be with Chase, and felt safe with him. She needed him. She got him. She ruined him. She left him in this world, empty and alone.

Shelia sipped her vodka and told her sexual things to give him to keep him, since she was not an expert, but believed if she could please Tom, he would have stayed.

"What would you tell me tonight, Shelia, about how to keep my husband?" I asked her out loud. Marisol walked in without my knowledge, as I was so focused on my fantasy.

"I would tell you that you should have fun with Daddy, and give him a big kiss on the lips!" Marisol answered as she played with my hair.

"What? A big kiss? Now, how big is this kiss?"

"It's this big." She opened her hands wide.

"Wow, that is some kiss. Then what should I do? Can he handle a kiss that big?" I asked her, as she continued to comb my hair.

"Then, tell him to move back. I miss Daddy not sleeping here anymore, and you do too," she said.

"How do you know that I miss him?" I asked her sarcastically.

"Because I hear you crying at night, and you call out for him."

I was shocked that she said that. I thought about him. I didn't know how loud my cry was, or that I was calling out for him. It was real; I missed Dylan. The door opened, Dylan entered the house, and I came downstairs.

"Oh, mi amor, oh my beautiful." He smiled and kissed my hand as I came close to him, and he escorted me to the door. Marisol went for a sleepover with Pri and Frannie, and they all waved as we got into the car and drove away. When we hit the end of the property, before we turned onto the main road, Dylan stopped the car and reached to grab my hand.

"Kiss me, Valerie," he said. He leaned in, I gave him a short kiss back, and held his face in my hand.

"Marisol told me I should give you a kiss tonight, so there you go."

"Oh, that Marisol. What else did she tell you to do to me?" he said laughing, as he took the turn onto the main road.

"I am not telling you. I just fulfilled one promise."

I smiled as he drove and held my hand. I sat back into the comfort of the leather chair, and felt the breeze of the sunroof open.

It was like old times again. We sat down at the restaurant, ordered champagne and gazed at each other over candlelight.

"How am I doing so far, Ms. Valerie?" He was nervous and tinkering with the silverware as he was afraid to wave his hands through his hair and mess it up.

"Why are you so nervous?" I asked him, in a sarcastic tone.

"Valerie, you are my wife that I am trying so dearly to win back. I need you in my life, I really need you. I love you, Valerie. I don't know how to stop that." He was sweating and trying to wipe it off when I wasn't looking.

"Relax, Dylan; if I wasn't interested, I wouldn't be here." We both smiled. Dinner was nice. The conversation was casual. Dylan ordered dessert that we shared. When it was over, he asked me for my hand across the table.

"Valerie, I have made many mistakes. I ask you for forgiveness. I want to be the husband you deserve and have asked me to be. I need you. I can't live without you. Valerie, will you marry me again?" He placed the red, cloth, lanyard ring the girls made for me when we went to Mexico on my finger. I had stopped wearing it, as it was faded and falling apart. Pri and Marisol gave it a facelift, and now it was a mix of pinks and bright red.

I looked him in the eyes and could see the genuine, kind spirit I met years ago at a Yankee game. I brought my hand over the hand he held in reassurance that I was happy.

"Dylan, this is a lot, really fast. It is hard to get over the fact that there was someone else. I accept your apology. I do want to marry you again. I just need to take this slow, and ease into it. I hope you can understand that?"

"Oh, mi amor, yes, yes," he said and kissed my hands.

"This is the other thing Marisol asked for," I whispered into his ear.

"That Marisol, she has good ideas." The morning came. Dylan showered. I found my spot in his back between the shoulder blades and wrapped my arms around his chest, and reached down just above his underwear line. We were back in sync.

Marisol came in from her night with the girls and ran up the stairs to greet us. She found us embracing in the bathroom and screamed, "I knew it!" and danced around the upstairs hallway.

*　　*　　*　　*　　*

"'For I know the plan I have for you,' declares
the Lord, 'plans to prosper you and not to harm
you, plans to give you hope and a future.'"
—Jeremiah, 29:11

John had a window of time to come home for the annual town barbecue, but he really came back during baseball season to see Clarissa. The family was back to normal. Dylan and I were happy again. Marisol was in Middle School, and she was excited to be allowed to wonder off with some friends for the special day. This day was bigger than Christmas for Dylan, where he overworked himself, but enjoyed each moment of it. I walked around and talked to all the vendors and neighbors as I waited for Dylan to break for the day. He was able to find me and startle me as he grabbed me from behind. We grabbed a few beers from the cooler, and went to retreat in the hammock under the shady trees.

"I miss this," Dylan said as he closed his eyes from the exhaustion of the event.

"Do you still think about Olivia?" I asked him.

"Every day," he replied. I snapped a picture of us in the same pose she took of us the first year I came to Texas, and posted it on every social media site I could think of with the caption, "We miss you, Olivia," in hopes that she would find us. Dylan took a quick nap as I ran my hands through his hair, and when he awoke, we spotted John and Clarissa skipping into the guesthouse.

"What do you think is going to happen with those two?" I asked Dylan.

"I don't know, but she does seem to keep his interest, that is for sure." John and Clarissa came over for breakfast. As usual, everyone sat around the island for eggs and bacon.

"I am heading back today, so when are you guys going to renew your vows?" John asked as we ate.

"We didn't really discuss it much. Valerie, did you have a time that you wanted it to be?" Dylan asked through coffee and bacon-chomping.

"I don't know, I just want everyone to be together, nothing crazy," I answered.

"Well, I had an idea. I am going to be in Vegas for a tournament next month. I have that Saturday off before we fly back on Sunday. Clarissa and I decided to get married. We want you to also renew your vows. What do you think?" John said as he held out Clarissa's hand to show off the ring.

"Well, congrats to both of you! You want us to be a part of the ceremony to renew our vows? That is awfully nice of you," Dylan said as I went to stand with him.

"I think it is lovely," I replied. We agreed to make it happen.

* * * * *

"Believe me, Believe me, I can't tell you why."

—Love is a Battlefield, Pat Benatar

Before we knew it, we were in Vegas, ready to walk John and Clarissa down the aisle. I was to renew my vows with Dylan. I was suddenly a parent giving away a son who I inherited and called my own.

They wanted it simple. As we were guests, we were also special guest stars, and happy with whatever they wanted to do. It was simple at the Luxor hotel, in a smaller catering room. Everyone we wanted was there. Clarissa's family, Tom and Brenda, Frannie and Sofia, our children, my childhood friend, Kellie, and a few of our neighbors, along with some of John's classmates. Clarissa was beautiful in her white, silk gown that her grandmother made for her. Her hair was back and she decided to not wear a veil. John was in a tux. Dylan stood next to him as his best man.

The ceremony was quick. They said their vows. John said he wanted, "A love just like Dylan and Valerie's." It was sweet. They placed rings on each other's finger, shared their first kiss, and walked back down the aisle as we all showered them with flowers. A woman appeared in the back of the room with dark sunglasses.

She was elegant, tall and wore a pink suit. As John and Clarissa made it to the backdoor, John lifted his arms in excitement and gave her a hug.

It was Olivia.

Dylan grabbed his chest and started to cry. He looked at me and gave me a hug. We made our way to them, and Dylan picked her up. She embraced the hug as deeply as he did.

"How did you find us? How did you know we were here, Olivia? How . . . oh, Olivia, this makes me so happy!" Dylan hugged her again and showered her with kisses. She laughed in excitement and teared up just the same at the amount of time that was lost from our lives together.

"Valerie posted the picture of you two at the barbecue, and I found it. She searched high and low to find me. She convinced me to come."

"I always believed we would see you again," I said. Olivia was now grown up and as beautiful as I pictured her to be. We all embraced until the pastor asked us to come back to renew our vows. She walked with us down the aisle. We were now the complete family we dreamed together it would be.

"Valerie, today I am blessed and excited that I have all that my heart desires. I am marrying the woman I love. I have back the daughter I lost so long ago. My son just got married, my kids are all with me, happy and healthy. God gave me the greatest gift. He gave me you. Valerie, you made all of this happen. I am forever grateful, and if I never wake up again, I will cherish this moment forever, knowing that I had a wonderful life."

"Dylan, I would do anything for you. I am blessed that we have a full family again. May we spend the rest of our lives together in peace and harmony as I never want to let you go. I love you, Dylan; you have my heart." We kissed and became one again. It was time to celebrate with the rest of our family. Pri had made me a bouquet of feathers that flew in the air as I walked. Each one felt like a memory from above. I looked at the ceiling and thanked Jesus, Madeline, Cal; even Shelia, Ashley; most of all, Lydia, who gave Olivia back to us on this day. It was warming and beautiful.

"Thank you, Jesus."

We danced, we broke bread, we clanged glasses, we all had a wonderful memory to keep with us. As the party was over, we walked to the hotel bar for some further drinks and celebrated for as long as the night allowed. I left Dylan to sit with Olivia as they had so much to catch up on. I headed to the bar to grab us some drinks. I heard a voice in the background, through the casino dings, and the loud music in the bar. Through the laughter of our crowd, I could hear him being rowdy, in an argument of sorts, and I could identify that voice. It was Christopher. I closed my eyes to hear the voice without distraction, and saw the memories flash before me, a wedding, being on the floor watching the lights glisten above us. I remember you.

The voice. I could feel the voice. I had to find it. I turned away from the bar and walked toward it. Dylan saw me as I looked confused and determined to find it. He got up and followed me into the hallway, and as he grabbed my arm from the back, he found him before I did.

"Are you fucking kidding me?" Dylan said as I stood there in amazement that he found me. Christopher found me. Dylan went over to him, grabbed him from his pack of friends, and punched him in the face. When he hit the ground, Dylan went down with him and continued the punches until everyone around pulled them apart. Dylan came over to me with blood on his shirt and on his hands.

"Valerie, are you serious? I can't believe I fell for your lies. I am done." He took off his ring and threw it at me, and ran off as the cops were coming the opposite way.

"Dylan, Dylan! I didn't know he was here! Dylan!"

I started to run after him, but with the heavy dress, heels, and cocktails consumed, he was gone. John, Clarissa, and Olivia came to find out what happened, and as the police attended to Christopher, I tried to run but was held back by police to tell them what happened. John went running for Dylan. All I could do was scream.

"Dylan, it is you! Dylan come back!"

But it was useless. He was gone. I fell to the ground and wept. I turned my head to see Christopher on the ground across from me. As our eyes met, I could see the blood dripping down his face. His nose was broken, his eyes mangled, and he curled himself as he spit up blood from the convulsions and stomach wounds. He tried to reach his hand out to me; then his body was sent into a seizure. The EMS came as quickly as they could to sweep him away, but his eyes opened again one last time

He mouthed, "Come with me," as he reached out his hand. I lay there and watched as I could not move from the screams over me, and amid the hysteria of what had happened. I turned to look up and could see the bright lights of the casino hallway. As I blinked my eyes, I could remember the first moments of when I entered in this world, missing the old world and confused. I couldn't see or hear; everything became blurry.

Dylan ran into the garage, got into his car, and raced away. He was drunk, and on a busy street he was unfamiliar with, he was running and not sure what he was running from. He took a wrong turn and slammed into a pole blocks away from the strip that was not very populated.

Dylan laid there with his face on the steering wheel. He faded to black.

Christopher was in the ambulance and regained consciousness as they performed CPR. He was raced to the hospital. They gave him a needle. He faded to black.

I could hear voices, I could hear Clarissa and John screaming. I could hear Marisol crying, Pri calming her down. I could see black.

"She is having a heart attack! My mom is having a heart attack, help!" John screamed out to the crowd. An ambulance came and pulled me onto a gurney, and swept me away to the hospital. I regained consciousness and went in for emergency surgery to release the blockage in my heart.

John called Dylan's cell phone over and over again. Sirens got closer and closer to his car, but Dylan laid there without moving. He could hear the noise get closer and closer. He lost blood; he lost tons of blood. They grabbed him. He still had a pulse.

"It is amazing this guy is still alive," the policeman said. The phone in his pocket rang and rang until the officer answered John's call, and told him the hospital they were headed to. I could feel the white light on me; I could hear the surgery being performed on me. I could see a man's face appear to lean over to me.

"Hello, Valerie, why are we here today?"

"Peter? Is it time, is it over already? So soon? It was so fast? I want to go back. I want to be with my love. Can you send me back to my love?" I was begging at the pearly gates to stay on this earth I didn't want to be on to begin with. I was just here for what felt like moments ago, but I remember being here.

"Valerie, you are not dying, you are merely just taking a visit. This is not your time; you are going back soon. So, you can be back with your family and your love. Do you know who your love is?" I thought I knew, but I didn't. I wanted to answer, and I couldn't.

"Exactly, Valerie, you don't know who your love is. Maybe now is the time to think about it. Goodbye, Valerie, I will be back when it is time for you to be here. Think about what you have learned in this life, Valerie. Think about who your love is. That person will always be in your heart and do what is right for you."

"Peter! Who is it? WHO?" and he was gone. Just like that, he was gone. I felt the strong, light beating on my face, and I could hear beeps coming from around me. I remember being in Mexico after my miscarriage, and the cold metal on the side of my face. I reached out my hands to find cold metal, and put my face to it. I needed to feel something. I needed to know I was alive.

"John! She is waking up!" Clarissa screamed in the hallway, as I started to move about in the bed. I could feel a strong hand on the other side.

"Good morning, sunshine," Tom said as he gave me a squeeze.

"Mommy!" Marisol exclaimed from behind him. She grabbed my arm. John came running into the room, and he grabbed my other hand with Clarissa.

"Mom, you are going to be okay, the doctor said you are going to be okay. Olivia, Pri, she is awake." Pri laid down Bingo, grabbed at my neck and pushed my hair away from my eyes as I tried to see.

"Dylan is in the other room, and so is Christopher. They are both recovering," John said. He became such an adult overnight. Marisol wandered into the hallway and into the other rooms as she was drawn there.

"Go and be with Dylan. He needs you," I said slowly to them. Tom stayed with me as they went to tend to Dylan.

"How are you doing, baby girl?" Tom said as he brushed my hair with his fingers.

"Tom, why didn't I ever call you Dad?"

"You did sometimes; I didn't need you to call me Dad. I needed you to let me be a part of your life."

"Why didn't you love Shelia? Why did she kill herself?"

"Your Mom was a very troubled woman. I couldn't love her because she didn't love herself. You can't love people if they don't love themselves. If you don't love yourself, you don't love God. He brought you here and created you. If you don't love yourself, it's as if you don't love him."

"Tom."

"Yes, dear."

"I love you."

"I know you do; I love you too."

"I love Shelia too," I said.

"Valerie, I am sure she heard you. Get some rest. You have a sick husband to attend too." I closed my eyes and woke up a few hours later to an empty room, and a strong feeling of thirst. A nurse came in moments later and greeted me.

"How is Dylan? How is Christopher? Are my children with Dylan? I need to see him."

"Yes, yes, I know you are very concerned. Christopher is in stable condition. Dylan, well, he lost a lot of blood. He has sustained head trauma and internal injuries. He is hanging in there the best he can. You can't get up just yet. We are trying to see what we can do to bring you together."

"Please, please, I need to see him."

"He is still unconscious; he won't be able to see you."

"But I need to touch him; I need to talk to him. He will hear my voice and wake up, I just know it. I need him." The nurse did her best to calm me down and console me.

"Please, I need him. Dylan! Dylan!" She pushed me back into the bed. I tried to scream and sit up.

"Mrs. Zavala, please sit back. You will hurt yourself. I will get you to him. Let me talk to the doctor." After some time, a team came and took my hospital bed out of the room, and wheeled me down the hall to Dylan. They placed me close enough that I could reach over to hold his hand. I leaned in to kiss it. The monitor continued to beat at the same pace.

"I love you, Dylan; I love you," I repeated as many times as I could. The girls and John sat around us and were in disbelief as to the state we were both in.

"Dylan, please wake up, please." Nothing. Marisol wandered out of the room and back to where Christopher was. She held his hand and sat with his daughter. He was in stable condition. She grabbed his hand. He squeezed it back. She went back to all the rooms, without anyone realizing she was doing it. She was drawn to Christopher. Every time she came in, he would get a little better, the heartbeat monitor would give a bit more excitement.

We sang to Dylan his favorite songs and hoped that he could hear us. He didn't respond. The beeps would stay the same, slow and far between each of them. When the night came, I moved myself up and attempted to get into his bed.

"Valerie, no, you can't!" John screamed.

"John, help me. Move him over, I need to be with him; I need to feel him, he needs me."

"You are crazy; you are going to hurt yourself."

"Then help me, John, I can't lose him." He moved Dylan over with the help of the sheets below him, and he carefully picked me up, and placed me next to him in the bed. I laid on my back next to him as we laid in the hospital bed in Mexico. I was able to kiss the side of his head, touch his chest.

"I love you, Dylan; I love you. It was always you." And the more I touched him, the beeps moved up. He was responding.

"Dylan, follow my voice, come to me. Come and find me, Dylan." I signaled for everyone to join in one by one and we did.

"Dad."

"Dylan."

"Come to us, we miss you, come find us, we love you." And he responded. Through rounds of this practice, he opened his eyes, but with the bright light, he closed them again. He gave me a squeeze to my hand and pulled it back into his chest.

"Valerie."

"Yes, Dylan, yes?" Then he closed his eyes; the monitor went beeping, his grip became weak. With me at his side, his children, his mother, and sister standing around his hospital bed. Doctors and nurses ran in to save him. The machine went on a long, continuous beep and the hand and body I was holding onto went limp—and Dylan was gone.

Marisol left the room and went in to see Christopher, and held his hand, and at that moment he opened his eyes.

"Hello, beautiful girl, he said to her." She smiled. She let go of his hand and came back into the room with myself and Dylan. I was carried back into my bed, and after everything was unhooked, they took Dylan's cold body under a white bedsheet out of the room. Each child said their goodbye and wept on each other as I lay in the hospital bed alone, now a widow. I felt empty.

I know that you loved me. I know you did what you had to do. Now it is time. Love yourself, the voice in my head said to me. It felt like Dylan.

Love yourself, I heard as I closed my eyes. I saw Madeline crying at the window, I saw Shelia, crying with her vodka in her bed. I saw Ashley crying as a young girl, watching me walk off with Chase.

Love yourself, the voice said again. I said it back to all of them.

"I choose to love myself," I said out loud.

*   *   *   *   *

"I pray you learn to trust
Have faith in both of us
And leave room in your heart for two."
—Precious, Depeche Mode

I was ready to leave the hospital. John and Clarissa went home to make arrangements for Dylan. Pri went to the farm with Frannie and Sofia. Marisol stayed with me and Tom as I was released.

"Mom?"

"Yes, Marisol?"

"Don't be mad; I made friends with Christopher. He needed someone; I wanted to be there for him, I don't know why. I just did. Are you mad?"

"No, Marisol, I am not mad. That is very kind of you. You have a big heart. Come, let's go say hello." I grabbed her hand. We walked down the hallway together. She had perfect brown hair and hazel eyes.

His smile was big, even after all that just happened.

"Hello," Christopher said as we entered the room. His daughter, Madison, was with him and helping him gather his things as he was also ready to leave.

"Hello, Christopher; hello, Madison. Did you ever meet my dad, Tom?" They shook hands; Tom waited by the doorway.

"This very special lady came to visit me this week. I am very grateful. She helped my recovery along with Madison. I had all my special ladies with me. I needed it." Christopher looked at Marisol; she was about his height now that she had grown so tall.

"She is a special lady. I can understand why she is so special to you. A daughter should always be special to her dad," I said, holding in tears that came from the years of secrets.

Marisol looked at me. Christopher smiled as he grabbed her and kissed her on the cheek.

"I knew it. I just knew it," Marisol said. He hugged Marisol. They both had a bond that they could now understand.

"So now, we don't have to all be strangers," I said and continued to cry.

"Valerie, when I said all my special ladies were here with me, I counted you as one of them," Christopher said as he grabbed my hand.

"I have to go and bury my husband, but I will make sure when that is over, you can all spend time together and get to know each other. I know these are crazy circumstances. I am sorry, I truly am. We all have learned how precious life is. I don't want to keep you apart any longer. Dylan needed Marisol; Marisol knew when you needed her. Now you need each other. So, you will all be together."

"Valerie."

"Yes?" I replied.

"I always knew you were an important part of my life."

*   *   *   *   *

The day was chilly. We set up chairs around the rose patch where Peanut was buried. Dylan always loved the chill in the air. I sat in the black chair and listened to the Minister give his final blessing over Dylan's coffin. I didn't know how to properly mourn Dylan, as I felt like he was still here with me. I could smell him as the wind blew, and I could hear him singing in the shower. I still look to see if he would come and sit next to me. I sat with John, who wept, and was being brave enough to stand up and talk about the man who raised and molded him.

"Dylan was not my father but the man who raised me. He gave me the family upbringing I would not have had. He let me look at life as a gift, and told me, every day, to tell the ones around you that you love them as often as possible. He wasn't perfect, but he was my best friend. My best man. The best dad I ever knew. Dylan, I hope you can hear me. I love you.

"In Spanish, there is a saying that 'one does not exist where your body is, but rather you exist where you are missed the most.' You will always be in my heart, as there is where I will miss you the most. I will believe you are always with me. Cheers to you," John said and lifted his hand to the crowd and to the coffin.

Olivia came to sit next to me and grabbed my hand, and with the hardship to watch each and every last person lay their rose on his coffin, it was finally my turn. I wasn't ready. Will I remember him in my next life? What will the moment be? Will it be the Yankee game? Will it be Mexico? Disney? Times in the barn? Barbecues? *Will you remember me, Dylan?* Olivia walked me to the coffin; I stood over it with my rose.

"Dylan, Dylan. I will follow you anywhere. Any lifetime. I won't forget about you. Don't forget about me. I love you; it was always you. It will always be you. May we meet again, one day, in Heaven." I kissed and dropped the rose onto the casket and walked away, with the help of Olivia, into the arms of John, Pri, Frannie, and Sofia.

*   *   *   *   *

I told the family my story of Christopher, my shame of Marisol's father, and holding it back from everyone. We had been through so much together, there were no judgements made. They all understood that I had to go and figure things out. Marisol had to go and live with her Dad to get to know him. I went to the rose patch and knelt down before them both.

"Dylan, I love you with all my heart. You are everything to me. I miss you so much. I know you know now that Marisol isn't your daughter, but you raised her. She will always think of you as her father. She loves you. I am so happy you got to see Olivia in your last moments of life.

"I am so blessed that I was able to tell you in front of family, friends, and God that I love you. I hope now you can see that I really did love you. But I made mistakes. I held Marisol's identity from you because you needed her, the news of Christopher that, one time, would have hurt you so badly. It would have ruined us. I needed you as much as you needed me. You saved me from a life of destruction. I will forever be grateful. I look at my mother and my sister; I can see that they didn't know how to love themselves. You helped me break that cycle.

"I loved Christopher, but I couldn't' be with him because I didn't love me. Dylan, you showed me how to love someone. You showed me unconditional love. You showed me how to love myself when I didn't know how. I was the true love I was chasing all this time. I love you, Dylan, so much. I will cherish your memory. I will follow you from this life to the next. I won't forget about you. I promise.

"Peanut, please take care of your Daddy as he loves you so much, as I do. May we all meet again one day in heaven. God, please watch over my loves. Amen." I signed the cross, and I headed to the airport with Marisol.

"Why won't you come to DC with me?" Marisol said, confused.

"You need to be with your dad. I went to live with my dad when I was your age, and I turned out okay. It will be great; you will make up for lost time."

"I will miss you. I will worry about you," Marisol said as she hugged me.

"We will Facetime, we won't be strangers. You can always come to see me. I will come to see you. I promise." We hugged, Marisol got on a plane to DC, I got on a plane to New York. I went to my hometown and walked around the park. I remember the fog and the mist from being a kid. I went to lay on the edge of the stone wall surrounding the tip of the harbor. It was so familiar to me. That day, the fog and mist lifted, and it was sunny. The birds are chirping.

I closed my eyes to soak in the sun. I could hear boys making noise in the water, the boats coming in and out of the basins. It was relaxing and peaceful. As I closed my eyes, I could see Dylan at our first wedding as we danced under the stars and twilight. It was magical. I could smell him as the wind picked up, and it made me smile. He gave me life again. I came to this life to feel again, to learn to love myself. He gave that to me.

"I love you, Dylan," I said out loud. "Until we meet again."

I could see Madeline call-up for dinner after her extra steamy kiss from Cal.

"Dinner!" she called. Shelia came down with Ashley. As they were about to sit down, the doorbell rang. Madeline went to the window to see a family outside.

"Hello!" she exclaimed.

"Is it too late for dinner?" they asked.

"Never!" Madeline replied. Dylan, Lydia, and Peanut went to join them at the kitchen table. They held hands and said a prayer before they broke bread. Everyone was smiling. I smiled to see them all together. My family was whole again. Shortly after, I heard my phone go off.

Come and be here with us.

It was time to go. I was done here. I took in another deep breath, and went back into my car. Among all the leaves, a feather caught onto my sleeve. I knew it was a message from above.

I got into my car and drove back to the airport, with a one-way ticket home.

About the Author

*D*ebby Kruszewski was born and raised in Westchester, New York. She decided to leave corporate America to pursue all the dreams she was told she could never achieve. Debby loves pizza, running with scissors, daily mass, mayonnaise, long walks on the beach, gifts from the Holy Spirit, sandwiches, Leatherstocking trail, ALPHA, adding items to your cart when you're not looking, acts of kindness, BMX, a good cry, *G-Men*, maisonnée, family and friends, cursing, being dangerous on the dance floor, adoration, Yankee games, happy hour, *The Catholic Guy Show*, red pants, *Lost*, *The Foo Fighters*, sunsets, a good joke that never dies, and the love God gives us every day.